THE SAFETY CURTAIN
AND OTHER STORIES

To My mum

On your 80th birthday 12th August 2013

With my fondest love as always.

Your daughter Jan
xxx

"You may take them to the devil!" Merryon said.

THE SAFETY CURTAIN

AND OTHER STORIES

by

ETHEL M. DELL

WILDSIDE PRESS

Published 2005 by Wildside Press, LLC

www.wildsidepress.com

CONTENTS

The Safety Curtain	7
The Experiment	72
Those Who Wait	106
The Eleventh Hour	116
The Place of Honour	180

The Safety Curtain

CHAPTER I

THE ESCAPE

A great shout of applause went through the crowded hall as the Dragon-Fly Dance came to an end, and the Dragon-Fly, with quivering, iridescent wings, flashed away.

It was the third encore. The dance was a marvellous one, a piece of dazzling intricacy, of swift and unexpected subtleties, of almost superhuman grace. It must have proved utterly exhausting to any ordinary being; but to that creature of fire and magic it was no more than a glittering fantasy, a whirl too swift for the eye to follow or the brain to grasp.

"Is it a boy or a girl?" asked a man in the front row.

"It's a boy, of course," said his neighbour, shortly.

He was the only member of the audience who did not take part in that third encore. He sat squarely in his seat throughout the uproar, watching the stage with piercing grey eyes that never varied in their stern directness. His brows were drawn above them—thick, straight brows that bespoke a formidable strength of purpose. He was plainly a man who was accustomed to hew his own way through life, despising the trodden paths, overcoming all obstacles by grim persistence.

Louder and louder swelled the tumult. It was evident that nothing but a repetition of the wonder-dance would content the audience. They yelled themselves hoarse for it; and when, light as air, incredibly swift, the green Dragon-Fly darted back, they outdid themselves in the madness of their welcome. The noise seemed to shake the building.

Only the man in the front row with the iron-grey eyes and iron-hard mouth made no movement or sound of any sort. He merely watched with unchanging intentness the face that gleamed, ashen-white, above the shimmering metallic green tights that clothed the dancer's slim body.

The noise ceased as the wild tarantella proceeded. There fell a deep hush, broken only by the silver notes of a flute played somewhere behind the curtain. The dancer's movements were wholly without sound. The quivering, whirling feet scarcely seemed to touch the floor, it was a dance of inspiration, possessing a strange and irresistible fascination, a weird and meteoric rush, that held the onlookers with bated breath.

It lasted for perhaps two minutes, that intense and trancelike stillness; then, like, a stone flung into glassy depths, a woman's scream rudely shattered it, a piercing, terror-stricken scream that brought the rapt audience back to earth with a shock as the liquid music of the flute suddenly ceased.

"Fire!" cried the voice. "Fire! Fire!"

There was an instant of horrified inaction, and in that instant a tongue of flame shot like a fiery serpent through the closed curtains behind the dancer. In a moment the cry was caught up and repeated in a dozen directions, and even as it went from mouth to mouth the safety-curtain began to descend.

The dancer was forgotten, swept as it were from the minds of the audience as an insect whose life was of no account. From the back of the stage came a roar like the roar of an open furnace. A great wave of heat rushed into the hall, and people turned like terrified, stampeding animals and made for the exits.

The Dragon-Fly still stood behind the footlights poised as if for flight, glancing this way and that, shimmering from head to foot in the awful glare that spread behind the descending curtain. It was evident that retreat behind the scenes was impossible, and in another moment or two that falling curtain would cut off the only way left.

But suddenly, before the dancer's hunted eyes, a man leapt forward. He held up his arms, making himself heard in clear command above the dreadful babel behind him.

"Quick!" he cried. "Jump!"

The wild eyes flashed down at him, wavered, and were caught in his compelling gaze. For a single instant—the last—the trembling, glittering figure seemed to hesitate, then like a streak of lightning leapt straight over the footlights into the outstretched arms.

They caught and held with unwavering iron strength. In the midst of a turmoil indescribable the Dragon-Fly hung quivering on the man's breast, the gauze wings shattered in that close, sustaining grip. The safety-curtain came down with a thud, shutting off the horrors behind, and a loud voice yelled through the building assuring the seething crowd of safety.

But panic had set in. The heat was terrific. People fought and struggled to reach the exits.

The dancer turned in the man's arms and raised a deathly face, gripping his shoulders with clinging, convulsive fingers. Two wild dark eyes looked up to his, desperately afraid, seeking reassurance.

He answered that look briefly with stern composure.

"Be still! I shall save you if I can."

The dancer's heart was beating in mad terror against his own, but at his words it seemed to grow a little calmer. Quiveringly the white lips spoke.

"There is a door—close to the stage—a little door—behind a green curtain—if we could reach it."

"Ah!" the man said.

His eyes went to the stage, from the proximity of which the audience had fled affrighted. He espied the curtain.

Only a few people intervened between him and it, and they were struggling to escape in the opposite direction.

"Quick!" gasped the dancer.

He turned, snatched up his great-coat, and wrapped it about the slight, boyish figure. The great dark eyes that shone out of the small white face thanked him for the action. The clinging hands slipped from his shoulders and clasped his arm. Together they faced the fearful heat that raged behind the safety-curtain.

They reached the small door, gasping. It was almost hidden by green drapery. But the dancer was evidently familiar with it. In a moment it was open. A great burst of smoke met them. The man drew back. But a quick hand closed upon his, drawing him on. He went blindly, feeling as if he were stepping into the heart of a furnace, yet strangely determined to go forward whatever came of it.

The smoke and the heat were frightful, suffocating in their intensity. The roar of the unseen flames seemed to fill the world.

The door swung to behind them. They stood in seething darkness.

But again the small clinging hand pulled upon the man.

"Quick!" the dancer cried again.

Choked and gasping, but resolute still, he followed. They ran through a passage that must have been on the very edge of the vortex of flame, for behind them ere they left it a red light glared.

It showed another door in front of them with which the dancer struggled a moment, then flung open. They burst through it together, and the cold night wind met them like an angel of deliverance.

The man gasped and gasped again, filling his parched lungs with its healing freshness. His companion uttered a strange, high laugh, and dragged him forth into the open.

They emerged into a narrow alley, surrounded by tall houses. The night was dark and wet. The rain pattered upon them as they staggered out into a space that seemed deserted. The sudden quiet after the awful turmoil they had just left was like the silence of death.

The man stood still and wiped the sweat in a dazed fashion from his face. The little dancer reeled back against the wall, panting desperately.

For a space neither moved. Then, terribly, the silence was rent by a crash and the roar of flames. An awful redness leapt across the darkness of the night, revealing each to each.

The dancer stood up suddenly and made an odd little gesture of farewell; then, swiftly, to the man's amazement, turned back towards the door through which they had burst but a few seconds before.

He stared for a moment—only a moment—not believing he saw aright, then with a single stride he reached and roughly seized the small, oddly-draped figure.

He heard a faint cry, and there ensued a sharp struggle against his hold; but he pinioned the thin young arms without ceremony, gripping them fast. In the awful, flickering glare above them his eyes shone downwards, dominant, relentless.

"Are you mad?" he said.

The small dark head was shaken vehemently, with gestures curiously suggestive of an imprisoned insect. It was as if wild wings fluttered against captivity.

And then all in a moment the struggling ceased, and in a low, eager voice the captive began to plead.

"Please, please let me go! You don't know—you don't understand. I came—because—because—you called. But I was wrong—I was wrong to come. You couldn't keep me—you wouldn't keep me—against my will!"

"Do you want to die, then?" the man demanded. "Are you tired of life?"

His eyes still shone piercingly down, but they read but little, for the dancer's were firmly closed against them, even while the dark cropped head nodded a strangely vigorous affirmative.

"Yes, that is it! I am so tired—so tired of life! Don't keep me! Let me go—while I have the strength!" The little, white, sharp-featured face, with its tight-shut eyes and childish, quivering mouth, was painfully pathetic. "Death can't be more dreadful than life," the low voice urged. "If I don't go back—I shall be so sorry afterwards. Why should one live—to suffer?"

It was piteously spoken, so piteously that for a moment the man seemed moved to compassion. His hold relaxed; but when the little form between his hands took swift advantage and strained afresh for freedom he instantly tightened his grip.

"No, No!" he said, harshly. "There are other things in life. You don't know what you are doing. You are not responsible."

The dark eyes opened upon him then—wide, reproachful, mysteriously far-seeing. "I shall not be responsible—if you make me live," said the Dragon-Fly, with the air of one risking a final desperate throw.

It was almost an open challenge, and it was accepted instantly, with grim decision. "Very well. The responsibility is mine," the man said briefly. "Come with me!"

His arm encircled the narrow shoulders. He drew his young companion unresisting from the spot. They left the glare of the furnace behind them, and threaded their way through dark and winding alleys back to the throbbing life of the city thoroughfares, back into the whirl and stress of that human existence which both had nearly quitted—and one had strenuously striven to quit—so short a time before.

CHAPTER II

NOBODY'S BUSINESS

"My name is Merryon," the man said, curtly. "I am a major in the Indian Army—home on leave. Now tell me about yourself!"

He delivered the information in the brief, aggressive fashion that seemed to be characteristic of him, and he looked over the head of his young visitor as he did so, almost as if he made the statement against his will.

The visitor, still clad in his great-coat, crouched like a dog on the hearthrug before the fire in Merryon's sitting-room, and gazed with wide, unblinking eyes into the flames.

After a few moments Merryon's eyes descended to the dark head and surveyed it critically. The collar of his coat was turned up all round it. It was glistening with rain-drops and looked like the head of some small, furry animal.

As if aware of that straight regard, the dancer presently

spoke, without turning or moving an eyelid.

"What you are doesn't matter to any one except yourself. And what I am doesn't matter either. It's just—nobody's business."

"I see," said Merryon.

A faint smile crossed his grim, hard-featured face. He sat down in a low chair near his guest and drew to his side a small table that bore a tray of refreshments. He poured out a glass of wine and held it towards the queer, elfin figure crouched upon his hearth.

The dark eyes suddenly flashed from the fire to his face. "Why do you offer me—that?" the dancer demanded, in a voice that was curiously vibrant, as though it strove to conceal some overwhelming emotion. "Why don't you give me—a man's drink?"

"Because I think this will suit you better," Merryon said; and he spoke with a gentleness that was oddly at variance with the frown that drew his brows.

The dark eyes stared up at him, scared and defiant, for the passage of several seconds; then, very suddenly, the tension went out of the white, pinched face. It screwed up like the face of a hurt child, and all in a moment the little, huddled figure collapsed on the floor at his feet, while sobs—a woman's quivering piteous sobs—filled the silence of the room.

Merryon's own face was a curious mixture of pity and constraint as he set down the glass and stooped forward over the shaking, anguished form.

"Look here, child!" he said, and whatever else was in his voice it certainly held none of the hardness habitual to it. "You're upset—unnerved. Don't cry so! Whatever you've been through, it's over. No one can make you go back. Do you understand? You're free!"

He laid his hand, with the clumsiness of one little accustomed to console, upon the bowed black head.

"Don't!" he said again. "Don't cry so! What the devil does it matter? You're safe enough with me. I'm not the sort of bounder to give you away."

She drew a little nearer to him. "You—you're not a bounder—at all," she assured him between her sobs. "You're just—a gentleman. That's what you are!"

"All right," said Merryon. "Leave off crying!"

He spoke with the same species of awkward kindliness that characterized his actions, and there must have been something strangely comforting in his speech, for the little dancer's tears ceased as abruptly as they had begun. She dashed a trembling hand across her eyes.

"Who's crying?" she said.

He uttered a brief, half-grudging laugh. "That's better. Now drink some wine! Yes, I insist! You must eat something, too. You look half-starved."

She accepted the wine, sitting in an acrobatic attitude on the floor facing him. She drank it, and an odd sparkle of mischief shot up in her great eyes. She surveyed him with an impish expression—much as a grasshopper might survey a toad.

"Are you married?" she inquired, unexpectedly.

"No," said Merryon, shortly. "Why?"

She gave a little laugh that had a catch in it. "I was only thinking that your wife wouldn't like me much. Women are so suspicious."

Merryon turned aside, and began to pour out a drink for himself. There was something strangely elusive about this little creature whom Fortune had flung to him. He wondered what he should do with her. Was she too old for a foundling hospital?

"How old are you?" he asked, abruptly.

She did not answer.

He looked at her, frowning.

"Don't!" she said. "It's ugly. I'm not quite forty. How old are you?"

"What?" said Merryon.

"Not—quite—forty," she said again, with extreme distinctness. "I'm small for my age, I know. But I shall never grow any more now. How old did you say you were?"

Merryon's eyes regarded her piercingly. "I should like the truth," he said, in his short, grim way.

She made a grimace that turned into an impish smile. "Then you must stick to the things that matter," she said. "That is— nobody's business."

He tried to look severe, but very curiously failed. He picked up a plate of sandwiches to mask a momentary confusion, and offered it to her.

Again, with simplicity, she accepted, and there fell a silence between them while she ate, her eyes again upon the fire. Her face, in repose, was the saddest thing he had ever seen. More than ever did she make him think of a child that had been hurt.

She finished her sandwich and sat for a while lost in thought. Merryon leaned back in his chair, watching her. The little, pointed features possessed no beauty, yet they had that which drew the attention irresistibly. The delicate charm of her dancing was somehow expressed in every line. There was fire, too,—a strange, bewitching fire,—behind the thick black lashes.

Very suddenly that fire was turned upon him again. With a swift, darting movement she knelt up in front of him, her clasped hands on his knees.

"Why did you save me just now?" she said. "Why wouldn't you let me die?"

He looked full at her. She vibrated like a winged creature on the verge of taking flight. But her eyes—her eyes sought his with a strange assurance, as though they saw in him a comrade.

"Why did you make me live when I wanted to die?" she insisted. "Is life so desirable? Have you found it so?"

His brows contracted at the last question, even while his mouth curved cynically. "Some people find it so," he said.

"But you?" she said, and there was almost accusation in her voice, "Have the gods been kind to you? Or have they thrown you the dregs—just the dregs?"

The passionate note in the words, subdued though it was, was not to be mistaken. It stirred him oddly, making him see her for the first time as a woman rather than as the fantastic being, half-elf, half-child, whom he had wrested from the very jaws of Death against her will. He leaned slowly forward, marking the deep, deep shadows about her eyes, the vivid red of her lips.

"What do you know about the dregs?" he said.

She beat her hands with a small, fierce movement on his knees, mutely refusing to answer.

"Ah, well," he said, "I don't know why I should answer either. But I will. Yes, I've had dregs—dregs—and nothing but dregs for the last fifteen years."

He spoke with a bitterness that he scarcely attempted to restrain, and the girl at his feet nodded—a wise little feminine nod.

"I knew you had. It comes harder to a man, doesn't it?"

"I don't know why it should," said Merryon, moodily.

"I do," said the Dragon-Fly. "It's because men were made to boss creation. See? You're one of the bosses, you are. You've been led to expect a lot, and because you haven't had it you feel you've been cheated. Life is like that. It's just a thing that mocks at you. I know."

She nodded again, and an odd, will-o'-the-wisp smile flitted over her face.

"You seem to know—something of life," the man said.

She uttered a queer choking laugh. "Life is a big, big swindle," she said. "The only happy people in the world are those who haven't found it out. But you—you say there are other things in life besides suffering. How did you know that if—if you've never had anything but dregs?"

"Ah!" Merryon said. "You have me there."

He was still looking full into those shadowy eyes with a curious, dawning fellowship in his own.

"You have me there," he repeated. "But I do know. I was happy enough once, till—" He stopped.

"Things went wrong?" insinuated the Dragon-Fly, sitting down on her heels in a childish attitude of attention.

"Yes," Merryon admitted, in his sullen fashion. "Things went wrong. I found I was the son of a thief. He's dead now, thank Heaven. But he dragged me under first. I've been at odds with life ever since."

"But a man can start again," said the Dragon-Fly, with her air of worldly wisdom.

"Oh, yes, I did that." Merryon's smile was one of exceeding bitterness. "I enlisted and went to South Africa. I hoped for death, and I won a commission instead."

The girl's eyes shone with interest. "But that was luck!" she said.

"Oh, yes; it was luck of a sort—the damnable, unsatisfactory sort. I entered the Indian Army, and I've got on. But socially I'm practically an outcast. They're polite to me, but they leave me outside. The man who rose from the ranks—the fellow with a shady past—fought shy of by the women, just tolerated by the men, covertly despised by the youngsters—that's the sort of person I am. It galled me once. I'm used to it now."

Merryon's grim voice went into grimmer silence. He was staring sombrely into the fire, almost as if he had forgotten his companion.

There fell a pause; then, "You poor dear!" said the Dragon-Fly, sympathetically. "But I expect you are like that, you know. I expect it's a bit your own fault."

He looked at her in surprise.

"No, I'm not meaning anything nasty," she assured him, with that quick smile of hers whose sweetness he was just beginning to realize. "But after a bad knockout like yours a man naturally looks for trouble. He gets suspicious, and a snub or two does the rest. He isn't taking any more. It's a pity you're not married. A woman would have known how to hold her own, and a bit over—for you."

"I wouldn't ask any woman to share the life I lead," said Merryon, with bitter emphasis. "Not that any woman would if I did. I'm not a ladies' man."

She laughed for the first time, and he started at the sound, for it was one of pure, girlish merriment.

"My! You are modest!" she said. "And yet you don't look it, somehow." She turned her right-hand palm upwards on his knee, tacitly inviting his. "You're a good one to talk of life being worth while, aren't you?" she said.

He accepted the frank invitation, faintly smiling. "Well, I know the good things are there," he said, "though I've missed them."

"You'll marry and be happy yet," she said, with confidence. "But I shouldn't put it off too long if I were you."

He shook his head. His hand still half-consciously grasped hers. "Ask a woman to marry the son of one of the most famous swindlers ever known? I think not," he said. "Why, even you—" His eyes regarded her, comprehended her. He stopped abruptly.

"What about me?" she said.

He hesitated, possessed by an odd embarrassment. The dark eyes were lifted quite openly to his. It came to him that they were accustomed to the stare of multitudes—they met his look so serenely, so impenetrably.

"I don't know how we got on to the subject of my affairs," he said, after a moment. "It seems to me that yours are the most important just now. Aren't you going to tell me anything about them?"

She gave a small, emphatic shake of the head. "I should have been dead by this time if you hadn't interfered," she said. "I haven't got any affairs."

"Then it's up to me to look after you," Merryon said, quietly.

But she shook her head at that more vigorously still. "You look after me!" Her voice trembled on a note of derision. "Sure, you're joking!" she protested. "I've looked after myself ever since I was eight."

"And made a success of it?" Merryon asked.

Her eyes shot swift defiance. "That's nobody's business but my own," she said. "You know what I think of life."

Merryon's hand closed slowly upon hers. "There seems to be a pair of us," he said. "You can't refuse to let me help you—for fellowship's sake."

The red lips trembled suddenly. The dark eyes fell before his for the first time. She spoke almost under her breath. "I'm too old—to take help from a man—like that."

He bent slightly towards her. "What has age to do with it?"

"Everything." Her eyes remained downcast; the hand he held was trying to wriggle free, but he would not suffer it.

"Circumstances alter cases," he said. "I accepted the responsibility when I saved you."

"But you haven't the least idea what to do with me," said the Dragon-Fly, with a forlorn smile. "You ought to have thought of that. You'll be going back to India soon. And I—and I—" She stopped, still stubbornly refusing to meet the man's eyes.

"I am going back next week," Merryon said.

"How fine to be you!" said the Dragon-Fly. "You wouldn't like to take me with you now as—as *valet de chambre*?"

He raised his brows momentarily. Then: "Would you come?" he asked, with a certain roughness, as though he suspected her of trifling.

She raised her eyes suddenly, kindled and eager. "Would I come!" she said, in a tone that said more than words.

"You would?" he said, and laid an abrupt hand on her shoulder. "You would, eh?"

She knelt up swiftly, the coat that enveloped her falling back, displaying the slim, boyish figure, the active, supple limbs. Her breathing came through parted lips.

"As your—your servant—your valet?" she panted.

His rough brows drew together. "My what? Good heavens, no! I could only take you in one capacity."

She started back from his hand. For a moment sheer horror looked out from her eyes. Then, almost in the same instant, they were veiled. She caught her breath, saying no word, only dumbly waiting.

"I could only take you as my wife," he said, still in that half-bantering, half-embarrassed fashion of his. "Will you come?"

She threw back her head and stared at him. "Marry you! What, really? Really?" she questioned, breathlessly.

"Merely for appearances' sake," said Merryon, with grim irony. "The regimental morals are somewhat easily offended, and an outsider like myself can't be too careful."

The girl was still staring at him, as though at some novel specimen of humanity that had never before crossed her path. Suddenly she leaned towards him, looking him full and straight in the eyes.

"What would you do if I said 'Yes'?" she questioned, in a small, tense whisper.

He looked back at her, half-interested, half amused. "Do, urchin? Why, marry you!" he said.

"Really marry me?" she urged. "Not make-believe?"

He stiffened at that. "Do you know what you're saying?" he demanded, sternly.

She sprang to her feet with a wild, startled movement; then, as he remained seated, paused, looking down at him sideways, half-doubtful, half-confiding. "But you can't be in earnest!" she said.

"I am in earnest." He raised his face to her with a certain doggedness, as though challenging her to detect in it aught but honesty. "I may be several kinds of a fool," he said, "but I am in earnest. I'm no great catch, but I'll marry you if you'll have me. I'll protect you, and I'll be good to you. I can't promise to make you happy, of course, but—anyway, I shan't make you miserable."

"But—but—" She still stood before him as though hovering on the edge of flight. Her lips were trembling, her whole form quivering and scintillating in the lamplight. She halted on the words as if uncertain how to proceed.

"What is it?" said Merryon.

And then, quite suddenly, his mood softened. He leaned slowly forward.

"You needn't be afraid of me," he said. "I'm not a heady youngster. I shan't gobble you up."

She laughed at that—a quick, nervous laugh. "And you won't beat me either? Promise!"

He frowned at her. "Beat you! I?"

She nodded several times, faintly smiling. "Yes, you, Mr. Monster! I'm sure you could."

He smiled also, somewhat grimly. "You're wrong, madam. I couldn't beat a child."

"Oh, my!" she said, and threw up her arms with a quivering laugh, dropping his coat in a heap on the floor. "How old do you think this child is?" she questioned, glancing down at him in her sidelong, speculative fashion.

He looked at her hard and straight, looked at the slim young body in its sheath of iridescent green that shimmered with every breath she drew, and very suddenly he rose.

She made a spring backwards, but she was too late. He caught and held her.

"Let me go!" she cried, her face crimson.

"But why?" Merryon's voice fell curt and direct. He held her firmly by the shoulders.

She struggled against him fiercely for a moment, then became suddenly still. "You're not a brute, are you?" she questioned, breathlessly. "You—you'll be good to me? You said so!"

He surveyed her grimly. "Yes, I will be good to you," he said. "But I'm not going to be fooled. Understand? If you marry me, you must play the part. I don't know how old you are. I don't greatly care. All I do care about is that you behave yourself as the wife of a man in my position should. You're old enough to know what that means, I suppose?"

He spoke impressively, but the effect of his words was not quite what he expected. The point of a very red tongue came suddenly from between the red lips, and instantly disappeared.

"That all?" she said. "Oh yes; I think I can do that. I'll try, anyway. And if you're not satisfied—well, you'll have to let me know. See? Now let me go, there's a good man! I don't like the feel of your hands."

He let her go in answer to the pleading of her eyes, and she slipped from his grasp like an eel, caught up the coat at her feet, and wriggled into it.

Then, impishly, she faced him, buttoning it with nimble fingers the while. "This is the garment of respectability," she declared. "It isn't much of a fit, is it? But I shall grow to it in time. Do you know, I believe I'm going to like being your wife?"

"Why?" said Merryon.

She laughed—that laugh of irrepressible gaiety that had surprised him before.

"Oh, just because I shall so love fighting your battles for you," she said. "It'll be grand sport."

"Think so?" said Merryon.

"Oh, you bet!" said the Dragon-Fly, with gay confidence. "Men never know how to fight. They're poor things—men!"

He himself laughed at that—his grim, grudging laugh. "It's a world of fools, Puck," he said.

"Or knaves," said the Dragon-Fly, wisely. And with that she stretched up her arms above her head and laughed again. "Now I know what it feels like," she said, "to have risen from the dead."

CHAPTER III

COMRADES

There came the flash of green wings in the cypresses and a raucous scream of jubilation as the boldest parakeet in the compound flew off with the choicest sweetmeat on the tiffin-table in the veranda. There were always sweets at tiffin in the major's bungalow. Mrs. Merryon loved sweets. She was wont to say that they were the best remedy for homesickness she knew.

Not that she ever was homesick. At least, no one ever suspected such a possibility, for she had a smile and a quip for all, and her laughter was the gayest in the station. She ran out now, half-dressed, from her bedroom, waving a towel at the marauder.

"That comes of being kind-hearted," she declared, in the deep voice that accorded so curiously with the frothy lightness of her personality. "Everyone takes advantage of it, sure."

Her eyes were grey and Irish, and they flashed over the scene dramatically, albeit there was no one to see and admire. For she was strangely captivating, and perhaps it was hardly to be expected that she should be quite unconscious of the fact.

"Much too taking to be good, dear," had been the verdict of the Commissioner's wife when she had first seen little Puck Merryon, the major's bride.

But then the Commissioner's wife, Mrs. Paget, was so severely plain in every way that perhaps she could scarcely be regarded as an impartial judge. She had never flirted with any one, and could not know the joys thereof.

Young Mrs. Merryon, on the other hand, flirted quite openly and very sweetly with every man she met. It was obviously her nature so to do. She had doubtless done it from her cradle, and would probably continue the practice to her grave.

"A born wheedler," the colonel called her; but his wife thought "saucy minx" a more appropriate term, and wondered how Major Merryon could put up with her shameless trifling.

As a matter of fact, Merryon wondered himself sometimes; for she flirted with him more than all in that charming, provocative way of hers, coaxed him, laughed at him, brilliantly eluded him. She would perch daintily on the arm of his chair when he was busy, but if he so much as laid a hand upon her she was gone in a flash like a whirling insect, not to return till he was too absorbed to pay any attention to her. And often as those daring red lips mocked him, they were never offered to his even in jest. Yet was she so finished a coquette that the omission was never obvious. It seemed the most natural thing in the world that she should evade all approach to intimacy. They were comrades—just comrades.

Everyone in the station wanted to know Merryon's bride. People had begun by being distant, but that phase was long past. Puck Merryon had stormed the citadel within a fortnight of her arrival, no one quite knew how. Everyone knew her now. She went everywhere, though never without her husband, who found himself dragged into gaieties for which he had scant liking, and sought after by people who had never seemed aware of him before. She had, in short, become the rage, and so gaily did she revel in her triumph that he could not bring himself to deny her the fruits thereof.

On that particular morning in March he had gone to an early parade without seeing her, for there had been a regimental ball the night before, and she had danced every dance. Dancing seemed her one passion, and to Merryon, who did not dance, the ball had been an unmitigated weariness. He had at last, in sheer boredom, joined a party of bridge-players, with the result that he had not seen much of his young wife throughout the evening.

Returning from the parade-ground, he wondered if he would find her up, and then caught sight of her waving away the marauders in scanty attire on the veranda.

He called a greeting to her, and she instantly vanished into her room. He made his way to the table set in the shade of the cluster-roses, and sat down to await her.

She remained invisible, but her voice at once accosted him. "Good-morning, Billikins! Tell the *khit* you're ready! I shall be out in two shakes."

None but she would have dreamed of bestowing so frivolous an appellation upon the sober Merryon. But from her it came so naturally that Merryon scarcely noticed it. He had been "Billikins" to her throughout the brief three months that had elapsed since their marriage. Of course, Mrs. Paget disapproved, but then Mrs. Paget was Mrs. Paget. She disapproved of everything young and gay.

Merryon gave the required order, and then sat in stolid patience to await his wife's coming. She did not keep him long. Very soon she came lightly out and joined him, an impudent smile on her sallow little face, dancing merriment in her eyes.

"Oh, poor old Billikins!" she said, commiseratingly. "You were bored last night, weren't you? I wonder if I could teach you to dance."

"I wonder," said Merryon.

His eyes dwelt upon her in her fresh white muslin. What a child she looked! Not pretty—no, not pretty; but what a magic smile she had!

She sat down at the table facing him, and leaned her elbows upon it. "I wonder if I could!" she said again, and then broke into her sudden laugh.

"What's the joke?" asked Merryon.

"Oh, nothing!" she said, recovering herself. "It suddenly came over me, that's all—poor old Mother Paget's face, supposing she had seen me last night."

"Didn't she see you last night? I thought you were more or less in the public eye," said Merryon.

"Oh, I meant after the dance," she explained. "I felt sort of wound up and excited after I got back. And I wanted to see if I could still do it. I'm glad to say I can," she ended, with another little laugh.

Her dark eyes shot him a tentative glance. "Can what?" asked Merryon.

"You'll be shocked if I tell you."

"What was it?" he said.

There was insistence in his tone—the insistence by which he had once compelled her to live against her will. Her eyelids fluttered a little as it reached her, but she cocked her small, pointed chin notwithstanding.

"Why should I tell you if I don't want to?" she demanded.

"Why shouldn't you want to?" he said.

The tip of her tongue shot out and in again. "Well, you never took me for a lady, did you?" she said, half-defiantly.

"What was it?" repeated Merryon, sticking to the point.

Again she grimaced at him, but she answered, "Oh, I only—after I'd had my bath—lay on the floor and ran round my head for a bit. It's not a bit difficult, once you've got the knack. But I got thinking of Mrs. Paget—she does amuse me, that woman. Only yesterday she asked me what Puck was short for, and I told her Elizabeth—and then I got laughing so that I had to stop."

Her face was flushed, and she was slightly breathless as she ended, but she stared across the table with brazen determination, like a naughty child expecting a slap.

Merryon's face, however, betrayed neither astonishment nor

disapproval. He even smiled a little as he said, "Perhaps you would like to give me lessons in that also? I've often wondered how it was done."

She smiled back at him with instant and obvious relief.

"No, I shan't do it again. It's not proper. But I will teach you to dance. I'd sooner dance with you than any of 'em."

It was naïvely spoken, so naïvely that Merryon's faint smile turned into something that was almost genial. What a youngster she was! Her freshness was a perpetual source of wonder to him when he remembered whence she had come to him.

"I am quite willing to be taught," he said. "But it must be in strict privacy."

She nodded gaily.

"Of course. You shall have a lesson tonight—when we get back from the Burtons' dinner. I'm real sorry you were bored, Billikins. You shan't be again."

That was her attitude always, half-maternal, half-quizzing, as if something about him amused her; yet always anxious to please him, always ready to set his wishes before her own, so long as he did not attempt to treat her seriously. She had left all that was serious in that other life that had ended with the fall of the safety-curtain on a certain night in England many æons ago. Her personality now was light as gossamer, irresponsible as thistledown. The deeper things of life passed her by. She seemed wholly unaware of them.

"You'll be quite an accomplished dancer by the time everyone comes back from the Hills," she remarked, balancing a fork on one slender brown finger. "We'll have a ball for two—every night."

"We!" said Merryon.

She glanced at him.

"I said 'we.'"

"I know you did." The man's voice had suddenly a dogged ring; he looked across at the vivid, piquant face with the suggestion of a frown between his eyes.

"Don't do that!" she said, lightly. "Never do that, Billikins! It's most unbecoming behaviour. What's the matter?"

"The matter?" he said, slowly. "The matter is that you are going to the Hills for the hot weather with the rest of the women, Puck. I can't keep you here."

She made a rude face at him.

"Preserve me from any cattery in the Hills!" she said. "I'm going to stay with you."

"You can't," said Merryon.

"I can," she said.

He frowned still more.

"Not if I say otherwise, Puck."

She snapped her fingers at him and laughed.

"I am in earnest," Merryon said. "I can't keep you here for the hot weather. It would probably kill you."

"What of that?" she said.

He ignored her frivolity.

"It can't be done," he said. "So you must make the best of it."

"Meaning you don't want me?" she demanded, unexpectedly.

"Not for the hot weather," said Merryon.

She sprang suddenly to her feet.

"I won't go, Billikins!" she declared, fiercely, "I just won't!"

He looked at her, sternly resolute.

"You must go," he said, with unwavering decision.

"You're tired of me! Is that it?" she demanded.

He raised his brows. "You haven't given me much opportunity to be that, have you?" he said.

A great wave of colour went over her face. She put up her hand as though instinctively to shield it.

"I've done my best to—to—to—" She stopped, became piteously silent, and suddenly he saw that she was crying behind the sheltering hand.

He softened almost in spite of himself.

"Come here, Puck!" he said.

She shook her head dumbly.

"Come here!" he repeated.

She came towards him slowly, as if against her will. He reached forward, still seated, and drew her to him.

She trembled at his touch, trembled and started away, yet in the end she yielded.

"Please," she whispered; "please!"

He put his arm round her very gently, yet with determination, making her stand beside him.

"Why don't you want to go to the Hills?" he said.

"I'd be frightened," she murmured.

"Frightened? Why?"

"I don't know," she said, vaguely.

"Yes, but you do know. You must know. Tell me." He spoke gently, but the stubborn note was in his voice and his hold was insistent. "Leave off crying and tell me!"

"I'm not crying," said Puck.

She uncovered her face and looked down at him through tears with a faintly mischievous smile.

"Tell me!" he reiterated. "Is it because you don't like the idea of leaving me?"

Her smile flashed full out upon him on the instant.

"Goodness, no! Whatever made you think that?" she demanded, briskly.

He was momentarily disconcerted, but he recovered himself at once.

"Then what is your objection to going?" he asked.

She turned and sat down conversationally on the corner of the table.

"Well, you know, Billikins, it's like this. When I married you—I did it out of pity. See? I was sorry for you. You seemed such a poor, helpless sort of creature. And I thought being married to me might help to improve your position a bit. You see my point, Billikins?"

"Oh, quite," he said. "Please go on!"

She went on, with butterfly gaiety.

"I worked hard—really hard—to get you out of your bog. It was a horrid deep one, wasn't it, Billikins? My! You were floundering! But I've pulled you out of it and dragged you up the bank a bit. You don't get sniffed at anything like you used, do you, Billikins? But I daren't leave you yet—I honestly daren't. You'd slip right back again directly my back was turned. And I should have the pleasure of starting the business all over again. I couldn't face it, my dear. It would be too disheartening."

"I see," said Merryon. There was just the suspicion of a smile among the rugged lines of his face. "Yes, I see your point. But I can show you another if you'll listen."

He was holding her two hands as she sat, as though he feared an attempt to escape. For though Puck sat quite still, it was with the stillness of a trapped creature that waits upon opportunity.

"Will you listen?" he said.

She nodded.

It was not an encouraging nod, but he proceeded.

"All the women go to the Hills for the hot weather. It's unspeakable here. No white woman could stand it. And we men get leave by turns to join them. There is nothing doing down here, no social round whatever. It's just stark duty. I can't lose much social status that way. It will serve my turn much better if you go up with the other women and continue to hold your own there. Not that I care a rap," he added, with masculine tactlessness. "I am no longer susceptible to snubs."

"Then I shan't go," she said at once, beginning to swing a restless foot.

"Yes, but you will go," he said. "I wish it."

"You want to get rid of me," said Puck, looking over his head with the eyes of a troubled child.

Merryon was silent. He was watching her with a kind of speculative curiosity. His hands were still locked upon hers.

Slowly her eyes came down to his.

"Billikins," she said, "let me stay down for a little!" Her lips were quivering. She kicked his chair agitatedly. "I don't want to go," she said, dismally. "Let me stay—anyhow—till I get ill!"

"No," Merryon said. "It can't be done, child. I can't risk that. Besides, there'd be no one to look after you."

She slipped to her feet in a flare of indignation. "You're a pig, Billikins! You're a pig!" she cried, and tore her hands free. "I've a good mind to run away from you and never come back. It's what you deserve, and what you'll get, if you aren't careful!"

She was gone with the words—gone like a flashing insect disturbing the silence for a moment, and leaving a deeper silence behind.

Merryon looked after her for a second or two, and then philosophically continued his meal. But the slight frown remained between his brows. The veranda seemed empty and colourless now that she was gone.

CHAPTER IV

FRIENDS

The Burtons' dinner-party was a very cheerful affair. The Burtons were young and newly married, and they liked to gather round them all the youth and gaiety of the station. It was for that reason that Puck's presence had been secured, for she was the life of every gathering; and her husband had been included in the invitation simply and solely because from the very outset she had refused to go anywhere without him. It was the only item of her behaviour of which worthy Mrs. Paget could conscientiously approve.

As a matter of fact Merryon had not the smallest desire to go, but he would not say so; and all through the evening he sat and watched his young wife with a curious hunger at his heart. He hated to think that he had hurt her.

There was no sign of depression about Puck, however, and he alone noticed that she never once glanced in his direction. She kept everyone up to a pitch of frivolity that certainly none would have attained without her, and an odd feeling began to stir in Merryon, a sensation of jealousy such as he had never before experienced. They seemed to forget, all of them, that this flashing, brilliant creature was his.

She seemed to have forgotten it also. Or was it only that deep-seated, inimitable coquetry of hers that prompted her thus to ignore him?

He could not decide; but throughout the evening the determination grew in him to make this one point clear to her. Trifle as she might, she must be made to understand that she belonged to him, and him alone. Comrades they might be, but he held a vested right in her, whether he chose to assert it or not.

They returned at length to their little gimcrack bungalow—the Match-box, as Puck called it—on foot under a blaze of stars. The distance was not great, and Puck despised rickshaws.

She flitted by his side in her airy way, chatting inconsequently, not troubling about response, as elusive as a fairy and—the man felt it in the rising fever of his veins—as maddeningly attractive.

They reached the bungalow. She went up the steps to the rose-twined veranda as though she floated on wings of gossamer. "The roses are all asleep, Billikins," she said. "They look like alabaster, don't they?"

She caught a cluster to her and held it against her cheek for a moment.

Merryon was close behind her. She seemed to realize his nearness quite suddenly, for she let the flowers go abruptly and flitted on.

He followed her till, at the farther end of the veranda, she turned and faced him. "Goodnight, Billikins," she said, lightly.

"What about that dancing-lesson?" he said.

She threw up her arms above her head with a curious gesture. They gleamed transparently white in the starlight. Her eyes shone like fire-flies.

"I thought you preferred dancing by yourself," she retorted.

"Why?" he said.

She laughed a soft, provocative laugh, and suddenly, without any warning, the cloak had fallen from her shoulders and she was dancing. There in the starlight, white-robed and wonderful, she danced as, it seemed to the man's fascinated senses, no human had ever danced before. She was like a white flame—a darting, fiery essence, soundless, all-absorbing, all-entrancing.

He watched her with pent breath, bound by the magic of her, caught, as it were, into the innermost circle of her being, burning in answer to her fire, yet so curiously enthralled as to be scarcely aware of the ever-mounting, ever-spreading heat. She was like a mocking spirit, a will-o'-the-wisp, luring him, luring him—whither?

The dance quickened, became a passionate whirl, so that suddenly he seemed to see a bright-winged insect caught in an endless web and battling for freedom. He almost saw the silvery strands of that web floating like gossamer in the starlight.

And then, with well-nigh miraculous suddenness, the struggle was over and the insect had darted free. He saw her flash away, and found the veranda empty.

Her cloak lay at his feet. He stooped with an odd sense of giddiness and picked it up. A fragrance of roses came to him with the touch of it, and for an instant he caught it up to his face. The sweetness seemed to intoxicate him.

There came a light, inconsequent laugh; sharply he turned. She had opened the window of his smoking-den and was standing in the entrance with impudent merriment in her eyes. There was triumph also in her pose—a triumph that sent a swirl of hot passion through him. He flung aside the cloak and strode towards her.

But she was gone on the instant, gone with a tinkle of maddening laughter. He blundered into the darkness of an empty room. But he was not the man to suffer defeat tamely. Momentarily baffled, he paused to light a lamp; then went from room to room of the little bungalow, locking each door that she might not elude him a second time. His blood was on fire, and he meant to find her.

In the end he came upon her wholly unexpectedly, standing on the veranda amongst the twining roses. She seemed to be awaiting him, though she made no movement towards him as he approached.

"Good-night, Billikins," she said, her voice very small and humble.

He came to her without haste, realizing that she had given the game into his hands. She did not shrink from him, but she raised an appealing face. And oddly the man's heart smote him. She looked so pathetically small and childish standing there.

But the blood was still running fiercely in his veins, and that momentary twinge did not cool him. Child she might be, but she had played with fire, and she alone was responsible for the conflagration that she had started.

He drew near to her; he took her, unresisting, into his arms.

She cowered down, hiding her face away from him. "Don't, Billikins! Please—please, Billikins!" she begged, incoherently. "You promised—you promised—"

"What did I promise?" he said.

"That you wouldn't—wouldn't"—she spoke breathlessly, for his hold was tightening upon her—"gobble me up," she ended, with a painful little laugh.

"I see." Merryon's voice was deep and low. "And you meantime are at liberty to play any fool game you like with me. Is that it?"

She was quivering from head to foot. She did not lift her face. "It wasn't—a fool game," she protested. "I did it because—because—you were so horrid this morning, so—so cold-blooded. And I—and I—wanted to see if—I could make you care."

"Make me care!" Merryon said the words over oddly to himself; and then, still fast holding her, he began to feel for the face that was so strenuously hidden from him.

She resisted him desperately. "Let me go!" she begged, piteously. "I'll be so good, Billikins. I'll go to the Hills. I'll do anything you like. Only let me go now! Billikins!"

She cried out sharply, for he had overcome her resistance by quiet force, had turned her white face up to his own.

"I am not cold-blooded tonight, Puck," he said. "Whatever you are—child or woman—gutter-snipe or angel—you are mine, all mine. And—I want you!"

The deep note vibrated in his voice; he stooped over her.

But she flung herself back over his arm, striving desperately to avoid him. "No—no—no!" she cried, wildly. "You mustn't, Billikins! Don't kiss me! Don't kiss me!"

She threw up a desperate hand, covering his mouth. "Don't—oh, don't!" she entreated, brokenly.

But the fire she had kindled she was powerless to quench. He would not be frustrated. He caught her hand away. He held her to his heart. He kissed the red lips hotly, with the savage freedom of a nature long restrained.

"Who has a greater right?" he said, with fiery exultation.

She did not answer him. But at the first touch of his lips upon her own she resisted no longer, only broke into agonized tears.

And suddenly Merryon came to himself—was furiously, overwhelmingly ashamed.

"God forgive me!" he said, and let her go.

She tottered a little, covering her face with her hands, sobbing like a hurt child. But she did not try to run away.

He flung round upon his heel and paced the veranda in fierce discomfort. Beast that he was—brute beast to have hurt her so! That piteous sobbing was more than he could bear.

Suddenly he turned back to her, came and stood beside her. "Puck—Puck, child!" he said.

His voice was soft and very urgent. He touched the bent, dark head with a hesitating caress.

She started away from him with a gasp of dismay; but he checked her.

"No, don't!" he said. "It's all right, dear. I'm not such a brute as I seem. Don't be afraid of me!"

There was more of pleading in his voice than he knew. She raised her head suddenly, and looked at him as if puzzled.

He pulled out his handkerchief and dabbed her wet cheeks with clumsy tenderness. "It's all right," he said again. "Don't cry! I hate to see you cry."

She gazed at him, still doubtful, still sobbing a little. "Oh, Billikins!" she said, tremulously, "why did you?"

"I don't know," he said. "I was mad. It was your own fault, in a way. You don't seem to realize that I'm as human as the rest of the world. But I don't defend myself. I was an infernal brute to let myself go like that."

"Oh, no, you weren't, Billikins!" Quite unexpectedly she answered him. "You couldn't help it. Men are like that. And I'm glad you're human. But—but"—she faltered a little—"I want to feel that you're safe, too. I've always felt—ever since I jumped into your arms that night—that you—that you were on the right side of the safety-curtain. You are, aren't you? Oh, please say you are! But I know you are." She held out her hands to him with a quivering gesture of confidence. "If you'll forgive me for—for fooling you," she said, "I'll forgive you—for being fooled. That's a fair offer, isn't it? Don't let's think any more about it!" Her rainbow smile transformed her face, but her eyes sought his anxiously.

He took the hands, but he did not attempt to draw her nearer. "Puck!" he said.

"What is it?" she whispered, trembling.

"Don't!" he said. "I won't hurt you. I wouldn't hurt a hair of your head. But, child, wouldn't it be safer—easier for both of us—if—if we lived together, instead of apart?"

He spoke almost under his breath. There was no hint of mastery about him at that moment, only a gentleness that pleaded with her as with a frightened child.

And Puck went nearer to him on the instant, as it were instinctively, almost involuntarily. "P'r'aps some day, Billikins!" she said, with a little, quivering laugh. "But not yet—not if I've got to go to the Hills away from you."

"When I follow you to the Hills, then," he said.

She freed one hand and, reaching up, lightly stroked his cheek. "P'r'aps, Billikins!" she said again. "But—you'll have to be awfully patient with me, because—because—" She paused, agitatedly; then went yet a little nearer to him. "You will be kind to me, won't you?" she pleaded.

He put his arm about her. "Always, dear," he said.

She raised her face. She was still trembling, but her action was one of resolute confidence. "Then let's be friends, Billikins!" she said.

It was a tacit invitation. He bent and gravely kissed her.

Her lips returned his kiss shyly, quiveringly. "You're the nicest man I ever met, Billikins," she said. "Good-night!"

She slipped from his encircling arm and was gone.

The man stood motionless where she had left him, wondering at himself, at her, at the whole rocking universe. She had kindled the Magic Fire in him indeed! His whole being was aglow. And yet—and yet—she had had her way with him. He had let her go.

Wherefore? Wherefore? The hot blood dinned in his ears. His hands clenched. And from very deep within him the answer came. Because he loved her.

CHAPTER V

THE WOMAN

Summer in the Plains! Pitiless, burning summer!

All day a blinding blaze of sun beat upon the wooden roof, forced a way through the shaded windows, lay like a blasting spell upon the parched compound. The cluster-roses had shrivelled and died long since. Their brown leaves still clung to the veranda and rattled desolately with a dry, scaly sound in the burning wind of dawn.

The green parakeets had ceased to look for sweets on the veranda. Nothing dainty ever made its appearance there. The Englishman who came and went with such grim endurance offered them no temptations.

Sometimes he spent the night on a *charpoy* on the veranda, lying motionless, though often sleepless, through the breathless, dragging hours. There had been sickness among the officers and Merryon, who was never sick, was doing the work of three men. He did it doggedly, with the stubborn determination characteristic of him; not cheerfully—no one ever accused Merryon of being cheerful—but efficiently and uncomplainingly. Other men cursed the heat, but he never took the trouble. He needed all his energies for what he had to do.

His own chance of leave had become very remote. There was so much sick leave that he could not be spared. Over that, also, he made no complaint. It was useless to grumble at the inevitable. There was not a man in the mess who could not be spared more easily than he.

For he was indomitable, unfailing, always fulfilling his duties with machine-like regularity, stern, impenetrable, hard as granite.

As to what lay behind that hardness, no one ever troubled to inquire. They took him for granted, much as if he had been a well-oiled engine guaranteed to surmount all obstacles. How he did it was nobody's business but his own. If he suffered in that appalling heat as other men suffered, no one knew of it. If he grew a little grimmer and a little gaunter, no one noticed. Everyone knew that whatever happened to others, he at least would hold on. Everyone described him as "hard as nails."

Each day seemed more intolerable than the last, each night a perceptible narrowing of the fiery circle in which they lived. They seemed to be drawing towards a culminating horror that grew hourly more palpable, more monstrously menacing—a horror that drained their strength even from afar.

"It's going to kill us this time," declared little Robey, the youngest subaltern, to whom the nights were a torment unspeakable. He had been within an ace of heat apoplexy more than once, and his nerves were stretched almost to breaking-point.

But Merryon went doggedly on, hewing his unswerving way through all. The monsoon was drawing near, and the whole tortured earth seemed to be waiting in dumb expectation.

Night after night a glassy moon came up, shining, immense and awful, through a thick haze of heat. Night after night Merryon lay on his veranda, smoking his pipe in stark endurance while the dreadful hours crept by. Sometimes he held a letter from his wife hard clenched in one powerful hand. She wrote to him frequently—short, airy epistles, wholly inconsequent, often provocatively meagre.

"There is a Captain Silvester here," she wrote once; "such a bounder. But he is literally the only man who can dance in the station. So what would you? Poor Mrs. Paget is so shocked!"

Feathery hints of this description were by no means unusual, but though Merryon sometimes frowned over them, they did not make him uneasy. His will-o'-the-wisp might beckon, but she would never allow herself to be caught. She never spoke of love in her letters, always ending demurely, "Yours sincerely, Puck." But now and then there was a small cross scratched impulsively underneath the name, and the letters that bore this token accompanied Merryon through his inferno whithersoever he went.

There came at last a night of terrible heat, when it seemed as if the world itself must burst into flames. A heavy storm rolled up, roared overhead for a space like a caged monster, and sullenly rolled away, without a single drop of rain to ease the awful tension of waiting that possessed all things.

Merryon left the mess early, tramping back over the dusty road, convinced that the downpour for which they all yearned was at hand. There was no moonlight that night, only a hot blackness, illumined now and then by a brilliant dart of lightning that shocked the senses and left behind a void indescribable, a darkness that could be felt. There was something savage in the atmosphere, something primitive and passionate that seemed to force itself upon him even against his will. His pulses were strung to a tropical intensity that made him aware of the man's blood in him, racing at fever heat through veins that felt swollen to bursting.

He entered his bungalow and flung off his clothes, took a plunge in a bath of tepid water, from which he emerged with a pricking sensation all over him that made the lightest touch a torture, and finally, keyed up to a pitch of sensitiveness that excited his own contempt, he pulled on some pyjamas and went out to his *charpoy* on the veranda.

He dismissed the *punkah* coolie, feeling his presence to be intolerable, and threw himself down with his coat flung open. The oppression of the atmosphere was as though a red-hot lid were being forced down upon the tortured earth. The blackness beyond the veranda was like a solid wall. Sleep was out of the question. He could not smoke. It was an effort even to breathe. He could only lie in torment and wait—and wait.

The flashes of lightning had become less frequent. A kind of waking dream began to move in his brain. A figure gradually grew upon that screen of darkness—an elf-like thing, intangible, transparent, a quivering, shadowy image, remote as the dawn.

Wide-eyed, he watched the vision, his pulses beating with a mad longing so fierce as to be utterly beyond his own control. It was as though he had drunk strong wine and had somehow slipped the leash of ordinary convention. The savagery of the night, the tropical intensity of it, had got into him. Half-naked, wholly primitive, he lay and waited—and waited.

For a while the vision hung before him, tantalizing him, maddening him, eluding him. Then came a flash of lightning, and it was gone.

He started up on the *charpoy*, every nerve tense as stretched wire.

"Come back!" he cried, hoarsely. "Come back!"

Again the lightning streaked the darkness.

There came a burst of thunder, and suddenly, through it and above it, he heard the far-distant roar of rain. He sprang to his feet. It was coming.

The seconds throbbed away. Something was moving in the compound, a subtle, awful Something. The trees and bushes quivered before it, the cluster-roses rattled their dead leaves wildly. But the man stood motionless in the light that fell across the veranda from the open window of his room, watching with eyes that shone with a fierce and glaring intensity for the return of his vision.

The fevered blood was hammering at his temples. For the

moment he was scarcely sane. The fearful strain of the past few weeks that had overwhelmed less hardy men had wrought upon him in a fashion more subtle but none the less compelling. They had been stricken down, whereas he had been strung to a pitch where bodily suffering had almost ceased to count. He had grown used to the torment, and now in this supreme moment it tore from him his civilization, but his physical strength remained untouched. He stood alert and ready, like a beast in a cage, waiting for whatever the gods might deign to throw him.

The tumult beyond that wall of blackness grew. It became a swirling uproar. The rose-vines were whipped from the veranda and flung writhing in all directions. The trees in the compound strove like terrified creatures in the grip of a giant. The heat of the blast was like tongues of flame blown from an immense furnace. Merryon's whole body seemed to be wrapped in fire. With a fierce movement, he stripped the coat from him and flung it into the room behind him. He was alone save for the devils that raged in that pandemonium. What did it matter how he met them?

And then, with the suddenness of a stupendous weight dropped from heaven, came rain, rain in torrents and billows, rain solid as the volume of Niagara, a crushing mighty force.

The tempest shrieked through the compound. The lightning glimmered, leapt, became continuous. The night was an inferno of thunder and violence.

And suddenly out of the inferno, out of the awful strife of elements, out of that frightful rainfall, there came—a woman!

CHAPTER VI

LOVERS

She came haltingly, clinging with both hands to the rail of the veranda, her white face staring upwards in terror and instinctive appeal. She was like an insect dragging itself away from destruction, with drenched and battered wings.

He saw her coming and stiffened. It was his vision returned to him, but till she came within reach of him he was afraid to move. He stood upright against the wall, every mad instinct of his blood fiercely awake and clamouring.

The noise and wind increased. It swirled along the veranda. She seemed afraid to quit her hold of the balustrade lest she should be swept away. But still she drew nearer to the lighted window, and at last, with desperate resolution, she tore herself free and sprang for shelter.

In that instant the man also sprang. He caught her in arms that almost expected to clasp emptiness, arms that crushed in a savage ecstasy of possession at the actual contact with a creature of flesh and blood. In the same moment the lamp in the room behind him flared up and went out.

There arose a frightened crying from his breast. For a few moments she fought like a mad thing for freedom. He felt her teeth set in his arm, and laughed aloud. Then very suddenly her struggles ceased. He became aware of a change in her. She gave her whole weight into his arms, and lay palpitating against his heart.

By the awful glare of the lightning he found her face uplifted to his. She was laughing, too, but in her eyes was such a passion of love as he had never looked upon before. In that moment he knew that she was his—wholly, completely, irrevocably his. And, stooping, he kissed the upturned lips with the fierce exultation of the conqueror.

Her arms slipped round his neck. She abandoned herself wholly to him. She gave him worship for worship, passion for passion.

Later, he awoke to the fact that she was drenched from head to foot. He drew her into his room and shut the window against the driving blast. She clung to him still.

"Isn't it dreadful?" she said, shuddering. "It's just as if Something Big is trying to get between us."

He closed the shutter also, and groped for matches. She accompanied him on his search, for she would not lose touch with him for a moment.

The lamp flared on her white, childish face, showing him wild joy and horror strangely mingled. Her great eyes laughed up at him.

"Billikins, darling! You aren't very decent, are you? I'm not decent either, Billikins. I'd like to take off all my clothes and dance on my head."

He laughed grimly. "You will certainly have to undress—the sooner the better."

She spread out her hands. "But I've nothing to wear, Billikins, nothing but what I've got on. I didn't know it was going to rain so. You'll have to lend me a suit of pyjamas, dear, while I get my things dried. You see"—she halted a little—"I came away in rather a hurry. I—was bored."

Merryon, oddly sobered by her utter dependence upon him, turned aside and foraged for brandy. She came close to him while he poured it out.

"It isn't for me, is it? I couldn't drink it, darling. I shouldn't know what was happening for the next twenty-four hours if I did."

"It doesn't matter whether you do or not," he said. "I shall be here to look after you."

She laughed at that, a little quivering laugh of sheer content. Her cheek was against his shoulder. "Live for ever, O king!" she said, and softly kissed it.

Then she caught sight of something on the arm below. "Oh, darling, did I do that?" she cried, in distress.

He put the arm about her. "It doesn't matter. I don't feel it," he said. "I've got you."

She lifted her lips to his again. "Billikins, darling, I didn't know it was you—at first, not till I heard you laugh. I'd rather die than hurt you. You know it, don't you?"

"Of course I know it," he said.

He caught her to him passionately for a moment, then slowly relaxed his hold. "Drink this, like a good child," he said, "and then you must get to bed. You are wet to the skin."

"I know I am," she said, "but I don't mind."

"I mind for you," he said.

She laughed up at him, her eyes like stars. "I was lucky to get in when I did," she said. "Wasn't the heat dreadful—and the lightning? I ran all the way from the station. I was just terrified at it all. But I kept thinking of you, dear—of you, and how—and how you'd kissed me that night when I was such a little idiot as to cry. Must I really drink it, Billikins? Ah, well, just to please you—anything to please you. But you must have one little sip first. Yes, darling, just one. That's to please your silly little wife, who wants to share everything with you now. There's my own boy! Now I'll drink every drop—every drop."

She began to drink, standing in the circle of his arm; then looked up at him with a quick grimace. "It's powerful strong, dear. You'll have to put me to bed double quick after this, or I shall be standing on my head in earnest."

He laughed a little. She leaned back against him.

"Yes, I know, darling. You're a man that likes to manage,

aren't you? Well, you can manage me and all that is mine for the rest of my natural life. I'm never going to leave you again, Billikins. That's understood, is it?"

His face sobered. "What possessed you to come back to this damnable place?" he said.

She laughed against his shoulder. "Now, Billikins, don't you start asking silly questions. I'll tell you as much as it's good for you to know all in good time. I came mainly because I wanted to. And that's the reason why I'm going to stay. See?"

She reached up an audacious finger and smoothed the faint frown from his forehead with her sunny, provocative smile.

"It'll have to be a joint management," she said. "There are so many things you mustn't do. Now, darling, I've finished the brandy to please you. So suppose you look out your prettiest suit of pyjamas, and I'll try and get into them." She broke into a giddy little laugh. "What would Mrs. Paget say? Can't you see her face? I can!"

She stopped suddenly, struck dumb by a terrible blast of wind that shook the bungalow to its foundations.

"Just hark to the wind and the rain, Billikins!" she whispered, as it swirled on. "Did you ever hear anything so awful? It's as if—as if God were very furious—about something. Do you think He is, dear? Do you?" She pressed close to him with white, pleading face upraised. "Do you believe in God, Billikins? Honestly now!"

The man hesitated, holding her fast in his arms, seeing only the quivering, childish mouth and beseeching eyes.

"You don't, do you?" she said. "I don't myself, Billikins. I think He's just a myth. Or anyhow—if He's there at all—He doesn't bother about the people who were born on the wrong side of the safety-curtain. There, darling! Kiss me once more—I love your kisses—I love them! And now go! Yes—yes, you must go—just while I make myself respectable. Yes, but you can leave the door ajar, dear heart! I want to feel you close at hand. I am yours—till I die—king and master!"

Her eyes were brimming with tears; he thought her overwrought and weary, and passed them by in silence.

And so through that night of wonder, of violence, and of storm, she lay against his heart, her arms wound about his neck with a closeness which even sleep could not relax.

Out of the storm she had come to him, like a driven bird seeking refuge; and through the fury of the storm he held her, compassing her with the fire of his passion.

"I am safe now," she murmured once, when he thought her sleeping. "I am quite—quite safe."

And he, fancying the raging of the storm had disturbed her, made hushing answer, "Quite safe, wife of my heart."

She trembled a little, and nestled closer to his breast.

CHAPTER VII

THE HONEYMOON

"You can't mean to let your wife stay here!" ejaculated the colonel, sharply. "You wouldn't do anything so mad!"

Merryon's hard mouth took a sterner downward curve. "My wife refuses to leave me, sir," he said.

"Good heavens above, Merryon!" The colonel's voice held a species of irritated derision. "Do you tell me you can't manage—a—a piece of thistledown like that?"

Merryon was silent, grimly, implacably silent. Plainly he had no intention of making such an admission.

"It's madness—criminal madness!" Colonel Davenant looked at him aggressively, obviously longing to pierce that stubborn calm with which Merryon had so long withstood the world.

But Merryon remained unmoved, though deep in his private soul he knew that the colonel was right, knew that he had decided upon a course of action that involved a risk which he dreaded to contemplate.

"Oh, look here, Merryon!" The colonel lost his temper after his own precipitate fashion. "Don't be such a confounded fool! Take a fortnight's leave—I can't spare you longer—and go back to the Hills with her! Make her settle down with my wife at Shamkura! Tell her you'll beat her if she doesn't!"

Merryon's grim face softened a little. "Thank you very much, sir! But you can't spare me even for so long. Moreover, that form of punishment wouldn't scare her. So, you see, it would come to the same thing in the end. She is determined to face what I face for the present."

"And you're determined to let her!" growled the colonel.

Merryon shrugged his shoulders.

"You'll probably lose her," the colonel persisted, gnawing

fiercely at his moustache. "Have you considered that?"

"I've considered everything," Merryon said, rather heavily. "But she came to me—through that inferno. I can't send her away again. She wouldn't go."

Colonel Davenant swore under his breath. "Let me talk to her!" he said, after a moment.

The ghost of a smile touched Merryon's face. "It's no good, sir. You can talk. You won't make any impression."

"But it's practically a matter of life and death, man!" insisted the colonel. "You can't afford any silly sentiment in an affair like this."

"I am not sentimental," Merryon said, and his lips twitched a little with the words. "But all the same, since she has set her heart on staying, she shall stay. I have promised that she shall."

"You are mad," the colonel declared. "Just think a minute! Think what your feelings will be if she dies!"

"I have thought, sir." The dogged note was in Merryon's voice again. His face was a mask of impenetrability. "If she dies, I shall at least have the satisfaction of knowing that I made her happy first."

It was his last word on the subject. He departed, leaving the colonel fuming.

That evening the latter called upon Mrs. Merryon. He found her sitting on her husband's knee smoking a Turkish cigarette, and though she abandoned this unconventional attitude to receive her visitor, he had a distinct impression that the two were in subtle communion throughout his stay.

"It's so very nice of you to take the trouble," she said, in her charming way, when he had made his most urgent representations. "But really it's much better for me to be with my husband here. I stayed at Shamkura just as long as I could possibly bear it, and then I just had to come back here. I don't think I shall get ill—really. And if I do"—she made a little foreign gesture of the hands—"I'll nurse myself."

As Merryon had foretold, it was useless to argue with her. She dismissed all argument with airy unreason. But yet the colonel could not find it in his heart to be angry with her. He was very angry with Merryon, so angry that for a whole fortnight he scarcely spoke to him.

But when the end of the fortnight came, and with it the first break in the rains, little Mrs. Merryon went smiling forth and returned his call.

"Are you still being cross with Billikins?" she asked him,

while her hand lay engagingly in his. "Because it's really not his fault, you know. If he sent me to Kamchatka, I should still come back."

"You wouldn't if you belonged to me," said Colonel Davenant, with a grudging smile.

She laughed and shook her head. "Perhaps I shouldn't—not unless I loved you as dearly as I love Billikins. But I think you needn't be cross about it. I'm quite well. If you don't believe me, you can look at my tongue."

She shot it out impudently, still laughing. And the colonel suddenly and paternally patted her cheek.

"You're a very naughty girl," he said. "But I suppose we shall have to make the best of you. Only, for Heaven's sake, don't go and get ill on the quiet! If you begin to feel queer, send for the doctor at the outset!"

He abandoned his attitude of disapproval towards Merryon after that interview, realizing possibly its injustice. He even declared in a letter to his wife that Mrs. Merryon was an engaging chit, with a will of her own that threatened to rule them all! Mrs. Davenant pursed her lips somewhat over the assertion, and remarked that Major Merryon's wife was plainly more at home with men than women. Captain Silvester was so openly out of temper over her absence that it was evident she had been "leading him on with utter heartlessness," and now, it seemed, she meant to have the whole mess at her beck and call.

As a matter of fact, Puck saw much more of the mess than she desired. It became the fashion among the younger officers to drop into the Merryons' bungalow at the end of the evening. Amusements were scarce, and Puck was a vigorous antidote to boredom. She always sparkled in society, and she was too sweet-natured to snub "the boys," as she called them. The smile of welcome was ever ready on her little, thin white face, the quick jest on her nimble tongue.

"We mustn't be piggy just because we are happy," she said to her husband once. "How are they to know we are having our honeymoon?" And then she nestled close to him, whispering, "It's quite the best honeymoon any woman ever had."

To which he could make but the one reply, pressing her to his heart and kissing the red lips that mocked so merrily when the world was looking on.

She had become the hub of his existence, and day by day he watched her anxiously, grasping his happiness with a feeling that it was too great to last.

The rains set in in earnest, and the reek of the Plains rose like an evil miasma to the turbid heavens. The atmosphere was as the interior of a steaming cauldron. Great toadstools spread like a loathsome disease over the compound. Fever was rife in the camp. Mosquitoes buzzed incessantly everywhere, and rats began to take refuge in the bungalow. Puck was privately terrified at rats, but she smothered her terror in her husband's presence and maintained a smiling front. They laid down poison for the rats, who died horribly in inaccessible places, making her wonder if they were not almost preferable alive. And then one night she discovered a small snake coiled in a corner of her bedroom.

She fled to Merryon in horror, and he and the *khitmutgar* slew the creature. But Puck's nerves were on edge from that day forward. She went through agonies of cold fear whenever she was left alone, and she feverishly encouraged the subalterns to visit her during her husband's absence on duty.

He raised no objection till he one day returned unexpectedly to find her dancing a hornpipe for the benefit of a small, admiring crowd to whom she had been administering tea.

She sprang like a child to meet him at his entrance, declaring the entertainment at an end; and the crowd soon melted away.

Then, somewhat grimly, Merryon took his wife to task.

She sat on the arm of his chair with her arms round his neck, swinging one leg while she listened. She was very docile, punctuating his remarks with soft kisses dropped inconsequently on the top of his head. When he ended, she slipped cosily down upon his knee and promised to be good.

It was not a very serious promise, and it was plainly proffered in a spirit of propitiation. Merryon pursued the matter no further, but he was vaguely dissatisfied. He had a feeling that she regarded his objections as the outcome of eccentric prudishness, or at the best an unreasonable fit of jealousy. She smoothed him down as though he had been a spoilt child, her own attitude supremely unabashed; and though he could not be angry with her, an uneasy sense of doubt pressed upon him. Utterly his own as he knew her to be, yet dimly, intangibly, he began to wonder what her outlook on life could be, how she regarded the tie that bound them. It was impossible to reason seriously with her. She floated out of his reach at the first touch.

So that curious honeymoon of theirs continued, love and passion crudely mingled, union without knowledge, flaming worship and blind possession.

"You are happy?" Merryon asked her once.

To which she made ardent answer, "Always happy in your arms, O king."

And Merryon was happy also, though, looking back later, it seemed to him that he snatched his happiness on the very edge of the pit, and that even at the time he must have been half-aware of it.

When, a month after her coming, the scourge of the Plains caught her, as was inevitable, he felt as if his new-found kingdom had begun already to depart from him.

For a few days Puck was seriously ill with malaria. She came through it with marvellous resolution, nursed by Merryon and his bearer, the general factotum of the establishment.

But it left her painfully weak and thin, and the colonel became again furiously insistent that she should leave the Plains till the rains were over.

Merryon, curiously enough, did not insist. Only one evening he took the little wasted body into his arms and begged her—actually begged her—to consent to go.

"I shall be with you for the first fortnight," he said. "It won't be more than a six-weeks' separation."

"Six weeks!" she protested, piteously.

"Perhaps less," he said. "I may be able to come to you for a day or two in the middle. Say you will go—and stay, sweetheart! Set my mind at rest!"

"But, darling, you may be ill. A thousand things may happen. And I couldn't go back to Shamkura. I couldn't!" said Puck, almost crying, clinging fast around his neck.

"But why not?" he questioned, gently. "Weren't they kind to you there? Weren't you happy?"

She clung faster. "Happy, Billikins! With that hateful Captain Silvester lying in wait to—to make love to me! I didn't tell you before. But that—that was why I left."

He frowned above her head. "You ought to have told me before, Puck."

She trembled in his arms. "It didn't seem to matter when once I'd got away; and I knew it would only make you cross."

"How did he make love to you?" demanded Merryon.

He tried to see her face, but she hid it resolutely against him. "Don't, Billikins! It doesn't matter now."

"It does matter," he said, sternly.

Puck was silent.

Merryon continued inexorably. "I suppose it was your own fault. You led him on."

She gave a little nervous laugh against his breast. "I never meant to, Billikins. I—I don't much like men—as a rule."

"You manage to conceal that fact very successfully," he said.

She laughed again rather piteously. "You don't know me," she whispered. "I'm not—like that—all through."

"I hope not," said Merryon, severely.

She turned her face slightly upwards and snuggled it into his neck. "You used not to mind," she said.

He held her close in his arms the while he steeled himself against her. "Well, I mind now," he said. "And I will have no more of it. Is that clearly understood?"

She assented dubiously, her lips softly kissing his neck. "It isn't—all my fault, Billikins," she whispered, wistfully, "that men treat me—lightly."

He set his teeth. "It must be your fault," he declared, firmly. "You can help it if you try."

She turned her face more fully to his. "How grim you look, darling! You haven't kissed me for quite five minutes."

"I feel more like whipping you," he said, grimly.

She leapt in his arms as if he had been about to put his words into action. "Oh, no!" she cried. "No, you wouldn't beat me, Billikins. You—you wouldn't, dear, would you?" Her great eyes, dilated and imploring, gazed into his for a long desperate second ere she gave herself back to him with a sobbing laugh. "You're not in earnest, of course. I'm silly to listen to you. Do kiss me, darling, and not frighten me anymore!"

He held her close, but still he did not comply with her request. "Did this Silvester ever kiss you?" he asked.

She shook her head vehemently, hiding her face.

"Look at me!" he said.

"No, Billikins!" she protested.

"Then tell me the truth!" he said.

"He kissed me—once, Billikins," came in distressed accents from his shoulder.

"And you?" Merryon's words sounded clipped and cold.

She shivered. "I ran right away to you. I—I didn't feel safe any more."

Merryon sat silent. Somehow he could not stir up his anger against her, albeit his inner consciousness told him that she had been to blame; but for the first time his passion was cooled. He held her without ardour, the while he wondered.

That night he awoke to the sound of her low sobbing at his side. His heart smote him. He put forth a comforting hand.

She crept into his arms. "Oh, Billikins," she whispered, "keep me with you! I'm not safe—by myself."

The man's soul stirred within him. Dimly he began to understand what his protection meant to her. It was her anchor, all she had to keep her from the whirlpools. Without it she was at the mercy of every wind that blew. Again cold doubt assailed him, but he put it forcibly away. He gathered her close, and kissed the tears from her face and the trouble from her heart.

CHAPTER VIII

THE MOUTH OF THE PIT

So Puck had her way and stayed.

She was evidently sublimely happy—at least in Merryon's society, but she did not pick up her strength very quickly, and but for her unfailing high spirits Merryon would have felt anxious about her. There seemed to be nothing of her. She was not like a creature of flesh and blood. Yet how utterly, how abundantly, she satisfied him! She poured out her love to him in a perpetual offering that never varied or grew less. She gave him freely, eagerly, glowingly, all she had to give. With passionate triumph she answered to his need. And that need was growing. He could not blind himself to the fact. His profession no longer filled his life. There were times when he even resented its demands upon him. The sick list was rapidly growing, and from morning till night his days were full.

Puck made no complaint. She was always waiting for him, however late the hour of his return. She was always in his arms the moment the dripping overcoat was removed. Sometimes he brought work back with him, and wrestled with regimental accounts and other details far into the night. It was not his work, but someone had to do it, and it had devolved upon him.

Puck never would go to bed without him. It was too lonely, she said; she was afraid of snakes, or rats, or bogies. She used to curl up on the *charpoy* in his room, clad in the airiest of wrappers, and doze the time away till he was ready.

One night she actually fell into a sound sleep thus, and he, finishing his work, sat on and on, watching her, loath to disturb her. There was deep pathos in her sleeping face. Lines that in her waking moments were never apparent were painfully noticeable in repose. She had the puzzled, wistful look of a child who has gone through trouble without understanding it—a hurt and piteous look.

He watched her thus till a sense of trespass came upon him, and then he rose, bent over her, and very tenderly lifted her.

She was alert on the instant, with a sharp movement of resistance. Then at once her arms went round his neck. "Oh, darling, is it you? Don't bother to carry me! You're so tired!"

He smiled at the idea, and she nestled against his heart, lifting soft lips to his.

He carried her to bed, and laid her down, but she would not let him go immediately. She yet clung about his neck, hiding her face against it.

He held her closely. "Good-night, little pal—little sweetheart," he said.

Her arms tightened. "Billikins!" she said.

He waited. "What is it, dear?"

She became a little agitated. He could feel her lips moving, but they said no audible word.

He waited in silence. And suddenly she raised her face and looked at him fully. There was a glory in her eyes such as he had never seen before.

"I dreamt last night that the wonderfullest thing happened," she said, her red lips quivering close to his own. "Billikins, what if—the dream came true?"

A hot wave of feeling went through him at her words. He crushed her to him, feeling the quick beat of her heart against his own, the throbbing surrender of her whole being to his. He kissed her burningly, with such a passion of devotion as had never before moved him.

She laughed rapturously. "Isn't it great, Billikins?" she said. "And I'd have missed it all if it hadn't been for you. Just think—if I hadn't jumped—before the safety-curtain—came—down!"

She was speaking between his kisses, and eventually they stopped her.

"Don't think," he said; "don't think!"

It was the beginning of a new era, the entrance of a new element into their lives. Perhaps till that night he had never looked upon her wholly in the light of wife. His blind passion for her had intoxicated him. She had been to him an elf from fairyland, a being elusive who offered him all the magic of her love, but upon whom he had no claims. But from that night his attitude towards her underwent a change. Very tenderly he took her into his own close keeping. She had become human in his eyes, no longer a wayward sprite, but a woman, eager-hearted, and his own. He gave her reverence because of that womanhood which he had only just begun to visualize in her. Out of his passion there had kindled a greater fire. All that she had in life she gave him, glorying in the gift, and in return he gave her love.

All through the days that followed he watched over her with unfailing devotion—a devotion that drew her nearer to him than she had ever been before. She was ever responsive to his mood, keenly susceptible to his every phase of feeling. But, curiously, she took no open notice of the change in him. She was sublimely happy, and like a child she lived upon happiness, asking no questions. He never saw her other than content.

Slowly that month of deadly rain wore on. The Plains had become a vast and fetid swamp, the atmosphere a weltering, steamy heat, charged with fever, leaden with despair.

But Puck was like a singing bird in the heart of the wilderness. She lived apart in a paradise of her own, and even the colonel had to relent again and bestow his grim smile upon her.

"Merryon's a lucky devil," he said, and everyone in the mess agreed with him.

But, "You wait!" said Macfarlane, the doctor, with gloomy emphasis. "There's more to come."

It was on a night of awful darkness that he uttered this prophecy, and his hearers were in too overwhelming a state of depression to debate the matter.

Merryon's bungalow was actually the only one in the station in which happiness reigned. They were sitting together in his den smoking a great many cigarettes, listening to the perpetual patter of the rain on the roof and the drip, drip, drip of it from gutter to veranda, superbly content and "completely weatherproof," as Puck expressed it.

"I hope none of the boys will turn up tonight," she said. "We haven't room for more than two, have we?"

"Oh, someone is sure to come," responded Merryon. "They'll be getting bored directly, and come along here for coffee."

"There's someone there now," said Puck, cocking her head. "I think I shall run along to bed and leave you to do the entertaining. Shall I?"

She looked at him with a mischievous smile, very bright-eyed and alert.

"It would be a quick method of getting rid of them," remarked Merryon.

She jumped up. "Very well, then. I'll go, shall I? Shall I, darling?"

He reached out a hand and grasped her wrist. "No," he said, deliberately, smiling up at her. "You'll stay and do your duty—unless you're tired," he added. "Are you?"

She stooped to bestow a swift caress upon his forehead. "My own Billikins!" she murmured. "You're the kindest husband that ever was. Of course, I'm going to stay."

She could scarcely have effected her escape had she so desired, for already a hand was on the door. She turned towards it with the roguish smile still upon her lips.

Merryon was looking at her at the moment. She interested him far more than the visitor, whom he guessed to be one of the subalterns. And so looking, he saw the smile freeze upon her face to a mask-like immobility. And very suddenly he remembered a man whom he had once seen killed on a battlefield—killed instantaneously—while laughing at some joke. The frozen mirth, the starting eyes, the awful vacancy where the soul had been—he saw them all again in the face of his wife.

"Great heavens, Puck! What is it?" he said, and sprang to his feet.

In the same instant she turned with the movement of one tearing herself free from an evil spell, and flung herself violently upon his breast. "Oh, Billikins, save me—save me!" she cried, and broke into hysterical sobbing.

His arms were about her in a second, sheltering her, sustaining her. His eyes went beyond her to the open door.

A man was standing there—a bulky, broad-featured, coarse-lipped man with keen black eyes that twinkled maliciously between thick lids, and a black beard that only served to emphasize an immensely heavy under-jaw. Merryon summed him up swiftly as a Portuguese American with more than a dash of darker blood in his composition.

He entered the room in a fashion that was almost insulting. It was evident that he was summing up Merryon also.

The latter waited for him, stiff with hostility, his arms still tightly clasping Puck's slight, cowering form. He spoke as the stranger advanced, in his voice a deep menace like the growl of an angry beast protecting its own.

"Who are you? And what do you want?"

The stranger's lips parted, showing a gleam of strong white teeth. "My name," he said, speaking in a peculiarly soft voice that somehow reminded Merryon of the hiss of a reptile, "is Leo Vulcan. You have heard of me? Perhaps not. I am better known in the Western Hemisphere. You ask me what I want?" He raised a brown, hairy hand and pointed straight at the girl in Merryon's arms. "I want—my wife!"

Puck's cry of anguish followed the announcement, and after it came silence—a tense, hard-breathing silence, broken only by her long-drawn, agonized sobbing.

Merryon's hold had tightened all unconsciously to a grip; and she was clinging to him wildly, convulsively, as she had never clung before. He could feel the horror that pulsed through her veins; it set his own blood racing at fever-speed.

Over her head he faced the stranger with eyes of steely hardness. "You have made a mistake," he said, briefly and sternly.

The other man's teeth gleamed again. He had a way of lifting his lip when talking which gave him an oddly bestial look. "I think not," he said. "Let the lady speak for herself! She will not—I think—deny me."

There was an intolerable sneer in the last sentence. A sudden awful doubt smote through Merryon. He turned to the girl sobbing at his breast.

"Puck," he said, "for Heaven's sake—what is this man to you?"

She did not answer him; perhaps she could not. Her distress was terrible to witness, utterly beyond all control.

But the newcomer was by no means disconcerted by it. He drew near with the utmost assurance.

"Allow me to deal with her!" he said, and reached out a hand to touch her.

But at that action Merryon's wrath burst into sudden flame. "Curse you, keep away!" he thundered. "Lay a finger on her at your peril!"

The other stood still, but his eyes gleamed evilly. "My good sir," he said, "you have not yet grasped the situation. It is not a pleasant one for you—for either of us; but it has got to be grasped. I do not happen to know under what circumstances you met this woman; but I do know that she was my lawful wife before the meeting took place. In whatever light you may be pleased to regard that fact, you must admit that legally she is my property, not yours!"

"Oh, no—no—no!" moaned Puck.

Merryon said nothing. He felt strangled, as if a ligature about his throat had forced all the blood to his brain and confined it there.

After a moment the bearded man continued: "You may not know it, but she is a dancer of some repute, a circumstance which she owes entirely to me. I picked her up, a mere child in the streets of London, turning cart-wheels for a living. I took her and trained her as an acrobat. She was known on the stage as Toby the Tumbler. Everyone took her for a boy. Later, she developed a talent for dancing. It was then that I decided to marry her. She desired the marriage even more than I did." Again he smiled his brutal smile.

"Oh, no!" sobbed Puck. "Oh, no!"

He passed on with a derisive sneer. "We were married about two years ago. She became popular in the halls very soon after, and it turned her head. You may have discovered yourself by this time that she is not always as tractable as she might be. I had to teach her obedience and respect, and eventually I succeeded. I conquered her—as I hoped—completely. However, six months ago she took advantage of a stage fire to give me the slip, and till recently I believed that she was dead. Then a friend of mine—Captain Silvester—met her out here in India a few weeks back at a place called Shamkura, and recognized her. Her dancing qualities are superb. I think she displayed them a little rashly if she really wished to remain hidden. He sent me the news, and I have come myself to claim her—and take her back."

"You can't take me back!" It was Puck's voice, but not as Merryon had ever heard it before. She flashed round like a hunted creature at bay, her eyes blazing a wild defiance into the mocking eyes opposite. "You can't take me back!" she repeated, with quivering insistence. "Our marriage was—no marriage! It was a sham—a sham! But even if—even if—it had been—a true marriage—you would have to—set me—free—now."

"And why?" said Vulcan, with his evil smile.

She was white to the lips, but she faced him unflinching. "There is—a reason," she said.

"In—deed!" He uttered a scoffing laugh of deadly insult. "The same reason, I presume, as that for which you married me?"

She flinched at that—flinched as if he had struck her across the face. "Oh, you brute!" she said, and shuddered back against Merryon's supporting arm. "You wicked brute!"

It was then that Merryon wrenched himself free from that paralysing constriction that bound him, and abruptly intervened.

"Puck," he said, "go! Leave us! I will deal with this matter in my own way."

She made no move to obey. Her face was hidden in her hands. But she was sobbing no longer, only sickly shuddering from head to foot.

He took her by the shoulder. "Go, child, go!" he urged.

But she shook her head. "It's no good," she said. "He has got—the whip-hand."

The utter despair of her tone pierced straight to his soul. She stood as one bent beneath a crushing burden, and he knew that her face was burning behind the sheltering hands.

He still held her with a certain stubbornness of possession, though she made no further attempt to cling to him.

"What do you mean by that?" he said, bending to her. "Tell me what you mean! Don't be afraid to tell me!"

She shook her head again. "I am bound," she said, dully, "bound hand and foot."

"You mean that you really are—married to him?" Merryon spoke the words as it were through closed lips. He had a feeling as of being caught in some crushing machinery, of being slowly and inevitably ground to shapeless atoms.

Puck lifted her head at length and spoke, not looking at him. "I went through a form of marriage with him," she said, "for the sake of—of—of—decency. I always loathed him. I always shall. He only wants me now because I am—I have been—valuable to him. When he first took me he seemed kind. I was nearly starved, quite desperate, and alone. He offered to teach me to be an acrobat, to make a living. I'd better have drowned myself." A little tremor of passion went through her voice; she paused to steady it, then went on. "He taught by fear—and cruelty. He opened my eyes to evil. He used to beat me, too—tie me up in the gymnasium—and beat me with a whip till—till I was nearly beside myself and ready to promise anything—anything, only to stop the torture. And so he got everything he wanted from me, and when I began to be successful as a dancer he—married me. I thought it would make things better. I didn't think, if I were his wife, he could go on ill-treating me quite so much. But I soon found my mistake. I soon found I was even more his slave than before. And then—just a week before the fire—another woman came, and told me that it was not a real marriage; that—that he had been through exactly the same form with her—and there was nothing in it."

She stopped again at sound of a low laugh from Vulcan. "Not quite the same form, my dear," he said. "Yours was as legal and binding as the English law could make it. I have the certificate with me to prove this. As you say, you were valuable to me then—as you will be again, and so I was careful that the contract should be complete in every particular. Now—if you have quite finished your—shall we call it confession?—I suggest that you should return to your lawful husband and leave this gentleman to console himself as soon as may be. It is growing late, and it is not my intention that you should spend another night under his protection."

He spoke slowly, with a curious, compelling emphasis, and as if in answer to that compulsion Puck's eyes came back to his.

"Oh, no!" she said, in a quick, frightened whisper. "No! I can't! I can't!"

Yet she made a movement towards him as if drawn irresistibly.

And at that movement, wholly involuntary as it was, something in Merryon's brain seemed to burst. He saw all things a burning, intolerable red. With a strangled oath he caught her back, held her violently—a prisoner in his arms.

"By God, no!" he said. "I'll kill you first!"

She turned in his embrace. She lifted her lips and passionately kissed him. "Yes, kill me! Kill me!" she cried to him. "I'd rather die!"

Again the stranger laughed, though his eyes were devilish. "You had better come without further trouble," he remarked. "You will only add to your punishment—which will be no light one as it is—by these hysterics. Do you wish to see my proofs?" He addressed Merryon with sudden open malignancy. "Or am I to take them to the colonel of your regiment?"

"You may take them to the devil!" Merryon said. He was holding her crushed to his heart. He flung his furious challenge over her head. "If the marriage was genuine you shall set her free. If it was not"—he paused, and ended in a voice half-choked with passion—"you can go to blazes!"

The other man showed his teeth in a wolfish snarl. "She is my wife," he said, in his slow, sibilant way. "I shall not set her free. And—wherever I go, she will go also."

"If you can take her, you infernal blackguard!" Merryon threw at him. "Now get out. Do you hear? Get out—if you don't want to be shot! Whatever happens tomorrow, I swear by God in heaven she shall not go with you tonight!"

The uncontrolled violence of his speech was terrible. His hold upon Puck was violent also, more violent than he knew. Her whole body lay a throbbing weight upon him, and he was not even aware of it.

"Go!" he reiterated, with eyes of leaping flame. "Go! or—" He left the sentence uncompleted. It was even more terrible than his flow of words had been. The whole man vibrated with a wrath that possessed him in a fashion so colossal as to render him actually sublime. He mastered the situation by the sheer, indomitable might of his fury. There was no standing against him. It would have been as easy to stem a racing torrent.

Vulcan, for all his insolence, realized the fact. The man's strength in that moment was gigantic, practically limitless. There was no coping with it. Still with the snarl upon his lips he turned away.

"You will pay for this, my wife," he said. "You will pay in full. When I punish, I punish well."

He reached the door and opened it, still leering back at the limp, girlish form in Merryon's arms.

"It will not be soon over," he said. "It will take many days, many nights, that punishment—till you have left off crying for mercy, or expecting it."

He was on the threshold. His eyes suddenly shot up with a gloating hatred to Merryon's.

"And you," he said, "will have the pleasure of knowing every night when you lie down alone that she is either writhing under the lash—a frequent exercise for a while, my good sir—or finding subtle comfort in my arms; both pleasant subjects for your dreams."

He was gone. The door closed slowly, noiselessly, upon his exit. There was no sound of departing feet.

But Merryon neither listened nor cared. He had turned Puck's deathly face upwards, and was covering it with burning, passionate kisses, drawing her back to life, as it were, by the fiery intensity of his worship.

CHAPTER IX

GREATER THAN DEATH

She came to life, weakly gasping. She opened her eyes upon him with the old, unwavering adoration in their depths. And then before his burning look hers sank. She hid her face against him with an inarticulate sound more anguished than any weeping.

The savagery went out of his hold. He drew her to the *charpoy* on which she had spent so many evenings waiting for him, and made her sit down.

She did not cling to him any longer; she only covered her face so that he should not see it, huddling herself together in a piteous heap, her black, curly head bowed over her knees in an overwhelming agony of humiliation.

Yet there was in the situation something that was curiously reminiscent of that night when she had leapt from the burning stage into the safety of his arms. Now, as then, she was utterly dependent upon the charity of his soul.

He turned from her and poured brandy and water into a glass. He came back and knelt beside her.

"Drink it, my darling!" he said.

She made a quick gesture as of surprised protest. She did not raise her head. It was as if an invisible hand were crushing her to the earth.

"Why don't you—kill me?" she said.

He laid his hand upon her bent head. "Because you are the salt of the earth to me," he said; "because I worship you."

She caught the hand with a little sound of passionate endearment, and laid her face down in it, her hot, quivering lips against his palm. "I love you so!" she said. "I love you so!"

He pressed her face slowly upwards. But she resisted. "No, no! I can't—meet—your—eyes."

"You need not be afraid," he said. "Once and for all, Puck, believe me when I tell you that this thing shall never—can never—come between us."

She caught her breath sharply; but still she refused to look up. "Then you don't understand," she said. "You—you—can't understand that—that—I was—his—his—" Her voice failed. She caught his hand in both her own, pressing it hard over her face, writhing in mute shame before him.

"Yes, I do understand," Merryon said, and his voice was

very quiet, full of a latent force that thrilled her magnetically. "I understand that when you were still a child this brute took possession of you, broke you to his will, did as he pleased with you. I understand that you were as helpless as a rabbit in the grip of a weasel. I understand that he was always an abomination and a curse to you, that when deliverance offered you seized it; and I do not forget that you would have preferred death if I would have let you die. Do you know, Puck"—his voice had softened by imperceptible degrees; he was bending towards her so that she could feel his breath on her neck while he spoke—"when I took it upon me to save you from yourself that night I knew—I guessed—what had happened to you? No, don't start like that! If there was anything to forgive I forgave you long ago. I understood. Believe me, though I am a man, I can understand."

He stopped. His hand was all wet with her tears. "Oh, darling!" she whispered. "Oh, darling!"

"Don't cry, sweetheart!" he said. "And don't be afraid any longer! I took you from your inferno. I learnt to love you—just as you were, dear, just as you were. You tried to keep me at a distance; do you remember? And then—you found life was too strong for you. You came back and gave yourself to me. Have you ever regretted it, my darling? Tell me that!"

"Never!" she sobbed. "Never! Your love—your love—has been—the safety-curtain—always—between me and—harm."

And then very suddenly she lifted her face, her streaming eyes, and met his look.

"But there's one thing, darling," she said, "which you must know. I loved you always—always—even before that monsoon night. But I came to you then because—because—I knew that I had been recognized, and—I was afraid—I was terrified—till—till I was safe in your arms."

"Ah! But you came to me," he said.

A sudden gleam of mirth shot through her woe. "My! That was a night, Billikins!" she said. And then the clouds came back upon her, overwhelming her. "Oh, what is there to laugh at? How could I laugh?"

He lifted the glass he held and drank from it, then offered it to her. "Drink with me!" he said.

She took, not the glass, but his wrist, and drank with her eyes upon his face.

When she had finished she drew his arms about her, and lay against his shoulder with closed eyes for a space, saying no word.

At last, with a little murmuring sigh, she spoke. "What is going to happen, Billikins?"

"God knows," he said.

But there was no note of dismay in his voice. His hold was strong and steadfast.

She stirred a little. "Do you believe in God?" she asked him, for the second time.

He had not answered her before; he answered her now without hesitation. "Yes, I do."

She lifted her head to look at him. "I wonder why?" she said.

He was silent for a moment; then, "Just because I can hold you in my arms," he said, "and feel that nothing else matters—or can matter again."

"You really feel that?" she said, quickly. "You really love me, dear?"

"That is love," he said, simply.

"Oh, darling!" Her breath came fast. "Then, if they try to take me from you—you will really do it—you won't be afraid?"

"Do what?" he questioned, sombrely.

"Kill me, Billikins," she answered, swiftly. "Kill me—sooner than let me go."

He bent his head. "Yes," he said. "My love is strong enough for that."

"But what would you do—afterwards?" she breathed, her lips raised to his.

A momentary surprise showed in his eyes. "Afterwards?" he questioned.

"After I was gone, darling?" she said, anxiously.

A very strange smile came over Merryon's face. He pressed her to him, his eyes gazing deep into hers. He kissed her, but not passionately, rather with reverence.

"Your afterwards will be mine, dear, wherever it is," he said. "If it comes to that—if there is any going—in that way—we go together."

The anxiety went out of her face in a second. She smiled back at him with utter confidence. "Oh, Billikins!" she said. "Oh, Billikins, that will be great!"

She went back into his arms, and lay there for a further space, saying no word. There was something sacred in the silence between them, something mysterious and wonderful. The drip, drip, drip of the ceaseless rain was the only sound in the stillness. They seemed to be alone together in a sanctuary that none other might enter, husband and wife, made one by the Bond Imperishable, waiting together for deliverance. They were the most precious moments that either had ever known, for in them they were more truly wedded in spirit than they had ever been before.

How long the great silence lasted neither could have said. It lay like a spell for awhile, and like a spell it passed.

Merryon moved at last, moved and looked down into his wife's eyes.

They met his instantly without a hint of shrinking; they even smiled. "It must be nearly bedtime," she said. "You are not going to be busy tonight?"

"Not tonight," he said.

"Then don't let's sit up any longer, darling," she said. "We can't either of us afford to lose our beauty sleep."

She rose with him, still with her shining eyes lifted to his, still with that brave gaiety sparkling in their depths. She gave his arm a tight little squeeze. "My, Billikins, how you've grown!" she said, admiringly. "You always were—pretty big. But tonight you're just—titanic!"

He smiled and touched her cheek, not speaking.

"You fill the world," she said.

He bent once more to kiss her. "You fill my heart," he said.

CHAPTER X

THE SACRIFICE

They went round the bungalow together to see to the fastenings of doors and windows. The *khitmutgar* had gone to his own quarters for the night, and they were quite alone. The drip, drip, drip of the rain was still the only sound, save when the far cry of a prowling jackal came weirdly through the night.

"It's more gruesome than usual somehow," said Puck, still fast clinging to her husband's arm. "I'm not a bit frightened, darling, only sort of creepy at the back. But there's nobody here but you and me, is there?"

"Nobody," said Merryon.

"And will you please come and see if there are any snakes or scorpions before I begin to undress?" she said. "The very fact of looking under my bed makes my hair stand on end."

He went with her and made a thorough investigation, finding nothing.

"That's all right," she said, with a sigh of relief. "And yet, somehow, I feel as if something is waiting round the corner to pounce out on us. Is it Fate, do you think? Or just my silly fancy?"

"I think it is probably your startled nerves, dear," he said, smiling a little.

She assented with a half-suppressed shudder. "But I'm sure something will happen directly," she said. "I'm sure. I'm sure."

"Well, I shall only be in the next room if it does," he said.

He was about to leave her, but she sprang after him, clinging to his arm. "And you won't be late, will you?" she pleaded. "I can't sleep without you. Ah, what is that? What is it? What is it?"

Her voice rose almost to a shriek. A sudden loud knocking had broken through the endless patter of the rain.

Merryon's face changed a very little. The iron-grey eyes became stony, quite expressionless. He stood a moment listening. Then, "Stay here!" he said, his voice very level and composed. "Yes, Puck, I wish it. Stay here!"

It was a distinct command, the most distinct he had ever given her. Her clinging hands slipped from his arm. She stood rigid, unprotesting, white as death.

The knocking was renewed with fevered energy as Merryon turned quietly to obey the summons. He closed the door upon his wife and went down the passage.

There was no haste in his movements as he slipped back the bolts, rather the studied deliberation of purpose of a man armed against all emergency. But the door burst inwards against him the moment he opened it, and one of his subalterns, young Harley, almost fell into his arms.

Merryon steadied him with the utmost composure. "Halloa, Harley! You, is it? What's all this noise about?"

The boy pulled himself together with an effort. He was white to the lips.

"There's cholera broken out," he said. "Forbes and Robey—both down—at their own bungalow. And they've got it at the barracks, too. Macfarlane's there. Can you come?"

"Of course—at once." Merryon pulled him forward. "Go in there and get a drink while I speak to my wife!"

He turned back to her door, but she met him on the threshold. Her eyes burned like stars in her little pale face.

"It's all right, Billikins," she said, and swallowed hard. "I heard. You've got to go to the barracks, haven't you, darling? I knew there was going to be—something. Well, you must take something to eat in your pocket. You'll want it before morning. And some brandy too. Give me your flask, darling, and I'll fill it!"

Her composure amazed him. He had expected anguished distress at the bare idea of his leaving her, but those brave, bright eyes of hers were actually smiling.

"Puck!" he said. "You—wonder!"

She made a small face at him. "Oh, you're not the only wonder in the world," she told him. "Run along and get yourself ready! My! You are going to be busy, aren't you?"

She nodded to him and ran into the drawing-room to young Harley. He heard her chatting there while he made swift preparations for departure, and he thanked Heaven that she realized so little the ghastly nature of the horror that had swept down upon them. He hoped the boy would have the sense to let her remain unenlightened. It was bad enough to have to leave her after the ordeal they had just faced together. He did not want her terrified on his account as well.

But when he joined them she was still smiling, eager only to provide for any possible want of his, not thinking of herself at all.

"I hope you will enjoy your picnic, Billikins," she said. "I'll shut the door after you, and I shall know it's properly fastened. Oh, yes, the *khit* will take care of me, Mr. Harley. He's such a brave man. He kills snakes without the smallest change of countenance. Good-night, Billikins! Take care of yourself. I suppose you'll come back sometime?"

She gave him the lightest caress imaginable, shook hands affectionately with young Harley, who was looking decidedly less pinched than he had upon arrival, and stood waving an energetic hand as they went away into the dripping dark.

"You didn't tell her—anything?" Merryon asked, as they plunged down the road.

"Not more than I could help, Major. But she seemed to know without." The lad spoke uncomfortably, as if against his will.

"She asked questions, then?" Merryon's voice was sharp.

"Yes, a few. She wanted to know about Forbes and Robey. Robey is awfully bad. I didn't tell her that."

"Who is looking after them?" Merryon asked.

"Only a native orderly now. The colonel and Macfarlane both had to go to the barracks. It's frightful there. About twenty cases already. Oh, hang this rain!" said Harley, bitterly.

"But couldn't they take them—Forbes, I mean, and Robey—to the hospital?" questioned Merryon.

"No. To tell you the truth, Robey is pegging out, poor fellow. It's always the best chaps that go first, though. Heaven knows, we may be all gone before this time tomorrow."

"Don't talk like a fool!" said Merryon, curtly.

And Harley said no more.

They pressed on through mud that was ankle-deep to the barracks.

There during all the nightmare hours that followed Merryon worked with the strength of ten. He gave no voluntary thought to his wife waiting for him in loneliness, but ever and anon those blazing eyes of hers rose before his mental vision, and he saw again that brave, sweet smile with which she had watched him go.

The morning found him haggard but indomitable, wrestling with the difficulties of establishing a camp a mile or more from the barracks out in the rain-drenched open. There had been fourteen deaths in the night, and seven men were still fighting a losing battle for their lives in the hospital. He had a native officer to help him in his task; young Harley was superintending the digging of graves, and the colonel had gone to the bungalow where the two stricken officers lay.

Dank and gruesome dawned the day, with the smell of rot in the air and the sense of death hovering over all. And there came to Merryon a sudden, overwhelming desire to go back to his bungalow beyond the fetid town and see how his wife was faring. She was the only white woman in the place, and the thought of her isolation came upon him now like a fiery torture.

It was the fiercest temptation he had ever known. Till that day his regimental duties had always been placed first with rigorous determination. Now for the first time he found himself torn by conflicting ties. The craving for news of her possessed him like a burning thirst. Yet he knew that some hours must elapse before he could honestly consider himself free to go.

He called an orderly at last, finding the suspense unendurable, and gave him a scribbled line to carry to his wife.

"Is all well, sweetheart? Send back word by bearer," he wrote, and told the man not to return without an answer.

The orderly departed, and for a while Merryon devoted

himself to the matter in hand, and crushed his anxiety into the background. But at the end of an hour he was chafing in a fever of impatience. What delayed the fellow? In Heaven's name, why was he so long?

Ghastly possibilities arose in his mind, fears unspeakable that he dared not face. He forced himself to attend to business, but the suspense was becoming intolerable. He began to realize that he could not stand it much longer.

He was nearing desperation when the colonel came unexpectedly upon the scene, unshaven and haggard as he was himself, but firm as a rock in the face of adversity.

He joined Merryon, and received the latter's report, grimly taciturn. They talked together for a space of needs and expediencies. The fell disease had got to be checked somehow. He spoke of recalling the officers on leave. There had been such a huge sick list that summer that they were reduced to less than half their normal strength.

"You're worth a good many," he said to Merryon, half-grudgingly, "but you can't work miracles. Besides, you've got—" He broke off abruptly. "How's your wife?"

"That's what I don't know, sir." Feverishly Merryon made answer. "I left her last night. She was well then. But since—I sent down an orderly over an hour ago. He's not come back."

"Confound it!" said the colonel, testily. "You'd better go yourself."

Merryon glanced swiftly round.

"Yes, go, go!" the colonel reiterated, irritably. "I'll relieve you for a spell. Go and satisfy yourself—and me! None but an infernal fool would have kept her here," he added, in a growling undertone, as Merryon lifted a hand in brief salute and started away through the sodden mists.

He went as he had never gone in his life before, and as he went the mists parted before him and a blinding ray of sunshine came smiting through the gap like the sword of the destroyer. The simile rushed through his mind and out again, even as the grey mist-curtain closed once more.

He reached the bungalow. It stood like a shrouded ghost, and the drip, drip, drip of the rain on the veranda came to him like a death-knell.

A gaunt figure met him almost on the threshold, and he recognized his messenger with a sharp sense of coming disaster. The man stood mutely at the salute.

"Well? Well? Speak!" he ordered, nearly beside himself with

anxiety. "Why didn't you come back with an answer?"

The man spoke with deep submission. "*Sahib*, there was no answer."

"What do you mean by that? What the—Here, let me pass!" cried Merryon, in a ferment. "There must have been—some sort of answer."

"No, *sahib*. No answer." The man spoke with inscrutable composure. "The *mem-sahib* has not come back," he said. "Let the *sahib* see for himself."

But Merryon had already burst into the bungalow; so he resumed his patient watch on the veranda, wholly undisturbed, supremely patient.

The *khitmutgar* came forward at his master's noisy entrance. There was a trace—just the shadow of a suggestion—of anxiety on his dignified face under the snow-white turban. He presented him with a note on a salver with a few murmured words and a deep salaam.

"For the *sahib's* hands alone," he said.

Merryon snatched up the note and opened it with shaking hands.

It was very brief, pathetically so, and as he read a great emptiness seemed to spread and spread around him in an ever-widening desolation.

"Good-bye, my Billikins!" Ah, the pitiful, childish scrawl she had made of it! "I've come to my senses, and I've gone back to him. I'm not worthy of any sacrifice of yours, dear. And it would have been a big sacrifice. You wouldn't like being dragged through the mud, but I'm used to it. It came to me just that moment that you said, 'Yes, of course,' when Mr. Harley came to call you back to duty. Duty is better than a worthless woman, my Billikins, and I was never fit to be anything more than a toy to you—a toy to play with and toss aside. And so good-bye, good-bye!"

The scrawl ended with a little cross at the bottom of the page. He looked up from it with eyes gone blind with pain and a stunned and awful sense of loss.

"When did the *mem-sahib* go?" he questioned, dully.

The *khitmutgar* bent his stately person. "The *mem-sahib* went in haste," he said, "an hour before midnight. Your servant followed her to the *dâk-bungalow* to protect her from *budmashes*, but she dismissed me ere she entered in. *Sahib*, I could do no more."

The man's eyes appealed for one instant, but fell the next

before the dumb despair that looked out of his master's.

There fell a terrible silence—a pause, as it were, of suspended vitality, while the iron bit deeper and deeper into tissues too numbed to feel.

Then, "Fetch me a drink!" said Merryon, curtly. "I must be getting back to duty."

And with soundless promptitude the man withdrew, thankful to make his escape.

CHAPTER XI

THE SACRED FIRE

"Well? Is she all right?" Almost angrily the colonel flung the question as his second-in-command came back heavy-footed through the rain. He had been through a nasty period of suspense himself during Merryon's absence.

Merryon nodded. His face was very pale and his lips seemed stiff.

"She has—gone, sir," he managed to say, after a moment.

"Gone, has she?" The colonel raised his brows in astonished interrogation. "What! Taken fright at last? Well, best thing she could do, all things considered. You ought to be very thankful."

He dismissed the subject for more pressing matters, and he never noticed the awful whiteness of Merryon's face or the deadly fixity of his look.

Macfarlane noticed both, coming up two hours later to report the death of one of the officers at the bungalow.

"For Heaven's sake, man, have some brandy!" he said, proffering a flask of his own. "You're looking pretty unhealthy. What is it? Feeling a bit off, eh?"

He held Merryon's wrist while he drank the brandy, regarding him with a troubled frown the while.

"What is the matter with you, man?" he said. "You're not frightening yourself? You wouldn't be such a fool!"

Merryon did not answer. He was never voluble. Today he seemed tongue-tied.

Macfarlane continued with an uneasy effort to hide a certain doubt stirring in his mind. "I hear there was a European died at the *dâk-bungalow* early this morning. I wanted to go round and see, but I haven't been able. It's fairly widespread, but there's no sense in getting scared. Halloa, Merryon!"

He broke off, staring. Merryon had given a great start. He looked like a man stabbed suddenly from a dream to full consciousness.

"A European—at the *dâk-bungalow*—dead, did you say?"

His words tumbled over each other; he gripped Macfarlane's shoulder and shook it with fierce impatience.

"So I heard. I don't know any details. How should I? Merryon, are you mad?" Macfarlane put up a quick hand to free himself, for the grip was painful. "He wasn't a friend of yours, I suppose? He wouldn't have been putting up there if he had been."

"No, no; not—a friend." The words came jerkily. Merryon was breathing in great spasms that shook him from head to foot. "Not—a friend!" he said again, and stopped, gazing before him with eyes curiously contracted as the eyes of one striving to discern something a long way off.

Macfarlane slipped a hand under his elbow. "Look here," he said, "you must have a rest. You can be spared for a bit now. Walk back with me to the hospital, and we will see how things are going there."

His hand closed urgently. He began to draw him away.

Merryon's eyes came back as it were out of space, and gave him a quick side-glance that was like the turn of a rapier. "I must go down to the *dâk-bungalow*," he said, with decision.

Swift protest rose to the doctor's lips, but it died there. He tightened his hold instead, and went with him.

The colonel looked round sharply at their approach, looked—and swore under his breath. "Yes, all right, major, you'd better go," he said. "Good-bye."

Merryon essayed a grim smile, but his ashen face only twisted convulsively, showing his set teeth. He hung on Macfarlane's shoulder while the first black cloud of agony possessed him and slowly passed.

Then, white and shaking, he stood up. "I'll get round to the *dâk* now, before I'm any worse. Don't come with me, Macfarlane! I'll take an orderly."

"I'm coming," said Macfarlane, stoutly.

But they did not get to the *dâk-bungalow*, or anywhere near it. Before they had covered twenty yards another frightful spasm of pain came upon Merryon, racking his whole being, depriving him of all his powers, wresting from him every faculty save that of suffering. He went down into a darkness that swallowed him, soul and body, blotting out all finite things, loosening his frantic clutch on life, sucking him down as it were into a frightful emptiness, where his only certainty of existence lay in the excruciating agonies that tore and convulsed him like devils in some inferno under the earth.

Of time and place and circumstance thereafter he became as completely unconscious as though they had ceased to be, though once or twice he was aware of a merciful hand that gave him opium to deaden—or was it only to prolong?—his suffering. And æons and eternities passed over him while he lay in the rigour of perpetual torments, not trying to escape, only writhing in futile anguish in the bitter dark of the prison-house.

Later, very much later, there came a time when the torture gradually ceased or became merged in a deathly coldness. During that stage his understanding began to come back to him like the light of a dying day. A vague and dreadful sense of loss began to oppress him, a feeling of nakedness as though the soul of him were already slipping free, passing into an appalling void, leaving an appalling void behind. He lay quite helpless and sinking, sinking—slowly, terribly sinking into an overwhelming sea of annihilation.

With all that was left of his failing strength he strove to cling to that dim light which he knew for his own individuality. The silence and the darkness broke over him in long, soundless waves; but each time he emerged again, cold, cold as death, but still aware of self, aware of existence, albeit the world he knew had dwindled to an infinitesimal smallness, as an object very far away, and floating ever farther and farther from his ken.

Vague paroxysms of pain still seized him from time to time, but they no longer affected him in the same way. The body alone agonized. The soul stood apart on the edge of that dreadful sea, shrinking afraid from the black, black depths and the cruel cold of the eternal night. He was terribly, crushingly alone.

Someone had once, twice, asked him a vital question about his belief in God. Then he had been warmly alive. He had held his wife close in his arms, and nothing else had mattered. But now—but now—he was very far from warmth and life. He was dying in loneliness. He was perishing in the outer dark, where no hand might reach and no voice console. He had believed—or thought he believed—in God. But now his faith was wearing very thin. Very soon it would crumble quite away, just as he himself was crumbling into the dreadful silence of the ages. His life—the brief passion called life—was over. Out of the dark it had come; into the dark it went. And no one to care—no one to cry farewell to him across that desolation of emptiness that was death! No one to kneel beside him and pray for light in that awful, all-encompassing dark!

Stay! Something had touched him even then. Or was it but his dying fancy? Red lips he had kissed and that had kissed him in return, eager arms that had clung and clung, eyes of burning adoration! Did they truly belong all to the past? Or were they here beside him even now—even now? Had he wandered backwards perchance into that strange, sweet heaven of love from which he had been so suddenly and terribly cast out? Ah, how he had loved her! How he had loved her! Very faintly there began to stir within him the old fiery longing that she, and she alone, had ever waked within him. He would worship her to the last flicker of his dying soul. But the darkness was spreading, spreading, like a yawning of a great gulf at his feet. Already he was slipping over the edge. The light was fading out of his sky.

It was the last dim instinct of nature that made him reach out a groping hand, and with lips that would scarcely move to whisper, "Puck!"

He did not expect an answer. The things of earth were done with. His life was passing swiftly, swiftly, like the sands running out of a glass. He had lost her already, and the world had sunk away, away, with all warmth and light and love.

Yet out of the darkness all suddenly there came a voice, eager, passionate, persistent. "I am here, Billikins! I am here! Come back to me, darling! Come back!"

He started at that voice, started and paused, holding back as it were on the very verge of the precipice. So she was there indeed! He could hear her sobbing breath. There came to him the consciousness of her hands clasping his, and the faintest, vaguest glow went through his ice-cold body. He tried, piteously weak as he was, to bend his fingers about hers.

And then there came the warmth of her lips upon them, kissing them with a fierce passion of tenderness, drawing them close as if to breathe her own vitality into his failing pulses.

"Open your eyes to me, darling!" she besought him. "See how I love you! And see how I want your love! I can't do without it, Billikins. It's my only safeguard. What! He is dead? I say he is not—he is not! Or if he is, he shall rise again. He shall come back. See! He is looking at me! How dare you say he is dead?"

The wild anguish of her voice reached him, pierced him, rousing him as no other power on earth could have roused him. Out of that deathly inertia he drew himself, inch by inch, as out of some clinging swamp. His hand found strength to tighten upon hers. He opened his eyes, leaden-lidded as they were, and saw her face all white and drawn, gazing into his own with such an agony of love, such a consuming fire of worship, that it seemed as if his whole being were drawn by it, warmed, comforted, revived.

She hung above him, fierce in her devotion, driving back the destroyer by the sheer burning intensity of her love. "You shan't die, Billikins!" she told him, passionately. "You can't die—now I am here!"

She stooped her face to his. He turned his lips instinctively to meet it, and suddenly it was as though a flame had kindled between them—hot, ardent, compelling. His dying pulses thrilled to it, his blood ran warmer.

"You—have—come—back!" he said, with slow articulation.

"My darling—my darling!" she made quivering answer. "Say I've come—in time!"

He tried to speak again, but could not. Yet the deathly cold was giving way like ice before the sun. He could feel his heart beating where before he had felt nothing. A hand that was not Puck's came out of the void beyond her and held a spoonful of spirit to his mouth. He swallowed it with difficulty, and was conscious of a greater warmth.

"There, my own boy, my own boy!" she murmured over him. "You're coming back to me. Say you're coming back!"

His lips quivered like a child's. He forced them to answer her. "If you—will—stay," he said.

"I will never leave you again, darling," she made swift answer. "Never, never again! You shall have all that you want—all—all!"

Her arms closed about him. He felt the warmth of her body, the passionate nearness of her soul; and therewith the flame that had kindled between them leaped to a great and burning glow, encompassing them both—the Sacred Fire.

A wonderful sense of comfort came upon him. He turned to her as a man turns to only one woman in all the world, and laid his head upon her breast.

"I only want—my wife," he said.

CHAPTER XII

FREEDOM

It took him many days to climb back up that slope down which he had slipped so swiftly in those few awful hours. Very slowly, with painful effort, but with unfailing purpose, he made his arduous way. And through it all Puck never left his side.

Alert and vigilant, very full of courage, very quick of understanding, she drew him, leaning on her, back to a life that had become strangely new to them both. They talked very little, for Merryon's strength was terribly low, and Macfarlane, still scarcely believing in the miracle that had been wrought under his eyes, forbade all but the simplest and briefest speech—a prohibition which Puck strenuously observed; for Puck, though she knew the miracle for an accomplished fact, was not taking any chances.

"Presently, darling; when you're stronger," was her invariable answer to any attempt on his part to elicit information as to the events that had immediately preceded his seizure. "There's nothing left to fret about. You're here—and I'm here. And that's all that matters."

If her lips quivered a little over the last assertion, she turned her head away that he might not see. For she was persistently cheery in his presence, full of tender humour, always undismayed.

He leaned upon her instinctively. She propped him so sturdily, with a strength so amazing and so steadfast. Sometimes she laughed softly at his weakness, as a mother might laugh at the first puny efforts of her baby to stand alone. And he knew that she loved his dependence upon her, even in a sense dreaded the time when his own strength should reassert itself, making hers weak by comparison.

But that time was coming, slowly yet very surely. The rains were lessening at last, and the cholera-fiend had been driven forth. Merryon was to go to the Hills on sick leave for several weeks. Colonel Davenant had awaked to the fact that his life was a valuable one, and his admiration for Mrs. Merryon was undisguised. He did not altogether understand her behaviour, but he was discreet enough not to seek that enlightenment which only one man in the world was ever to receive.

To that man on the night before their departure came Puck, very pale and resolute, with shining, unwavering eyes. She knelt down before him with small hands tightly clasped.

"I'm going to say something dreadful, Billikins," she said.

He looked at her for a moment or two in silence.

Then, "I know what you are going to say," he said.

She shook her head. "Oh, no, you don't, darling. It's something that'll make you frightfully angry."

The faintest gleam of a smile crossed Merryon's face. "With you?" he said.

She nodded, and suddenly her eyes were brimming with tears. "Yes, with me."

He put his hand on her shoulder. "I tell you, I know what it is," he said, with a certain stubbornness.

She turned her cheek for a moment to caress the hand; then suddenly all her strength went from her. She sank down on the floor at his feet, huddled together in a woeful heap, just as she had been on that first night when the safety-curtain had dropped behind her.

"You'll never forgive me!" she sobbed. "But I knew—I knew—I always knew!"

"Knew what, child?" He was stooping over her. His hand, trembling still with weakness, was on her head. "But, no, don't tell me!" he said, and his voice was deeply tender. "The fellow is dead, isn't he?"

"Oh, yes, he's dead." Quiveringly, between piteous sobs, she answered him. "He—was dying before I reached him—that dreadful night. He just—had strength left—to curse me! And I am cursed! I am cursed!"

She flung out her arms wildly, clasping his feet.

He stooped lower over her. "Hush—hush!" he said.

She did not seem to hear. "I let you take me—I stained your honour—I wasn't a free woman. I tried to think I was; but in my heart—I always knew—I always knew! I wouldn't have your love at first—because I knew. And I came to you—that monsoon night—chiefly because—I wanted—when he came after me—as I knew he would come—to force him—to set me—free."

Through bitter sobbing the confession came; in bitter sobbing it ended.

But still Merryon's hand was on her head, still his face was bent above her, grave and sad and pitiful, the face of a strong man enduring grief.

After a little, haltingly, she spoke again. "And I wasn't

coming back to you—ever. Only—someone—a *syce*—told me you had been stricken down. And then I had to come. I couldn't leave you to die. That's all—that's all! I'm going now. And I shan't come back. I'm not—your wife. You're quite, quite free. And I'll never—bring shame on you—again."

Her straining hands tightened. She kissed, the feet she clasped. "I'm a wicked, wicked woman," she said. "I was born—on the wrong side—of the safety-curtain. That's no—excuse; only—to make you understand."

She would have withdrawn herself then, but his hands held her. She covered her face, kneeling between them.

"Why do you want me to understand?" he said, his voice very low.

She quivered at the question, making no attempt to answer, just weeping silently there in his hold.

He leaned towards her, albeit he was trembling with weakness. "Puck, listen!" he said. "I do understand."

She caught her breath and became quite still.

"Listen again!" he said. "What is done—is done; and nothing can alter it. But—your future is mine. You have forfeited the right to leave me."

She uncovered her face in a flash to gaze at him as one confounded.

He met the look with eyes that held her own. "I say it," he said. "You have forfeited the right. You say I am free. Am I free?"

She nodded, still with her eyes on his. "I have—no claim on you," she whispered, brokenly.

His hands tightened; he brought her nearer to him. "And when that dream of yours comes true," he said, "what then? What then?"

Her face quivered painfully at the question. She swallowed once or twice spasmodically, like a hurt child trying not to cry.

"That's—nobody's business but mine," she said.

A very curious smile drew Merryon's mouth. "I thought I had had something to do with it," he said. "I think I am entitled to part-ownership, anyway."

She shook her head, albeit she was very close to his breast. "You're not, Billikins!" she declared, with vehemence. "You only say that—out of pity. And I don't want pity. I—I'd rather you hated me than that! Miles rather!"

His arms went round her. He uttered a queer, passionate laugh and drew her to his heart. "And what if I offer you—

love?" he said. "Have you no use for that either, my wife—my wife?"

She turned and clung to him, clung fast and desperately, as a drowning person clings to a spar. "But I'm not, Billikins! I'm not!" she whispered, with her face hidden.

"You shall be," he made steadfast answer. "Before God you shall be."

"Ah, do you believe in God?" she murmured.

"I do," he said, firmly.

She gave a little sob. "Oh, Billikins, so do I. At least, I think I do; but I'm half afraid, even now, though I did try to do—the right thing. I shall only know for certain—when the dream comes true." Her face came upwards, her lips moved softly against his neck. "Darling," she whispered, "don't you hope—it'll be—a boy?"

He bent his head mutely. Somehow speech was difficult.

But Puck was not wanting speech of him just then. She turned her red lips to his. "But even if it's a girl, darling, it won't matter, for she'll be born on the right side of the safety-curtain now, thanks to your goodness, your generosity."

He stopped her sharply. "Puck! Puck!"

Their lips met. Puck was sobbing a little and smiling at the same time.

"Your love is the safety-curtain, Billikins darling," she whispered, softly. "And I'm going to thank God for it—every day of my life."

"My darling!" he said. "My wife!"

Her eyes shone up to his through tears. "Oh, do you realize," she said, "that we have risen from the dead?"

The Experiment

CHAPTER I

ON TRIAL

"I really don't know why I accepted him. But somehow it was done before I knew. He waltzes so divinely that it intoxicates me, and then I naturally cease to be responsible for my actions."

Doris Fielding leant back luxuriously, her hands clasped behind her head.

"I can't think what he wants to marry me for," she said reflectively. "I am quite sure I don't want to marry him."

"Then, my dear child, what possessed you to accept him?" remonstrated her friend, Vera Abingdon, from behind the tea-table.

"That's just what I don't know," said Doris, a little smile twitching the corner of her mouth. "However, it doesn't signify greatly. I don't mind being engaged for a little while if he is good, but I certainly shan't go on if I don't like it. It's in the nature of an experiment, you see; and it really is necessary, for there is absolutely no other way of testing the situation."

She glanced at her friend and burst into a gay peal of laughter. No one knew how utterly charming this girl could be till she laughed.

"Oh, don't look so shocked, please!" she begged. "I know I'm flippant, flighty, and foolish, but really I'm not a bit wicked. Ask Phil if I am. He has known me all my life."

"I do not need to ask him, Dot." Vera spoke with some gravity notwithstanding. "I have never for a moment thought you wicked. But I do sometimes think you are rather heartless."

Doris opened her blue eyes wide.

"Oh, why? I am sure I am not. It really isn't my fault that I have been engaged two or three times before. Directly I begin to get pleasantly intimate with any one he proposes, and how can I possibly know, unless I am on terms of intimacy, whether I should like to marry him or not? I am sure I don't want to be engaged to any one for any length of time. It's as bad as being cast up on a desert island with only one wretched man to speak to. As a matter of fact, what you call heartlessness is sheer broad-mindedness on my part. I admit that I do occasionally sail near the wind. It's fun, and I like it. But I never do any harm—any real harm I mean. I always put my helm over in time. And I must protect myself somehow against fortune-hunters."

Vera was silent. This high-spirited young cousin of her husband's was often a sore anxiety to her. She had had sole charge of the girl for the past three years and had found it no light responsibility.

"Cheer up, darling!" besought Doris. "There is not the smallest cause for a wrinkled brow. Perhaps the experiment will turn out a success this time. Who knows? And even if it doesn't, no one will be any the worse. I am sure Vivian Caryl will never break his heart for me."

But Vera Abingdon shook her head.

"I don't like you to be so wild, Dot. It makes people think lightly of you. And you know how angry Phil was last time."

Dot snapped her fingers airily and rose.

"Who cares for Phil? Besides, it really was not my fault last time, whatever any one may say. Are you going to ask my *fiancé* down to Rivermead for Easter? Because if so, I do beg you won't tell everybody we are engaged. It is quite an informal arrangement, and perhaps, considering all the circumstances, the less said about it the better."

She stopped and kissed Vera's grave face, laughed again as though she could not help it, and flitted like a butterfly from the room.

CHAPTER II

HIS INTENTIONS

"Where is Doris?" asked Phil Abingdon, looking round upon the guests assembled in his drawing-room at Rivermead. "We are all waiting for her."

"I think we had better go in without her," said his wife, with her nervous smile. "She arranged to motor down with Mrs. Lockyard and her party this afternoon. Possibly they have persuaded her to dine with them."

"She would never do that surely," said Phil, with an

involuntary glance at Vivian Caryl who had just entered.

"If you are talking about my *fiancé*, I think it more than probable that she would," the latter remarked. "Mrs. Lockyard's place is just across the river, I understand? Shall I punt over and fetch Doris?"

"No, no!" broke in his hostess anxiously. "I am sure she wouldn't come if you did. Besides—"

"Oh, as to that," said Vivian Caryl, with a grim smile, "I think, with all deference to your opinion, that the odds would be in my favour. However, let us dine first, if you prefer it."

Mrs. Abingdon did prefer it, and said so hastily. She seemed to have a morbid dread of a rupture between Doris Fielding and her *fiancé*, a feeling with which Caryl quite obviously had no sympathy. There was nothing very remarkable about the man save this somewhat supercilious demeanour which had caused Vera to marvel many times at Doris's choice.

They went in to dinner without further discussion. Caryl sat on Vera's left, and amazed her by his utter unconcern regarding the absentee. He seemed to be in excellent spirits, and his dry humour provoked a good deal of merriment.

She led the way back to the drawing-room as soon as possible. There was a billiard-room beyond to which the members of her party speedily betook themselves, and here most of the men joined them soon after. Neither Caryl nor Abingdon was with them, and Vera counted the minutes of their absence with a sinking heart while her guests buzzed all unheeding around her.

It was close upon ten o'clock when she saw her husband's face for a moment in the doorway. He made a rapid sign to her, and with a murmured excuse she went to him, closing the door behind her.

Caryl was standing with him, calm as ever, though she fancied that his eyes were a little wider than usual and his bearing less supercilious.

Her husband, she saw at a glance, was both angry and agitated.

"She has gone off somewhere with that bounder Brandon," he said. "They got down to tea, and went off again in the motor afterwards, Mrs. Lockyard doesn't seem to know for certain where."

"Phil!" she exclaimed in consternation, and added with her eyes on Caryl, "What is to be done? What can be done?"

Caryl made quiet reply:

"There was some talk of Wynhampton. I am going there now on your husband's motor-bicycle. If I do not find her there—"

He paused, and on the instant a girl's high peal of laughter rang through the house. The drawing-room door was flung back, and Doris herself stood on the threshold.

"Goodness!" she cried. "What a solemn conclave! You can't think how funny you all look! Do tell me what it is all about!"

She stood before them, the motor-veil thrown back from her dainty face, her slight figure quivering with merriment.

Vera hastened to meet her with outstretched hands.

"Oh, my dear, you can't think how anxious we have been about you."

Doris took her by the shoulders and lightly kissed her.

"Silly! Why? You know I always come up smiling. Why, Phil, you are looking positively green! Have you been anxious, too? I am indeed honoured."

She swept him a curtsey, her face all dimples and laughter.

"We've had the jolliest time," she declared. "We motored to Wynhampton and saw the last of the races. After that, we dined at a dear little place with a duckpond at the bottom of the garden. And finally we returned—it ought to have been by moonlight, only there was no moon. Where is everyone? In the billiard-room? I want some milk and soda frightfully. Vivian, you might, like the good sort you are, go and get me some."

She bestowed a dazzling smile upon her *fiancé* and offered him one finger by way of salutation.

Abingdon, who had been waiting to get in a word, here exploded with some violence and told his young cousin in no measured terms what he thought of her conduct.

She listened with her head on one side, her eyes brimful of mischief, and finally with an airy gesture turned to Caryl.

"Don't you want to scold me, too? I am sure you do. You had better be quick or there will be nothing left to say."

Abingdon turned on his heel and walked away. He was thoroughly angry and made no attempt to hide it. His wife lingered a moment irresolute, then softly followed him. And as the door closed, Caryl looked very steadily into the girl's flushed face and spoke:

"All I have to say is this. Maurice Brandon is no fit escort for any woman who values her reputation. And I here and now forbid you most strictly, most emphatically, ever to go out with him alone again."

He paused. She was looking straight back at him with her

chin in the air.

"Dear me!" she said. "Do you really? And who gave you the right to dictate to me?"

"You yourself," he answered quietly.

"Indeed! May I ask when?"

He stiffened a little, but his face did not alter.

"When you promised to be my wife," he said.

Her eyes blazed instant defiance.

"An engagement can be broken off!" she declared recklessly.

"By mutual consent," said Caryl drily.

"That is absurd," she rejoined. "You couldn't possibly hold me to it against my will."

"I am quite capable of doing so," he told her coolly, "if I think it worth my while."

"Worth your while!" she exclaimed, staring at him as if she doubted his sanity.

"Even so," he said. "When I have fully satisfied myself that a heartless little flirt like you can be transformed into a virtuous and amiable wife. It may prove a difficult process, I admit, and perhaps not altogether a pleasant one. But I shall not shirk it on that account."

He leant back against the mantelpiece with a gesture that plainly said that so far as he was concerned the matter was ended.

But it was not so with Doris. She stood before him for several seconds absolutely motionless, all the vivid colour gone from her face, her blue eyes blazing with speechless fury. At length, with a sudden, fierce movement, she tore the ring he had given her from her finger and held it out to him.

"Take it!" she said, her voice high-pitched and tremulous. "This is the end!"

He did not stir a muscle.

"Not yet, I think," he said.

She flashed a single glance at him in which pride and uncertainty were strangely mingled, then made a sudden swoop towards the fire. He read her intention in a second, and stooping swiftly caught her hand. The ring shot from her hold, gleamed in a shining curve in the firelight, and fell with a tinkle among the ashes of the fender.

Caryl did not utter a word, but his face was fixed and grim as, still tightly gripping the hand he had caught, he knelt and groped among the half-dead embers for the ring it had wantonly flung there. When he found it he rose.

"Before you do anything of that sort again," he said, "let me advise you to stop and think. It will do you no harm, and may save trouble."

He took her left hand, paused a moment, and then deliberately fitted the ring back upon her finger. She made no resistance, for she was instinctively aware that he would brook no morefrom her just then. She was in fact horribly scared, though his voice was still perfectly quiet and even. Something in his touch had set her heart beating, something electric, something terrifying. She dared not meet his eyes.

He dropped her hand almost contemptuously. There was nothing lover-like about him at that moment.

"And remember," he said, "that no experiment can ever prove a success unless it is given a fair trial. You will continue to be engaged to me until I set you free. Is that understood?"

She did not answer him. She was pulling at the loose ends of her veil with restless fingers, her face downcast and very pale.

"Doris!" he said.

She glanced up at him sharply.

"I am rather tired," she said, and her voice quivered a little. "Do you mind if I say good-night?"

"Answer me first," he said.

She shook her head.

"I forget what you asked me. It doesn't matter, does it? There's someone coming, and I don't want to be caught. Good-night!"

She whisked round with the words before he could realize her intention, and in a moment was at the door. She waved a hand to him airily as she disappeared. And Caryl was left to wonder if her somewhat precipitate departure could be regarded as a sign of defeat or merely a postponement of the struggle.

CHAPTER III

THE KNIGHT ERRANT

It was the afternoon of Easter Day, and a marvellous peace lay upon all things.

Maurice Brandon, a look of supreme boredom on his

handsome face, had just sauntered down to the river bank. A belt of daffodils nodded to him from the shrubbery on the farther shore. He stood and stared at them absently while he idly smoked a cigarette.

Finally, after a long and quite unprofitable inspection, he turned aside to investigate a boathouse under the willows on Mrs. Lockyard's side of the stream. He found the door unlocked, and discovered within a somewhat dilapidated punt. This, after considerable exertion, he managed to drag forth and finally to run into the water. The craft seemed seaworthy, and he proceeded to forage for a punt-pole.

Fully equipped at length, he stepped on board and poled himself out from the shore. Arrived at the farther bank, he calmly disembarked and tied up under the willows. He paused a few seconds to light another cigarette, then turned from the river and sauntered up the path between the high box hedges.

The garden was deserted, and he pursued his way unmolested till he came within sight of the house. Here for the first time he stopped to take deliberate stock of his surroundings. Standing in the shelter of a giant rhododendron, he saw two figures emerge and walk along the narrow gravelled terrace before the house. As he watched, they reached the farther end and turned. He recognized them both. They were Caryl and his host Abingdon.

For a few moments they stood talking, then went away together round an angle of the house.

Scarcely had they disappeared before a girl's light figure appeared at an upstairs window. Doris's mischievous face peeped forth, wearing her gayest, most impudent grimace.

There was no one else in sight, and with instant decision Brandon stepped into full view, and without the faintest suggestion of concealment began to stroll up the winding path.

She heard his footsteps on the gravel, and turned her eyes upon him with a swift start of recognition.

He raised his hand in airy salute, and he heard her low murmur of laughter as she waved him a hasty sign to await her in the shrubbery from which he had just emerged.

"Did you actually come across the river?" said Doris. "Whatever made you do that?"

"I said I should come and fetch you, you know, if you didn't turn up," he said.

She laughed.

"Do you always keep your word?"

"To you—always," he assured her.

Her merry face coloured a little, but she met his eyes with absolute candour.

"And now that you have come what can we do? Are you going to take me on the river? It looks rather dangerous."

"It is dangerous," Brandon said coolly, "but I think I can get you over in safety if you will allow me to try. In any case, I won't let you drown."

"I shall be furious if anything happens," she told him—"if you splash me even. So beware!"

He pushed out from the bank with a laugh. It was evident that her threat did not greatly impress him.

As for Doris, she was evidently enjoying the adventure, and the risks that attended it only added to its charm. There was something about this man that fascinated her, a freedom and a daring to which her own reckless spirit could not fail to respond. He was the most interesting plaything she had had for a long time. She had no fear that he would ever make the mistake of taking her seriously.

They reached the opposite bank in safety, and he handed her ashore with considerable *empressement*.

"I have a confession to make," he said, as they walked up to the house.

"Oh, I know what it is," she returned carelessly. "Mrs. Lockyard did not expect me and has gone out."

He nodded.

"You are taking it awfully well. One would almost think you didn't mind."

She laughed.

"I never mind anything so long as I am not bored."

"Nor do I," said Brandon. "We seem to have a good deal in common. But what puzzles me—"

He broke off. They had reached the open French window that led into Mrs. Lockyard's drawing-room. He stood aside for her to enter.

"Well?" she said, as she passed him. "What is this weighty problem?"

He followed her in.

"What puzzles me," he said, "is how a girl with your natural independence and love of freedom can endure to remain unmarried."

She opened her eyes wide in astonishment.

"My good sir, you have expressed the exact reason in words which could not have been better chosen. Independence, love of freedom, and a very strong preference for going my own way."

He laughed a little.

"Yes, but you would have all these things a thousand times multiplied if you were married. Look at all the restraints and restrictions to which girls are subjected where married women simply please themselves. Why, you are absolutely hedged round with conventions. You can scarcely go for a ride with a man of your acquaintance in broad daylight without endangering your reputation. What would they say—your cousin and Mrs. Abingdon—if they knew that you were here with me now? They would hold up their hands in horror."

The girl's thoughts flashed suddenly to Caryl. How much freedom might she expect from him?

"It's all very well," she said, with a touch of petulance, "but easy-going husbands don't grow on every gooseberry-bush. I have never yet met the man who wouldn't want to arrange my life in every detail if I married him."

"Yes, you have," said Brandon.

He spoke with deliberate emphasis, and she knew that as he spoke he looked at her in a manner that there could be no mistaking. Her heart quickened a little, and she felt the colour rise in her face.

"Do you know that I am engaged to Vivian Caryl?" she said.

"Perfectly," he answered. "I also know that you have not the smallest intention of marrying him."

She frowned, but did not contradict him.

He continued with considerable assurance:

"He is not the man to make you happy, and I think you know it. My only wonder is that you didn't realize it earlier—before you became engaged to him."

"My engagement was only an experiment," she said quickly.

"And therefore easily broken," he rejoined. "Why don't you put a stop to it?"

She hesitated.

He bent towards her.

"Do you mean to say that he is cad enough to hold you against your will?"

Still she hesitated, half-afraid to speak openly.

He leant nearer; he took her hand.

"My dear child," he said, "don't for Heaven's sake give in to such tyranny as that, and be made miserable for the rest of your life. Oh, I grant you he is the sort of fellow who would make what is called a good husband, but not the sort of husband you want. He would keep you in order, shackle you at every turn. Marry him, and it will be good-bye to liberty—even such liberty as you have now—forever."

Her face had changed. She was very pale.

"I know all that," she said, speaking rapidly, with headlong impulse. "But, don't you see how difficult it is for me? They are all on his side, and he is so horribly strong. Oh, I was a fool I know to accept him. But we were waltzing and it came so suddenly. I never stopped to think. I wish I could get away now, but I can't."

"I can tell you of a way," said Brandon.

She glanced at him.

"Oh, yes, I know. But I can't be engaged to two people at once. I couldn't face it. I detest scenes."

"There need be no scene," he said. "You have only to come to me and give me the right to defend you. I ask for nothing better. Even Caryl would scarcely have the impertinence to dispute it. As my wife you will be absolutely secure from any interference."

She was gazing at him wide-eyed.

"Do you mean a runaway marriage?" she questioned slowly.

He drew nearer still, and possessed himself of her hands.

"Yes, just that," he said. "It would take a little courage, but you have plenty of that. And the rest I would see to. It wouldn't be so very difficult, you know. Mrs. Lockyard would help us, and you would be absolutely safe with me. I haven't much to offer you, I admit. I'm as poor as a church mouse. But at least you would find me"—he smiled into her startled eyes—"a very easy-going husband, I assure you."

"Oh, I don't know!" Doris said. "I don't know!"

Yet still she left her hands in his and still she listened to him. That airy reference of his to his poverty affected her favourably. He would scarcely have made it, she told herself, with an unconscious effort to silence unacknowledged misgivings, if her fortune had been the sole attraction.

"Look here," he said, breaking in upon these hasty meditations, "I don't want you to do anything in a hurry. Take a little while to think it over. Let me know tomorrow. I am not leaving till the evening. You shall do nothing, so far as I am concerned, against your will. I want you, now and always, to do exactly as you like. You believe that?"

"I quite believe you mean it at the present moment," she said with a decidedly doubtful smile.

"It will be so always," said Brandon, "whether you believe it or not."

And with considerable ceremony he raised her hands to his lips and deliberately kissed them. It seemed to Doris at that moment that even so headlong a scheme as this was not without its very material advantages. There were so many drawbacks to being betrothed.

CHAPTER IV

AT CLOSE QUARTERS

When Doris descended to breakfast on the following morning she found an animated party in the dining-room discussing the best means of spending the day. Abingdon himself and most of his guests were in favour of attending an aviation meeting at Wynhampton a few miles away.

Caryl was not present, but as she passed through the hall a little later, he came in at the front door.

"I was just coming to you," he remarked, pausing to flick the ash from his cigarette before closing the door. "I have been making arrangements for you to drive to Wynhampton with me."

Doris made a stiff movement that seemed almost mechanical. But the next moment she recovered her self-control. Why was she afraid of this man, she asked herself desperately? No man had ever managed to frighten her before.

"I think I should prefer to go in the motor," she said, and smiled with quivering lips. "Get Phil to drive with you. He likes the dog-cart better than I do."

"I have talked it over with him," Caryl responded gravely. "He agrees with me that this is the best arrangement."

There was to be no escape then. Once more the stronger will prevailed. Without another word she turned from him and went upstairs. She might have defied him, but she knew in her heart that he could compass his ends in spite of her. And she was afraid.

She had a moment of absolute panic as she mounted into the high cart. He handed her up, and his grasp, close and firm, seemed to her eloquent of that deadly resolution with which he mastered her.

For the first half-mile he said nothing whatever, being fully occupied with the animal he was driving—a skittish young mare impatient of restraint.

Doris on her side sat in unbroken silence, enduring the strain with a set face, dreading the moment when he should have leisure to speak.

He was evidently in no hurry to do so. Or was it possible that he found some difficulty in choosing his words?

At length he turned his head and spoke.

"I secured this interview," he said, "because there is an important point which I want to discuss with you."

"What is it?"

She nerved herself to meet his look, but her eyes fell before its steady mastery almost instantly.

"About our wedding," he said in his calm, deliberate voice. "I should like to have the day fixed."

Her heart gave a great thump of dismay.

"Do you really mean to hunt me down then and—and marry me against my will?" she said, almost panting out the words.

Caryl turned his eyes back to the mare.

"I mean to marry you—yes," he said. "I think you forget that you accepted me of your own accord."

"I was mad!" she broke in passionately.

"People in love are never wholly sane," he remarked cynically.

"I was never in love with you!" she cried. "Never, never!"

He raised his eyebrows.

"Nevertheless you will marry me," he said.

"Why?" she gasped back furiously. "Why should I marry you? You know I hate you, and you—you—surely you must hate me?"

"No," he said with extreme deliberation, "strange as it may seem, I don't."

Something in the words quelled her anger. Abruptly she abandoned the struggle and fell silent, her face averted.

"And so," he proceeded, "we may as well decide upon the wedding-day without further argument."

"And, if—if I refuse?" she murmured rather incoherently.

"You will not refuse," he said with a finality so absolute that her last hope went out like an extinguished candle.

She seized her courage with both hands and turned to him.

"You will give me a little while to think it over?"

"Why?" said Caryl.

"Because I—I can't possibly decide upon the spur of the moment," she said confusedly.

Was he going to refuse her even this small request? It almost seemed that he was.

"How long will it take you?" he asked. "Will you give me an answer tonight?"

Her heart leapt to a sudden hope called to life by his words.

"Tomorrow!" she said quickly.

"I said tonight."

"Very well," she rejoined, yielding. "Tonight, if you prefer it."

"Thanks. I do."

They were his last words on the subject. He seemed to think it ended there, and there was nothing more to be said.

As for Doris, she sat by his side, outwardly calm but inwardly shaken to the depths. To be thus firmly caught in the meshes of her own net was an experience so new and so terrifying that she was utterly at a loss as to how to cope with it. Yet there was a chance, one ray of hope to help her. There was Major Brandon, the man who had offered her freedom. He was to have his answer today. For the first time she began seriously to ponder what that answer should be.

CHAPTER V

THE WAY TO FREEDOM

So far as Doris was concerned the aviation meeting was not a success. There were some wonderful exhibitions of flying, but she was too preoccupied to pay more than a very superficial attention to what she saw.

They lunched at a great hotel overlooking the aviation ground. The place was crowded, and they experienced some difficulty in finding places. Eventually Doris found herself seated at a square table with Caryl and two others in the middle of the great room.

She was studying a menu as a pretext for avoiding conversation with her *fiancé*, when a man's voice murmured hurriedly in her ear:

"Will you allow me for a moment please? The lady who has just left this table thinks she must have dropped one of her gloves under it."

Doris pushed back her chair and would have risen, but the speaker was already on his knees and laid a hasty, restraining hand upon her. It found hers and, under cover of the tablecloth, pressed a screw of paper into her fingers.

The next instant he emerged, very red in the face, but triumphant, a lady's gauntlet glove in his hand.

"Awfully obliged!" he declared. "Sorry to have disturbed you. Thought I should find it here."

He smiled, bowed, and departed, leaving Doris amazed at his audacity. She had met this young man often at Mrs. Lockyard's house, where he was invariably referred to as "the little Fricker boy."

She threw a furtive glance at Caryl, but he had plainly noticed nothing. With an uneasy sense of shame she slipped the note into her glove.

She perused it on the earliest opportunity. It contained but one sentence:

"If you still wish for freedom, you can find it down by the river at any hour tonight."

There was no signature of any sort; none was needed, She hid the message away again, and for the rest of the afternoon she was almost feverishly gay to hide the turmoil of indecision at her heart.

She saw little of Caryl after luncheon, but he re-appeared again in time to drive her back in the dog-cart as they had come. She found him very quiet and preoccupied, on the return journey, but his presence no longer dismayed her. It was the consciousness that a way of escape was open to her that emboldened her.

They were nearing the end of the drive, when he at length laid aside his preoccupation and spoke:

"Have you made up your mind yet?"

That query of his was the turning point with her. Had he shown the smallest sign of relenting from his grim purpose, had he so much as couched his question in terms of kindness, he might have melted her even then; for she was impulsive ever and quick to respond to any warmth. But the coldness of his question, the unyielding mastery of his manner, impelled her to final rebellion. In the moment that intervened between his question and her reply her decision was made.

"You shall have my answer tonight," she said.

He turned from her without a word, and a little wonder quivered through her as to the meaning of his silence. She was glad when they reached Rivermead and she could take refuge in her own room.

Here once more she read Brandon's message; read it with a thumping heart, but no thought of drawing back. It was the only way out for her.

She dressed for dinner, and then made a few hasty preparations for her flight. She laid no elaborate plans for effecting it, for she anticipated no difficulty. The night would be dark, and she could rely upon her ingenuity for the rest. Failure was unthinkable.

When they rose from the table she waited for Vera and slipped a hand into her arm.

"Do make an excuse for me," she whispered. "I have had a dreadful day, and I can't stand any more. I am going upstairs."

"My dear!" murmured back Vera, by way of protest.

Nevertheless she made the excuse almost as soon as they entered the drawing-room, and Doris fled upstairs on winged feet. At the head she met Caryl about to descend; almost collided with him. He had evidently been up to his room to fetch something.

He stood aside for her at once.

"You are not retiring yet?" he asked.

She scarcely glanced at him. She would not give herself time to be disconcerted.

"I am coming down again," she said, and ran on.

Barely a quarter of an hour after the encounter with Caryl, dressed in a long dark motoring coat and closely veiled, she slipped down the back stairs that led to the servants' quarters, stood listening against a baize door that led into the front hall, then whisked it open and fled across to open the conservatory door, noiseless as a shadow.

The conservatory was in semi-darkness. She expected to see no one; looked for no one. A moment she paused by the door that led into the garden, and in that pause she heard a slight sound. It might have been anything. It probably was a creak from one of the wicker chairs that stood in a corner. Whatever its origin, it startled her to greater haste. She fumbled at the door and pulled it open.

A gust of wind and rain blew in upon her, but she was scarcely aware of it. In another moment she had softly closed the door again and was scudding across the terrace to the steps that led towards the river path.

As she reached it a light shone out in front of her, wavered, and was gone.

"This way to freedom, lady mine," said Brandon's voice close to her, and she heard in it the laugh he did not utter. "Mind you don't tumble in."

His hand touched her arm, closed upon it, drew her to his side. In another instant it encircled her, but she pushed him vehemently away.

"Let us go!" she said feverishly. "Let us go!"

"Come along then," he said gaily. "The boat is just here. You'll have to hold the lantern. Mind how you get on board."

As he pushed out from the bank, he told her something of his arrangements.

"There's a motor waiting—not the one Polly usually hires, but it's quite a decent little car. By the way, she has gone straight up to Town from Wynhampton; said we should do our eloping best alone. We shan't be quite alone, though, for Fricker is going to drive us. But he's a negligible quantity, eh? His only virtue is that he isn't afraid of driving in the dark."

"You will take me to Mrs. Lockyard?" said Doris quickly.

"Of course. She is at her flat, she and Mrs. Fricker. We shall be there soon after midnight, all being well. Confound this stream! It swirls like a mill-race."

He fell silent, and devoted all his attention to reaching the farther bank.

Doris sat with the lantern in her hands, striving desperately to control her nervous excitement. Her absence could not have been discovered yet, she was sure, but she was in a fever of anxiety notwithstanding. She would not feel safe until she was actually on the road.

The boat bumped at last against the bank, and she drew a breath of relief. The journey had seemed interminable.

Suddenly through the windy darkness there came to them the hoot of a motor-horn.

"That's all right," said Brandon cheerily. "That's Fricker, wanting to know if all's well."

He hurried her over the wet grass, skirted the house by a

side-path that ran between dripping laurels, and brought her out finally into the little front garden.

A glare of acetylene lamps met them abruptly as they emerged, dazzling them for the moment. The buzz of a motor engine also greeted them, and a smell of petrol hung in the wet air.

As her eyes accustomed themselves to the brightness, Doris made out a small closed motor-car, with a masked chauffeur seated at the wheel.

"Good little Fricker!" said Brandon, slapping the chauffeur's shoulder as he passed. "So you've got your steam up! Straight ahead then, and as fast as you like. Don't get run in, that's all."

He handed Doris into the car, followed her, and slammed the door.

The next moment they passed swiftly out on to the road, and Doris knew that the die was cast. She stood finally committed to this, the wildest, most desperate venture of her life.

CHAPTER VI

A MASTER STROKE

"Here beginneth," laughed Brandon, sliding his arm around her as she sat tense in every nerve gazing at the rain-blurred window.

She did not heed him; it was almost as if she had not heard. Her hands were tightly clasped upon one another, and her face was turned from him. There was no lamp inside the car, the only illumination proceeding from those without, showing them the driver huddled over the wheel, but shedding little light into the interior.

He tightened his arm about her, laying his other hand upon her clasped ones.

"By Jove, little girl, you're cold!" he said.

She was—cold as ice. She parted her fingers stiffly to free them from his grasp.

"I—I'm quite comfortable," she assured him, without turning her head. "Please don't trouble about me."

But he was not to be thus discouraged.

"You can't be comfortable," he argued. "Why, you're

shivering. Let me see what I can do to make things better."

He tried to draw her to him, but she resisted almost angrily.

"Oh, do leave me alone! I'm not uncomfortable. I'm only thinking."

"Well, don't be silly!" he urged. "It's no use thinking at this stage. The thing is done now, and well done. We shall be man and wife by this time tomorrow. We'll go to Paris, eh, and have no end of a spree."

"Perhaps," she said, not looking at him or yielding an inch to his persuasion.

It was plain that for some reason she desired to be left in peace, and after a brief struggle with himself, Brandon decided that he would be wise to let her have her way. He leant back and crossed his arms in silence.

The car sped along at a pace which he found highly satisfactory. He had absolute faith in Fricker's driving and knowledge of the roads.

They had been travelling for the greater part of an hour, when Doris at length relaxed from her tense attitude and lay back in her corner, nestling into it with a long shiver.

Brandon was instantly on the alert.

"I'm sure you are cold. Here's a rug here. Let me—"

"Oh, do please leave me alone!" she said, with a sob. "I'm so horribly tired."

Beseechingly almost she laid her hand upon his arm with the words.

The touch fired him. He considered that he had been patient long enough. Abruptly he caught her to him.

"Come, I say," he said, half-laughing, half in savage earnest, "I can't have you crying on what's almost our wedding trip!"

He certainly did not expect the absolutely furious resistance with which she met his action. She thrust him from her with the strength of frenzy.

"How dare you?" she cried passionately. "How dare you touch me, you—you hateful cad?"

For the moment, such was his astonishment, he suffered her to escape from his hold. Then, called into activity by her unreasoning fury, the devil in him leapt suddenly up and took possession. With a snarling laugh he gripped her by the arms, holding her by brutal force.

"You little wild cat!" he said in a voice that shook between anger and amusement. "So this is your gratitude, is it? I am to give all and receive nothing for my pains. Then let me make it quite clear to you here and now that that is not my intention. I will be kind to you, but you must be kind to me, too. The benefit is to be mutual."

It was premature. In his heart he knew it, but she had provoked him to it and there was no turning back now. He resented the provocation, that was all, and it made him the more brutally inclined towards her.

As for Doris, she fought and tore at his grasp like a mad creature; and when he mastered her, when, still laughing between his teeth, he forced her face upwards and kissed it fiercely and violently, she shrieked between his kisses, shrieked and shrieked again.

The sudden grinding of the brake recalled Brandon to his senses. The fool was actually stopping the car. He relinquished his hold upon the girl to dash his hand against the window in front.

"Drive on, curse you, drive on!" he shouted through the glass. "I'll let you know if we want to stop."

But the car stopped in spite of him. The chauffeur, shining from head to foot in his oil-skins, sprang to the ground. A moment and he was at the door, had wrenched it open, and was peering within.

"What are you gaping there for, you fool?" raved Brandon, his hand upon Doris, who was suddenly straining forward. "It's all right, I tell you. Go on."

"I am going on," the chauffeur responded calmly through his mask. "But I am not taking you any farther, Major Brandon. So tumble out at once, you dirty, thieving hound!"

The words, the tone, the attitude, flashed such a revelation upon Doris that she cried out in amazement, and then with a revulsion of feeling so great that it deprived her of all speech she threw herself forward and clung to the masked chauffeur in an agony of tears.

Brandon was staring at him with dropped jaw.

"Who the blazes are you?" he said.

"You know me, I think," the chauffeur responded quietly. He was pressing Doris back into her seat with absolute steadiness. "We have met before. I was present at your first wedding ten years ago, and—as a junior counsel—I helped to divorce you a few months after. My name is Vivian Caryl."

He freed a hand to push up his mask. His pale face with its heavy-lidded eyes stared, supremely contemptuous, into Brandon's suffused countenance. His composure was somehow disconcerting.

"Suppose you get out," he suggested. "I can talk to you then in a language you will understand."

"Curse you!" bawled Brandon. "Where's Fricker?"

Caryl shrugged his shoulders.

"You have seen him since I have. Are you going to get out? Ah, I thought you would."

He stood aside to allow him to do so, and then stepped back to shut the door. He did not utter a word to the girl cowering within, but that action of his was a mute command. She crouched in the dark and listened, but she did not dare to follow or to flee.

CHAPTER VII

THE MAN AT THE WHEEL

When Caryl came back to the motor his handkerchief was bound about the knuckles of his right hand, and his face wore a faint smile that had in it more of grimness than humour.

He paused at the open window and looked in on Doris without opening the door. The sound of the rain pattering heavily upon his shoulders filled in a silence that she found terrible. He spoke at length:

"You had better shut the window, the rain is coming in."

That was all, spoken in his customary drawl without a hint of anger or reproach. They cut her hard, those few words of his. It was as if he deemed her unworthy even of his contempt.

She raised her white face.

"What—are you going to do?" she managed to ask through her quivering lips.

"I am going to take you to the nearest town—to Bramfield to spend the rest of the night. It is getting late, you know—past midnight already."

"Bramfield!" she echoed with a start. "Then—then we have been going north all this time?"

"We have been going north," he said.

She glanced around. Her eyes were hunted.

"No," said Caryl. "I haven't killed him. He is sitting under the hedge about fifty yards up the road, thinking things over."

He opened the door then abruptly, and she held her breath and became still and tense with apprehension. But he only pulled up the window, closed the door again with a sharp click, and left her. When she dared to breathe again the car was in motion.

She took no interest in her surroundings. Her destination had become a matter of such secondary importance that she gave it no consideration whatever. What mattered, all that mattered, was that she was now in the hands and absolutely at the mercy of the man whom she feared as she feared no one else on earth, the man with whom in her mad coquetry she had dared to trifle.

The car was stopping. It came to a standstill almost imperceptibly, and Caryl stepped into the road. Tensely she watched him; but he did not so much as glance her way. He turned aside to a little gate in a high hedge of laurel, and passed within, leaving her alone in the night.

Soon she heard his deliberate footfalls returning. In a moment he had reached the door, his hand was upon it. She turned stiffly towards him as it opened.

He spoke at once in his calm, unmoved voice:

"A very old friend of mine lives here. She will put you up for the night and see to your comfort. Will you get out?"

Mutely she did so, feeling curiously weak and unstrung. He put his arm around her, and led her into the dim cottage garden.

They went up a tiled path to an open door from which the light of a single candle gleamed fitfully in the draught. She stumbled at the doorstep, but he held her up. He was almost carrying her.

As they entered, an old woman, bent and indescribably wrinkled, rose from her knees before a deep old-fashioned fireplace on the other side of the little kitchen, and came to meet them. She had evidently just coaxed a dying fire back to life.

"Ah, poor dear," she said at sight of the girl's exhausted face. "She looks more dead than alive. Bring her to the fire, Master Vivian. I'll soon have some hot milk for the poor lamb."

Caryl led her to an armchair that stood on one side of the blaze, and made her sit down. Then, stooping, he took one of her nerveless hands and held it closely in his own.

He did not speak to her, and she was relieved by his forbearance. As the warmth of his grasp gradually communicated itself to her numbed fingers, she felt her racing pulses grow steadier; but she was glad when he laid her hand down quietly in her lap and turned away.

He bent over her again in a few minutes with a cup of steaming milk. She took it from him, tasted it, and shuddered.

"There is brandy in it."

"Yes," said Caryl.

She turned her head away.

"I don't want it. I hate brandy."

He put his hand on her shoulder.

"You had better drink it all the same," he said.

She glanced at him, caught her breath sharply, then dumbly gave way. He kept his hand upon her while she drank, and only removed it to take the empty cup.

After that, standing gravely before her, he spoke again.

"I am going on into the town now with the motor, and I shall put up there. My old nurse will take care of you. I shall come back in the morning."

CHAPTER VIII

THE SURRENDER OF THE CITADEL

Old Mrs. Maynard, sweeping her brick floor with wide-open door through which the April sunlight streamed gloriously, nodded to herself a good many times over the doings of the night. A very discreet creature was Mrs. Maynard, faithful to the very heart of her, but she would not have been mortal had she not been intensely curious to know what were the circumstances that had led Vivian Caryl to bring to her door that shrinking, exhausted girl who still lay sleeping in the room above.

When Doris awoke in response to her deferential knock, only the reticence of the trained servant greeted her. The motherliness of the night before had completely vanished.

Doris was glad of it. She had to steel herself for the coming interview with Caryl; she had to face the result of her headlong actions with as firm a front as she could assume. She needed all her strength, and she could not have borne sympathy just then.

She thanked Mrs. Maynard for her attentions and saw her withdraw with relief. Then, having nibbled very half-heartedly at the breakfast provided, she arose with a great sigh, and began to prepare for whatever might lie before her.

Dressed at length, she sat down by the open window to wait—and wonder.

The click of the garden gate fell suddenly across her meditations, and she drew back sharply out of sight. He was entering.

She heard his leisurely footfall on the tiles and then his quiet voice below. Her heart began to thump with thick, uncertain beats. She was horribly afraid.

Yet when she heard the old woman ascending the stairs, she had the courage to go to the door and open it.

Mr. Caryl was in the parlour, she was told. He would be glad to see her at her convenience.

"I will go to him," she said, and forthwith descended to meet her fate.

He stood by the window when she entered, but wheeled round at once with his back to the light. She felt that this did not make much difference. She knew exactly how he was looking—cold, self-contained, implacable as granite. She had seldom seen him look otherwise. His face was a perpetual mask to her. It was this very inscrutability of his that had first waked in her the desire to see him among her retinue of slaves.

She went forward slowly, striving to attain at least a semblance of composure. At first it seemed that he would wait for her where he was; then unexpectedly he moved to meet her. He took her hand into his own, and she shrank a little involuntarily. His touch unnerved her.

"You have slept?" he asked. "You are better?"

Something in his tone made her glance upwards, catching her breath. But she decided instantly that she had been mistaken. He would not, he could not, mean to be kind at such a moment.

She made answer with an assumption of pride. She dared not let herself be natural just then.

"I am quite well. There was nothing wrong with me last night. I was only tired."

He suffered her hand to slip from his.

"I wonder what you think of doing," he said quietly. "Have you made any plans?"

The hot blood rushed to her face before she was aware of it. She turned it sharply aside.

"Am I to have a voice in the matter?" she said, her voice very low. "You did not think it worth while to consult me last night."

"You were scarcely in a fit state to be consulted," he answered gravely. "That is why I postponed the discussion. But I was then—as I am now—entirely at your disposal. I will take you back to your people at once if you wish it."

She made a quick, passionate gesture of protest, and moved away from him.

"Have you any alternative in your mind?" he asked.

She remained with her back to him.

"I shall go away," she said, a sudden note of recklessness in her voice. "I shall travel."

"Alone?" he questioned.

"Yes, alone." This time her voice rang defiance. She wheeled round quivering from head to foot. "But for you," she said, "but for your unwarrantable interference I should never have been placed in this hateful, this impossible, position. I should have been with my friends in London. It would have been my wedding-day."

The attack was plainly unexpected. Even Caryl was taken by surprise. But the next moment he was ready for her.

"Then by all means," he said, "let me take you to your friends in London. Doubtless your chivalrous lover has found his way thither long ere this."

She stamped like a little fury.

"Do you think I would marry him—now? Do you think I would marry any one after—after what happened last night? Oh, I hate you—I hate you all!"

Her voice broke. She covered her face, with tempestuous sobbing, and sank into a chair.

Caryl stood silent, biting his lip as if in irresolution. He did not try to comfort her.

After a while, her weeping still continuing, he leant across the table.

"Doris," he said, "leave off crying and listen to me. I know it is out of the question for you to marry that scoundrel whom I had the pleasure of thrashing last night. It always has been out of the question. That is one reason why I have been keeping such a hold upon you. Now that you admit the impossibility of it, I set you free. But you will be wise to think well before you accept your freedom from me. You are in an intolerable position, and I am quite powerless to help you unless you place yourself unreservedly in my hands and give me the right to protect you. It means a good deal, I know. It means, Doris, the sacrifice of your independence. But it also means a safe haven, peace, comfort, if not happiness. You may not love me. I never seriously thought that you did. But if you will give me your trust—I shall try to be satisfied with that."

Love! She had never heard the word on his lips before. It sent a curious thrill through her to hear it then. She had listened to him with her face hidden, though her tears had ceased. But as he ended, she slowly raised her head and looked at him.

"Are you asking me to marry you?" she said.

"I am," said Caryl.

She lowered her eyes from his, and began to trace a design on the table-cloth with one finger.

"I don't want to marry you," she said at length.

"I know," said Caryl.

She did not look up.

"No, you don't know. That's just it. You think you know everything. But you don't. For instance, you think you know why I ran away with Major Brandon. But you don't. You never will know—unless I tell you, probably not even then."

She broke off with an abrupt sigh, and leant back in her chair.

"One thing I do thank you for," she said irrelevantly. "And that is that you didn't take me back to Rivermead last night. Have they, I wonder, any idea where I am?"

"I left a message for your cousin before I left," Caryl said.

"Oh, then he knew—?"

"He knew that I had you under my protection," Caryl told her grimly. "I did not go into details. It was unnecessary. Only Flicker knew the details. I marked him down in the afternoon, after the incident at luncheon."

She opened her eyes.

"Then you guessed—?"

"I knew he did not find the missing glove under the table," said Caryl quietly. "I did not need any further evidence than that. I knew, moreover, that you had not devoted the whole of the previous afternoon to your correspondence. I was waiting for your cousin in the conservatory when you joined Brandon in the garden."

"And you—you were in the conservatory last night when I went through. I—I felt there was someone there."

"Yes," he answered. "I waited to see you go."

"Why didn't you stop me?"

For an instant her eyes challenged his.

He stood up, straightening himself slowly.

"It would not have answered my purpose," he told her steadily.

She stood up also, her face gone suddenly white.

"You chose this means of—of forcing me to marry you?"

"I chose this means—the only means to my hand—of opening your eyes," he said. "It has not perhaps been over successful. You are still blind to much that you ought to see. But you will understand these things better presently."

"Presently?" she faltered.

"When you are my wife," he said.

She flashed him a swift glance.

"I am to marry you then?"

He held out his hand to her across the table.

"Will you marry me, Doris?"

She hesitated for a single instant, her eyes downcast. Then suddenly, without speaking, she put her hand into his, glad that, notwithstanding the overwhelming strength of his position, he had allowed her the honours of war.

CHAPTER IX

THE WILLING CAPTIVE

"And so you were obliged to marry your *bête noire* after all! My dear, it has been the talk of the town. Come, sit down, and tell me all about it. I am burning to hear how it came about."

Doris's old friend, Mrs. Lockyard, paused to flick the ash from her cigarette, and to laugh slyly at the girl's face of discomfiture.

Doris also held a cigarette between her fingers, but she was only toying with it restlessly.

"There isn't much to tell," she said. "We were married by special licence. I was not obliged to marry him. I chose to do so."

Mrs. Lockyard laughed again, not very pleasantly.

"And left poor Maurice in the lurch. That was rather cruel of you after all his chivalrous efforts to deliver you from bondage. And he so hard up, too."

A flush of anger rose in the girl's face. She tilted her chin with the old proud gesture.

"I should not have married him in any case," she said. "He made that quite impossible by his own act. He—was not so chivalrous as I thought."

A gleam of malice shone for a moment in Mrs. Lockyard's eyes, and just a hint of it was perceptible in her voice as she made response.

"One has to make allowances sometimes. All men are not made after the pattern of your chosen lord and master. He, I grant you, is hard as granite and about as impassive. Still I mustn't depreciate your prize since it was of your own choosing. Let me wish you instead every happiness."

"He was not impassive that night," said Doris quickly, with a sharp inward sense of injustice.

"No?" questioned Mrs. Lockyard.

"No. At least—Major Brandon did not find him so." Doris's blue eyes took fire at the recollection. "He gave him his deserts," she said, with a certain exultation. "He thrashed him."

"Oh, my dear, he would have done that in any case. That was an old, old score paid off at last. Forgive me for depriving you of this small gratification. But that debt was contracted many years ago when you were scarcely out of your cradle. Your presence was a mere incident. You were the opportunity, not the cause."

"I don't know what you mean," said Doris, looking her straight in the face.

"No? Well, my dear, it isn't my business to enlighten you. If you really want to know, I must refer you to your husband. Surely that is Mrs. Fricker over there. You will not mind if she joins us?"

"I am going!" Doris announced abruptly—"I really only looked in to see if there were any letters."

She dropped her cigarette with determination and turned to the nearest door.

It was true that she had run into the club for her correspondence, but having met Mrs. Lockyard she had been almost compelled to linger, albeit unwillingly. Now from the depths of her soul she regretted the impulse that had borne her thither. She vowed to herself that she would not enter the club again so long as Mrs. Lockyard remained in town.

Three weeks had elapsed since her marriage; three weeks of shopping in Paris with Caryl somewhere in the background, looking on but never advising.

He had been very kind on the whole, she was fain to admit,

but she was further from understanding him now than she had ever been. He had retired into his shell so completely that it seemed unlikely that he would ever again emerge, and she did not dare to make the first advance.

Her return to London had been one of the greatest ordeals she had ever faced, but she had endured it unflinchingly, and had found that London had already almost forgotten the eccentricity of her marriage. In the height of the season memories are short.

Caryl had taken a flat overlooking the river, and here they had settled down. He spent the greater part of his day at the Law Courts, and Doris found herself thrown a good deal upon her own resources. In happier days this had been her ideal, but for some reason it did not now content her.

Returning from her encounter with Mrs. Lockyard at the club, she told herself with sudden petulance that life in town had lost all charm for her.

Entering the dainty sitting-room that looked on to the river, she dropped into a chair by the window and stared out with her chin in her hands. The river was a blaze of gold. A line of long black barges was drifting down-stream in the wake of a noisy steam-tug. She watched them absently, sick at heart.

Gradually the shining water grew blurred and dim. Its beauty wholly passed her by, or if she saw it, it was only in vivid contrast to the darkness in her soul. For a little, wide-eyed, she resisted the impulse that tugged at her heart-strings; but at last in sheer weariness she gave in. What did it matter, a tear more or less? There was no one to know or care. And tears were sometimes a relief. She bowed her head upon the sill and wept.

"Why, Doris!" a quiet voice said.

She started, started violently, and sprang upright.

Caryl was standing slightly behind her, his hand on the back of her chair, but as she rose he came forward and stood beside her.

"What is it?" he said. "Why are you crying?"

"I'm not!" she declared vehemently. "I wasn't! You—you startled me—that's all."

She turned her back on him and hastily dabbed her eyes. She was furious with him for coming upon her thus.

He stood at the window, looking out upon the long, black barges in silence.

After a few seconds of desperate effort she controlled herself and turned round.

"I never heard you come in. I—must have been asleep."

He did not look at her, or attempt to refute the statement.

"I thought you were going to be out this afternoon," he said.

"So I was. So I have been. I went to the club to get my letters."

"Didn't you find any one there to talk to?" he asked.

"No one," she answered somewhat hastily; then, moved by some impulse she could not have explained, "That is, no one that counts. I saw Mrs. Lockyard."

"Doesn't she count?" asked Caryl, still with his eyes on the river.

"I hate the woman!" Doris declared passionately.

He turned slowly round.

"What has she been saying to you?"

"Nothing."

Again he made no comment on the obvious lie.

"Look here," he said. "Can't we go out somewhere tonight? There is a new play at the Regency. They say it's good. Shall we go?"

The suggestion was quite unexpected; she looked at him in surprise.

"I have promised Vera to dine there," she said.

"Ring her up and say you can't," said Caryl.

She hesitated.

"I must make some excuse if I do. What shall I say?"

"Say I want you," he said, and suddenly that rare smile of his for which she had wholly ceased to look flashed across his face, "and tell the truth for once."

She did not see him again till she entered the dining-room an hour later. He was waiting for her there, and as she came in he presented her with a spray of lilies.

Again in astonishment she looked up at him.

"Don't you like them?" he said.

"Of course I do. But—but—"

Her answer tailed off in confusion. Her lip quivered uncontrollably, and she turned quickly away.

Caryl was plainly unaware of anything unusual in her demeanour. He talked throughout dinner in his calm, effortless drawl, and gradually under its soothing influence she recovered herself.

She enjoyed the play that followed. It was a simple romance, well staged, and superbly acted. She breathed a sigh of regret when it was over.

Driving home again with Caryl, she thanked him impulsively for taking her.

"You weren't bored?" he asked.

"Of course not," she said.

She would have said more, but something restrained her. A sudden shyness descended upon her that lasted till they reached the flat.

She left Caryl at the outer door and turned into the room overlooking the river. The window was open as she had left it, and the air blew in sweetly upon her over the water. She had dropped her wrap from her shoulders, and she shivered a little as she stood, but a feeling of suspense kept her motionless.

Caryl had entered the room behind her. She wondered if he would pause at the table where a tray of refreshments was standing. He did not, and her nerves tingled and quivered as he passed it by.

He joined her at the window, and they stood together for several seconds looking out upon the great river with its myriad lights.

She had not the faintest idea as to what was passing in his mind, but her heart-beats quickened in his silence to such a tumult that at last she could bear it no longer. She turned back into the room.

He followed her instantly, and she fancied that he sighed.

"Won't you have anything before you go?" he said.

She shook her head.

"Good-night!" she said almost inaudibly.

For a moment—no longer—her hand lay in his. She did not look at him. There was something in his touch that thrilled through her like an electric current.

But his grave "Good-night!" had in it nothing startling, and by the time she reached her own room she had begun to ask herself what cause there had been for her agitation. She was sure he must have thought her very strange, very abrupt, even ungracious.

And at that her heart smote her, for he had been kinder that evening than ever before. The fragrance of the lilies at her breast reminded her how kind.

She bent her head to them, and suddenly, as though the flowers exhaled some potent charm, impulse—blind, domineering impulse—took possession of her.

She turned swiftly to the door, and in a moment her feet were bearing her, almost without her voluntary effort, back to the room she had left.

The door was unlatched. She pushed it open, entering impetuously. And she came upon Caryl suddenly—as he had come upon her that afternoon—sunk in a chair by the window, with his head in his hands.

He rose instantly at her entrance, rose and closed the window; then lowered the blind very quietly, very slowly, and finally turned round to her.

"What is it? You have forgotten something?"

Except that he was paler than usual, his face bore no trace of emotion. He looked at her with his heavy eyes gravely, with unfailing patience.

For an instant she stood irresolute, afraid; then again that urging impulse drove her forward. She moved close to him.

"I only came back to say—I only wanted to tell you—Vivian, I—I was horrid to you this afternoon. Forgive me!"

She stretched out her trembling hands to him, and he took them, held them fast, then sharply let them go.

"My dear," he said, "you were in trouble, and I intruded upon you. It was no case for forgiveness."

But she would not accept his indulgence.

"I was horrid," she protested, with a catch in her voice. "Why are you so patient with me? You never used to be."

He did not answer her. He seemed to regard the question as superfluous.

She drew a little nearer. Her fingers fastened quivering upon his coat.

"Don't be too kind to me, Vivian," she said, her voice trembling. "It—it isn't good for me."

He took her by the wrists and drew her hands away.

"You want to tell me something," he said. "What is it?"

She glanced upwards, meeting his look with sudden resolution.

"You asked me this afternoon why I was crying," she said. "And I—I lied to you. You asked me, too, what Mrs. Lockyard said to me. And I lied again. I will tell you now, if—if you will listen to me."

Caryl was still holding her wrists. There was a hint of sternness in his attitude.

"Well?" he said quietly. "What did she say?"

"She said"—Doris spoke with an effort—"she said, or rather she hinted, that there was an old grudge between you and Major Brandon, a matter with which I was in no way concerned, an affair of many years' standing. She said that was why you followed him up and—thrashed him that night. She implied that I didn't count at all. She made me wonder if—if—"—she was speaking almost inarticulately, with bent head—"if perhaps it was only to satisfy this ancient grudge that you married me."

Her words went into silence. She could not look him in the face. If he had not held her wrists so firmly she would have been tempted to turn and flee. As it was, she could only stand before him in quivering suspense.

He moved at length, moved suddenly and disconcertingly, freeing one hand to turn her face quietly upwards. She did not resist him, but she shrank as she met his eyes. She fancied she had never seen him look so grim.

"And that was why you were crying?" he asked, deliberately searching her reluctant eyes.

"That was—one reason," she acknowledged faintly.

"Then there was something more than that?"

"Yes." She laid her hand pleadingly on his arm, and he released her. "I will tell you," she said tremulously, keeping her face upturned to his. "At least, I will try. But it's very difficult because—"

She began to falter under his look.

"Because," he said slowly, "you have no confidence in me. That I can well understand. You married me more or less under compulsion, and when a wife is no more than a guest in her husband's house, confidence between them, of any description, is almost an impossibility."

He spoke without anger, but with a sadness that pierced her to the heart; and having so spoken he leant his arm upon the mantelpiece, turning slightly from her.

"I will tell you," he said, his voice very quiet and even, "exactly what Mrs. Lockyard was hinting at. Ten years ago I was engaged to a girl—like you in many ways—gay, impulsive, bewitching. I was young in those days, romantic, too. I worshipped her as a goddess. I was utterly blind to her failings. They simply didn't exist for me. She rewarded me by running away with Maurice Brandon. I knew he was a blackguard, but how much of a blackguard I did not realize till later. However, I didn't trust him even then, and I followed them and insisted that they should be married in my presence. Six months later I heard from her. He had treated her abominably, had finally deserted her, and she was trying to get a divorce. I did my best to help her, and eventually she obtained it." He paused a moment, then went on with bent head, "I never saw her after she gained her freedom. She went to her people, and very soon after—she died."

Again he paused, then slowly straightened himself.

"I never cared for any woman after that," he said, "until I met you. As for Brandon, he kept out of my way, and I had no object in seeking him. In fact, I took no interest in his doings till I found that you were in Mrs. Lockyard's set. That, I admit, was something of a shock. And then when I found that you liked the man—"

"Oh, don't!" she broke in. "Don't! I was mad ever to tolerate him. Let me forget it! Please let me forget it!"

She spoke passionately, and as if her emotion drew him he turned fully round to her.

"If you could have forgotten him sooner," he said, with a touch of sternness, "you would not find yourself tied now to a man you never loved."

The effect of his words was utterly unexpected. She started as one stricken, wounded in a vital place, and clasped her hands tightly against her breast, crushing the flowers that drooped there.

"It is a lie!" she cried wildly. "It is a lie!"

"What is a lie?"

He took a step towards her, for she was swaying as she stood; but she flung out her hands, keeping him from her.

Her face was working convulsively. She turned and moved unsteadily away from him, groping out before her as she went. So groping, she reached the door, and blindly sought the handle. But before she found it he spoke in a tone that had subtly altered:

"Doris!"

Her hands fell. She stood suddenly still, listening.

"Come here!" he said.

He crossed the room and reached her.

"Look at me!" he said.

She refused for a little, trembling all over. Then suddenly as he waited she threw back her head and met his eyes. She was sobbing like a child that has been hurt.

He bent towards her, looking closely, closely into her quivering face.

"So," he said, "it was a lie, was it? But, my own girl, how was I to know? Why on earth didn't you say so before?"

She broke into a laugh that had in it the sound of tears.

"How could I? You never asked. How could I?"

"Shall I ask you now?" he said.

She stretched up her arms and clasped his neck.

"No," she whispered back. "Take me—take everything—for granted. It's the only way, if you want to turn a heartless little flirt like me into—into a virtuous and amiable wife!"

And so, clinging to him, her lips met his in the first kiss that had ever passed between them.

Those Who Wait

A faint draught from the hills found its way through the wide-flung door as the sun went down. It fluttered the papers on the table, and stirred a cartoon upon the wall with a dry rustling as of wind in corn.

The man who sat at the table turned his face as it were mechanically towards that blessed breath from the snows. His chin was propped on his hand. He seemed to be waiting.

The light failed very quickly, and he presently reached out and drew a reading-lamp towards him. The flame he kindled flickered upward, throwing weird shadows upon his lean, brown face, making the sunken hollows of his eyes look cavernous.

He turned the light away so that it streamed upon the open doorway. Then he resumed his former position of sphinx-like waiting, his chin upon his hand.

Half an hour passed. The day was dead. Beyond the radius of the lamp there hung a pall of thick darkness—a fearful, clinging darkness that seemed to wrap the whole earth. The heat was intense, unstirred by any breeze. Only now and then the cartoon on the wall moved as if at the touch of ghostly fingers, and each time there came that mocking whisper that was like wind in corn.

At length there sounded through the night the dull throbbing of a horse's feet, and the man who sat waiting raised his head. A gleam of expectancy shone in his sombre eyes. Some of the rigidity went out of his attitude.

Nearer came the hoofs and nearer yet, and with them, mingling rhythmically, a tenor voice that sang.

As it reached him the man at the table pulled out a drawer with a sharp jerk. His hand sought something within it, but his eyes never left the curtain of darkness that the open doorway framed.

Slowly, very slowly at last, he withdrew his hand empty; but he only partially closed the drawer.

The voice without was nearer now, was close at hand. The horse's hoofs had ceased to sound. There came the ring of spurred heels without, a man's hand tapped upon the doorpost, a man's figure showed suddenly against the darkness.

"Hallo, Conyers! Still in the land of the living? Ye gods, what a fiendish night! Many thanks for the beacon! It's kept me straight for more than half the way."

He entered carelessly, the lamplight full upon him—a handsome, straight-limbed young Hercules—tossed down his riding-whip, and looked round for a drink.

"Here you are!" said Conyers, turning the rays of the lamp full upon some glasses on the table.

"Ah, good! I'm as dry as a smoked herring. You must drink too, though. Yes, I insist. I have a toast to propose, so be sociable for once. What have you got in that drawer?"

Conyers locked the drawer abruptly, and jerked out the key.

"What do you want to know for?"

His visitor grinned boyishly.

"Don't be bashful, old chap! I always guessed you kept her there. We'll drink her health, too, in a minute. But first of all"—he was splashing soda-water impetuously out of a syphon as he spoke—"first of all—quite ready, I say? It's a grand occasion—here's to the best of good fellows, that genius, that inventor of guns, John Conyers! Old chap, your fortune's made. Here's to it! Hip—hip—hooray!"

His shout was like the blare of a bull. Conyers rose, crossed to the door, and closed it.

Returning, he halted by his visitor's side, and shook him by the shoulder.

"Stop rotting, Palliser!" he said rather shortly.

Young Palliser wheeled with a gigantic laugh, and seized him by the arms.

"You old fool, Jack! Can't you see I'm in earnest? Drink, man, drink, and I'll tell you all about it. That gun of yours is going to be an enormous success—stupendous—greater even than I hoped. It's true, by the powers! Don't look so dazed. All comes to those who wait, don't you know. I always told you so."

"To be sure, so you did." The man's words came jerkily. They had an odd, detached sound, almost as though he were speaking in his sleep. He turned away from Palliser, and took up his untouched glass.

But the next instant it slipped through his fingers, and crashed upon the table edge. The spilt liquid streamed across the floor.

Palliser stared for an instant, then thrust forward his own glass.

"Steady does it, old boy! Try both hands for a change. It's this infernal heat."

He turned with the words, and picked up a paper from the table, frowning over it absently, and whistling below his breath.

When he finally looked round again his face cleared.

"Ah, that's better! Sit down, and we'll talk. By Jove, isn't it colossal? They told me over at the fort that I was a fool to come across tonight. But I simply couldn't keep you waiting another night. Besides, I knew you would expect me."

Conyers' grim face softened a little. He could scarcely have said how he had ever come to be the chosen friend of young Hugh Palliser. The intimacy had been none of his seeking.

They had met at the club on the occasion of one of his rare appearances there, and the younger man, whose sociable habit it was to know everyone, had scraped acquaintance with him.

No one knew much about Conyers. He was not fond of society, and, as a natural consequence, society was not fond of him. He occupied the humble position of a subordinate clerk in an engineer's office. The work was hard, but it did not bring him prosperity. He was one of those men who go silently on week after week, year after year, till their very existence comes almost to be overlooked by those about them. He never seemed to suffer as other men suffered from the scorching heat of that tropical corner of the Indian Empire. He was always there, whatever happened to the rest of the world; but he never pushed himself forward. He seemed to lack ambition. There were even some who said he lacked brains as well.

But Palliser was not of these. His quick eyes had detected at a glance something that others had never taken the trouble to discover. From the very beginning he had been aware of a force that contained itself in this silent man. He had become interested, scarcely knowing why; and, having at length overcome the prickly hedge of reserve which was at first opposed to his advances, he had entered the private place which it defended, and found within—what he certainly had not expected to find—a genius.

It was nearly three months now since Conyers, in a moment of unusual expansion, had laid before him the invention at which he had been working for so many silent years. The thing even then, though complete in all essentials, had lacked finish, and this final touch young Palliser, himself a gunner with a positive passion for guns, had been able to supply. He had seen the value of the invention and had given it his ardent support. He had, moreover, friends in high places, and could obtain a fair and thorough investigation of the idea.

This he had accomplished, with a result that had transcended his high hopes, on his friend's behalf; and he now proceeded to pour out his information with an accompanying stream of congratulation, to which Conyers sat and listened with scarcely the movement of an eyelid.

Hugh Palliser found his impassivity by no means disappointing. He was used to it. He had even expected it. That momentary unsteadiness on Conyers' part had astonished him far more.

Concluding his narration he laid the official correspondence before him, and got up to open the door. The night was black and terrible, the heat came in overwhelming puffs, as though blown from a blast furnace. He leaned against the doorpost and wiped his forehead. The oppression of the atmosphere was like a tangible, crushing weight. Behind him the paper on the wall rustled vaguely, but there was no other sound. After several minutes he turned briskly back again into the room, whistling a sentimental ditty below his breath.

"Well, old chap, it was worth waiting for, eh? And now, I suppose, you'll be making a bee-line for home, you lucky beggar. I shan't be long after you, that's one comfort. Pity we can't go together. I suppose you can't wait till the winter."

"No, my boy. I'm afraid I can't." Conyers spoke with a faint smile, his eyes still fixed upon the blue official paper that held his destiny. "I'm going home forthwith, and be damned to everything and everybody—except you. It's an understood thing, you know, Palliser, that we are partners in this deal."

"Oh, rot!" exclaimed Palliser impetuously. "I don't agree to that. I did nothing but polish the thing up. You'd have done it yourself if I hadn't."

"In the course of a few more years," put in Conyers drily.

"Rot!" said Palliser again. "Besides, I don't want any pelf. I've quite as much as is good for me, more than I want. That's why I'm going to get married. You'll be going the same way yourself now, I suppose?"

"You have no reason whatever for thinking so," responded Conyers.

Palliser laughed lightheartedly and sat down on the table. "Oh, haven't I? What about that mysterious locked drawer of yours? Don't be shy, I say! You had it open when I came in. Show her to me like a good chap! I won't tell a soul."

"That's not where I keep my love-tokens," said Conyers, with a grim twist of the mouth that was not a smile.

"What then?" asked Palliser eagerly. "Not another invention?"

"No." Conyers inserted the key in the lock again, turned it, and pulled open the drawer. "See for yourself as you are so anxious."

Palliser leaned across the table and looked. The next instant his glance flashed upwards, and their eyes met.

There was a sharply-defined pause. Then, "You'd never be fool enough for that, Jack!" ejaculated Palliser, with vehemence.

"I'm fool enough for anything," said Conyers, with his cynical smile.

"But you wouldn't," the other protested almost incoherently. "A fellow like you—I don't believe it!"

"It's loaded," observed Conyers quietly. "No, leave it alone, Hugh! It can remain so for the present. There is not the smallest danger of its going off—or I shouldn't have shown it to you."

He closed the drawer again, looking steadily into Hugh Palliser's face.

"I've had it by me for years," he said, "just in case the Fates should have one more trick in store for me. But apparently they haven't, though it's never safe to assume anything."

"Oh, don't talk like an idiot!" broke in Palliser heatedly. "I've no patience with that sort of thing. Do you expect me to believe that a fellow like you—a fellow who knows how to wait for his luck—would give way to a cowardly impulse and destroy himself all in a moment because things didn't go quite straight? Man alive! I know you better than that; or if I don't, I've never known you at all."

"Ah! Perhaps not!" said Conyers.

Once more he turned the key and withdrew it. He pushed back his chair so that his face was in shadow.

"You don't know everything, you know, Hugh," he said.

"Have a smoke," said Palliser, "and tell me what you are driving at."

He threw himself into a bamboo chair by the open door, the light streaming full upon him, revealing in every line of him the arrogant splendour of his youth. He looked like a young Greek god with the world at his feet.

Conyers surveyed him with his faint, cynical smile. "No," he said, "you certainly don't know everything, my son. You never have come a cropper in your life."

"Haven't I, though?" Hugh sat up, eager to refute this criticism. "That's all you know about it. I suppose you think you have had the monopoly of hard knocks. Most people do."

"I am not like most people," Conyers asserted deliberately. "But you needn't tell me that you have ever been right under, my boy. For you never have."

"Depends what you call going under," protested Palliser. "I've been down a good many times, Heaven knows. And I've had to wait—as you have—all the best years of my life."

"Your best years are to come," rejoined Conyers. "Mine are over."

"Oh, rot, man! Rot—rot—rot! Why, you are just coming into your own! Have another drink and give me the toast of your heart!" Hugh Palliser sprang impulsively to his feet. "Let me mix it! You can't—you shan't be melancholy tonight of all nights."

But Conyers stayed his hand.

"Only one more drink tonight, boy!" he said. "And that not yet. Sit down and smoke. I'm not melancholy, but I can't rejoice prematurely. It's not my way."

"Prematurely!" echoed Hugh, pointing to the official envelope.

"Yes, prematurely," Conyers repeated. "I may be as rich as Croesus, and yet not win my heart's desire."

"Oh, I know that," said Hugh quickly. "I've been through it myself. It's infernal to have everything else under the sun and yet to lack the one thing—the one essential—the one woman."

He sat down again, abruptly thoughtful. Conyers smoked silently, with his face in the shadow.

Suddenly Hugh looked across at him.

"You think I'm too much of an infant to understand," he said. "I'm nearly thirty, but that's a detail."

"I'm forty-five," said Conyers.

"Well, well!" Hugh frowned impatiently. "It's a detail, as I said before. Who cares for a year more or less?"

"Which means," observed Conyers, with his dry smile, "that the one woman is older than you are."

"She is," Palliser admitted recklessly. "She is five years older. But what of it? Who cares? We were made for each other. What earthly difference does it make?"

"It's no one's business but your own," remarked Conyers through a haze of smoke.

"Of course it isn't. It never has been." Hugh yet sounded in some fashion indignant. "There never was any other possibility for me after I met her. I waited for her six mortal years. I'd have waited all my life. But she gave in at last. I think she realized that it was sheer waste of time to go on."

"What was she waiting for?" The question came with a certain weariness of intonation, as though the speaker were somewhat bored; but Hugh Palliser was too engrossed to notice.

He stretched his arms wide with a swift and passionate gesture.

"She was waiting for a scamp," he declared.

"It is maddening to think of—the sweetest woman on earth, Conyers, wasting her spring and her summer over a myth, an illusion. It was an affair of fifteen years ago. The fellow came to grief and disappointed her. She told me all about it on the day she promised to marry me. I believe her heart was nearly broken at the time, but she has got over it—thank Heaven!—at last. Poor Damaris! My Damaris!"

He ceased to speak, and a dull roar of thunder came out of the night like the voice of a giant in anguish.

Hugh began to smoke, still busy with his thoughts.

"Yes," he said presently, "I believe she would actually have waited all her life for the fellow if he had asked it of her. Luckily he didn't go so far as that. He was utterly unworthy of her. I think she sees it now. His father was imprisoned for forgery, and no doubt he was in the know, though it couldn't be brought home to him. He was ruined, of course, and he disappeared, just dropped out, when the crash came. He had been on the verge of proposing to her immediately before. And she would have had him too. She cared."

He sent a cloud of smoke upwards with savage vigour.

"It's damnable to think of her suffering for a worthless brute like that!" he exclaimed. "She had such faith in him too. Year after year she was expecting him to go back to her, and she kept me at arm's length, till at last she came to see that both our lives were being sacrificed to a miserable dream. Well, it's my innings now, anyway. And we are going to be superbly happy to make up for it."

Again he flung out his arms with a wide gesture, and again out of the night there came a long roll of thunder that was like the menace of a tortured thing. A flicker of lightning gleamed through the open door for a moment, and Conyers' dark face was made visible. He had ceased to smoke, and was staring with fixed, inscrutable eyes into the darkness. He did not flinch from the lightning; it was as if he did not see it.

"What would she do, I wonder, if the prodigal returned," he
 d quietly. "Would she be glad—or sorry?"

"He never will," returned Hugh quickly. "He never can—after fifteen years. Think of it! Besides—she wouldn't have him if he did."

"Women are proverbially faithful," remarked Conyers cynically.

"She will stick to me now," Hugh returned with confidence. "The other fellow is probably dead. In any case, he has no shadow of a right over her. He never even asked her to wait for him."

"Possibly he thought that she would wait without being asked," said Conyers, still cynical.

"Well, she has ceased to care for him now," asserted Hugh. "She told me so herself."

The man opposite shifted his position ever so slightly. "And you are satisfied with that?" he said.

"Of course I am. Why not?" There was almost a challenge in Hugh's voice.

"And if he came back?" persisted the other. "You would still be satisfied?"

Hugh sprang to his feet with a movement of fierce impatience. "I believe I should shoot him!" he said vindictively. He looked like a splendid wild animal suddenly awakened. "I tell you, Conyers," he declared passionately, "I could kill him with my hands if he came between us now."

Conyers, his chin on his hand, looked him up and down as though appraising his strength.

Suddenly he sat bolt upright and spoke—spoke briefly, sternly, harshly, as a man speaks in the presence of his enemy. At the same instant a frightful crash of thunder swept the words away as though they had never been uttered.

In the absolute pandemonium of sound that followed, Hugh Palliser, with a face gone suddenly white, went over to his friend and stood behind him, his hands upon his shoulders.

But Conyers sat quite motionless, staring forth at the leaping lightning, rigid, sphinx-like. He did not seem aware of the man behind him, till, as the uproar began to subside, Hugh bent and spoke.

"Do you know, old chap, I'm scared!" he said, with a faint, shamed laugh. "I feel as if there were devils abroad. Speak to me, will you, and tell me I'm a fool!"

"You are," said Conyers, without turning.

"That lightning is too much for my nerves," said Hugh uneasily. "It's almost red. What was it you said just now? I couldn't hear a word."

"It doesn't matter," said Conyers.

"But what was it? I want to know."

The gleam in the fixed eyes leaped to sudden terrible flame, shone hotly for a few seconds, then died utterly away. "I don't remember," said Conyers quietly. "It couldn't have been anything of importance. Have a drink! You will have to be getting back as soon as this is over."

Hugh helped himself with a hand that was not altogether steady. There had come a lull in the tempest. The cartoon on the wall was fluttering like a caged thing. He glanced at it, then looked at it closely. It was a reproduction of Doré's picture of Satan falling from heaven.

"It isn't meant for you surely!" he said.

Conyers laughed and got to his feet. "It isn't much like me, is it?"

Hugh looked at him uncertainly. "I never noticed it before. It might have been you years ago."

"Ah, perhaps," said Conyers. "Why don't you drink? I thought you were going to give me a toast."

Hugh's mood changed magically. He raised his glass high. "Here's to your eternal welfare, dear fellow! I drink to your heart's desire."

Conyers waited till Hugh had drained his glass before he lifted his own.

Then, "I drink to the one woman," he said, and emptied it at a draught.

The storm was over, and a horse's feet clattered away into the darkness, mingling rhythmically with a cheery tenor voice.

In the room with the open door a man's figure stood for a long while motionless.

When he moved at length it was to open the locked drawer of the writing-table. His right hand felt within it, closed upon something that lay there; and then he paused.

Several minutes crawled away.

From afar there came the long rumble of thunder. But it was not this that he heard as he stood wrestling with the fiercest temptation he had ever known.

Stiffly at last he stooped, peered into the drawer, finally ?ed it with an unfaltering hand. The struggle was over.

"For your sake, Damaris!" he said aloud, and he spoke without cynicism. "I should know how to wait by now—even for death—which is all I have to wait for."

And with that he pulled the fluttering paper from the wall, crushed it in his hand, and went out heavily into the night.

This story was originally issued in the *Red Magazine*.

The Eleventh Hour

CHAPTER I

HIS OWN GROUND

"Oh, to be a farmer's wife!"

Doris Elliot paused, punt-pole in hand, to look across a field of corn-sheaves with eyes of shining appreciation.

Her companion, stretched luxuriously on his back on a pile of cushions, smiled a contemplative smile and made no comment.

The girl's look came down to him after a moment. She regarded him with friendly contempt.

"You're very lazy, Hugh," she said.

"I know it," said Hugh Chesyl comfortably.

She dropped the pole into the water and drove the punt towards the bank. "It's a pity you're such a slacker," she said.

He removed his cigarette momentarily. "You wouldn't like me any better if I weren't," he said.

"Indeed I should—miles!"

"No, you wouldn't." His smile became more pronounced. "If I were more energetic, I should be for ever pestering you to marry me. And, you know, you wouldn't like that. As it is, I take 'No,' for an answer and rest content."

Doris was silent. Her slim, white-clad figure was bent to the task of bringing the punt to a pleasant anchorage in an inviting hollow in the grassy shore. Hugh Chesyl clasped his hands behind his head and watched her with placid admiration.

The small brown hands were very capable. They knew exactly what to do, and did it with precision. When they had finally secured the punt, with him in it, to the bank he sat up.

"Are we going to have tea here? What a charming spot! Sweetly romantic, isn't it? I wonder why you particularly want to be a farmer's wife?"

Doris's pointed chin still looked slightly scornful. "You wouldn't wonder if you took the trouble to reflect, Mr. Chesyl," she said.

He laughed easily. "Oh, don't ask me to do that! You know at a sluggish brain mine is. I can quite understand your not ting to marry me, but why you should want to marry a farmer—like Jeff Ironside—I cannot see."

"Who is Jeff Ironside?" she demanded.

"He's the chap who owns this property. Didn't you know? A frightfully energetic person; prosperous, too, for a wonder. But an absolute tinker, my dear. I shouldn't marry him—all his fair acres notwithstanding—if I were you. I don't think the county would approve."

Doris snapped her fingers with supreme contempt. "That for the county! What a snob you are!"

"Am I?" said Hugh. "I didn't know."

She nodded severely. "Do you mind moving your legs? I want to get at the tea-basket."

"Don't mention it!" he said accommodatingly. "Are you going to give me tea now? How nice! You are looking awfully pretty today, do you know? I can't think how you do it. There isn't a feature in your face worth mentioning, but, notwithstanding, you make an entrancing whole."

Doris sternly repressed a smile. "Please don't take the trouble to be complimentary."

Hugh groaned. "There's no pleasing you. And still you haven't let me into the secret as to why you want to be a farmer's wife."

Doris was unpacking the tea-things energetically. "You never understand anything without being told," she said. "Don't you know that I positively hate the life I live now?"

"I can quite believe it," said Hugh Chesyl. "But, if you will allow me to say so, I think your remedy would be worse than the disease. Your utmost ingenuity will fail to persuade me that the life of a farmer's wife would suit you."

"I should like the simplicity of it," she maintained.

"And getting up at five in the morning to make the butter? And having a hulking brute of a husband—like Jeff Ironside—tramping into your kitchen with his muddy boots and beastly clothes (which you would have to mend) just when you had got things into good order? I can see you doing it!" Hugh Chesyl's speech went into his easy, high-bred laugh. "You of all people—the dainty and disdainful Miss Elliot, for whom no man is good enough!"

"I don't know why you say that." There was quick protest in the girl's voice. She clattered the cups and saucers as if something in the lazy argument had exasperated her. "I like a man who is a man—the hard, outdoor, wholesome kind—who isn't afraid of taking a little trouble—who knows what he wants and how to get it. I shouldn't quarrel with him on the score of muddy boots. I should be only glad that he had enough of the real thing in him to go out in all weathers and not to care."

"All of which is aimed at me," said Hugh to the trees above him. "I'm afraid I'm boring you more than usual this afternoon."

"You can't help it," said Doris.

Hugh Chesyl's good-looking face crumpled a little, then smoothed itself again to its usual placid expression. "Ah, well!" he said equably, "we won't quarrel about it. Let's have some tea!"

He sat up in the punt and looked across at her; but she would not meet his eyes, and there ensued a considerable pause before he said gently, "I'm sorry you are not happy, you know."

"Are you?" she said.

"Yes. That's why I want you to marry me."

"Should I be any happier if I did?" said Doris, with a smile that was somehow slightly piteous.

"I don't know." Hugh Chesyl's voice was as pleasantly vague as his personality. "I shouldn't get in your way at all, and, at least, you would have a home of your own."

"To be miserable in," said Doris, with suppressed vehemence.

"I don't know why you should be miserable," he said. "You wouldn't have anything to do that you didn't like."

She uttered a laugh that caught her breath as if it had been a sob. "Oh, don't talk about it, Hugh! I should be bored—bored to death. I want the real thing—the real thing—not a polite substitute."

"Sorry," said Hugh imperturbably. "I have offered the utmost of which I am capable. May I have my tea here, please? It's less trouble than scrambling ashore."

She acceded to his request without protest; but she stepped on to the bank herself, and sat down with her back to a cornsheaf. Very young and slender she looked sitting there with the sunshine on her brown, elf-like face, but she was by no means without dignity. There was a fairy queenliness about her that imparted an indescribable charm to her every movement. Her eyes were grey and fearless.

"How lovely to own a field like this!" she said. "And plough it and sow it and watch it grow up, and then cut it and turn it into sheaves! How proud the man who owns it must be!"

Something stirred on the other side of the sheaf, and she

started a little and glanced backwards. "What's that?"

"A rat probably," said Hugh Chesyl serenely from his couch in the punt. "I expect the place is full of 'em. Won't you continue your rhapsody? The man who owns this particular field is a miller as well as a farmer. He grinds his own grain."

"Oh, is he that man?" Eagerly she broke in. "Does he live in that perfectly exquisite old red-brick house on the water with the wheel turning all day long? Oh, isn't he lucky?"

"I doubt if he thinks so," said Hugh Chesyl. "I've never met a contented farmer yet."

"I don't like people to be too contented," said Doris perversely. "It's a sign of laziness and—yes—weakness of purpose."

"Oh, is it?" Again he uttered his good-tempered laugh; then, as he began to drink his tea, he gradually sobered. "Has anything happened lately to make you specially discontented with your lot?" he asked presently.

Doris's brows contracted. "Things are always happening. My stepmother gets more unbearable every day. I sometimes think I will go and work for my living, but my father won't hear of it. And what can I do? I haven't qualified for anything. The only thing open to me is to fill a post of unpaid companion to a rich and elderly cousin who would put up with me but doesn't much want me. She lives at Kensington, too, and I can breathe only in the country."

"Poor little girl!" said Hugh kindly.

"Oh, don't pity me!" she said quickly. "You can't do anything to help. And I shouldn't grumble to you if there were anyone else to grumble to." She leaned back against her sheaf with her eyes on the sunlit water below. "I suppose I shall just go on in the same old way till something happens. Anyhow, I can't see my way out at present. It's such a shame to be unhappy, too, when life might be so ecstatic."

"How could life be ecstatic?" asked Hugh, passing up his cup to be refilled.

She threw him a quick glance. "You wouldn't understand if I were to tell you," she said. "It never could be—for you."

He sighed. "I know I'm very limited. But it's a mistake to expect too much from life, believe me. Ask but little, and perhaps—if you're lucky—you won't be disappointed."

"I would rather have nothing than that," she said quickly.

Hugh Chesyl turned and regarded her curiously. "Would you really?" he said.

She nodded several times emphatically. "Yes; just live my own life out-of-doors and do without everything else." She pulled a long stalk of corn from the sheaf against which she rested and looked at it thoughtfully. Her eyes were downcast, and the man in the punt could not see the deep shadow of pain they held. "If I can't have corn," she said slowly, with the air of one pronouncing sentence, "I won't have husks. I will die of starvation sooner."

And with that very suddenly she rose and walked round the sheaf.

The movement was abrupt, so abrupt that Hugh Chesyl lifted his brows in astonishment. He was still more surprised a moment later when he heard her clear, girlish voice raised in admonition.

"I don't think it's very nice of you to lie there listening and not to let us know."

Hugh sat upright in the punt. Who on earth was it that she was reproving thus?

The next moment he saw. A huge man with the frame of a bull rose from behind the sheaf and confronted his young companion. He had his hat in his hand, and the afternoon sun fell full upon his uncovered head, revealing a rugged, clean-shaven face that had in it a good deal of British strength and a suspicion of gipsy alertness. To Chesyl's further amazement he did not appear in the least abashed by the encounter.

"I'm sorry I overheard you," he said, with blunt deference. "I was half-asleep at first. Afterwards, I didn't like to intrude."

Doris's grey eyes looked him up and down for a moment or two in silence, and a flush rose in her tanned face. It seemed to Hugh that she was likely to become the more embarrassed of the two, and he wondered if he ought to go to the rescue.

Then swiftly Doris collected her forces. "I suppose you know you are trespassing?" she said.

At that Hugh laid himself very suddenly down again in the bottom of the boat, and left her to fight her own battles.

The man on the bank looked down at his small assailant with a face of grim decorum. "No, I didn't know," he said.

"Well, you are," said Doris. "All this ground is private property. You can see for yourself. It's a cornfield."

The intruder's eyes travelled over the upstanding sheaves, passed gravely over the man in the punt, and came back to the girl. "Yes; I see," he said stolidly.

"Then don't you think you'd better go?" she said.

He put his hat on somewhat abruptly. "Yes. I think I had better," he said, and with that he turned on his heel and walked away through the stubble.

"Such impertinence!" said Doris, as she stepped down the bank to her companion.

"It was rather," said Hugh.

She looked at him somewhat sharply. "I don't see that there is anything to laugh at," she said.

"Don't you?" said Hugh.

"No. Why are you laughing?"

Hugh explained. "It only struck me as being a little funny that you should order the man off his own ground in that cavalier fashion."

"Hugh!" Genuine dismay shone in the girl's eyes. "That wasn't—wasn't—"

"Jeff Ironside? Yes, it was," said Hugh. "I wonder you have never come across him before. He works like a nigger."

"Hugh!" Doris collapsed upon the bank in sheer horror. "I have seen him before—seen him several times. I thought he was just—a labourer—till today."

"Oh, no," said Hugh. "He's just your hard, outdoor, wholesome farmer. Fine animal, isn't he? Always reminds me of a prize bull."

"How frightful!" said Doris with a gasp. "It's the worst *faux pas* I have ever made."

"Cheer up!" said Hugh consolingly. "No doubt he was flattered by the little attention. He took it very well."

"That doesn't make matters any better," said Doris. "I almost wish he hadn't."

Whereupon Hugh laughed again. "Oh, don't wish that! I should think he would be quite a nasty animal when roused. I shouldn't have cared to fight him on your behalf. He could wipe the earth with me were he so minded."

Doris's eyes, critical though not unkindly, rested upon him as he lay. "Yes," she said thoughtfully, "I should almost think he could."

CHAPTER II

THE PLOUGHMAN

It was on a day six weeks later that Doris Elliot next found herself upon the scene of her discomfiture. She had ridden from her home three miles distant very early on a morning of September to join a meeting of the foxhounds and go cub-hunting. There had been a heavy fall of rain, and the ground was wet and slippery.

The field that had been all yellow with the shocks of corn was now in process of being ploughed, and her horse Hector sank up to the fetlocks at every stride, a fact which he resented with obvious impatience. She guided him down to the edge of the river where the ground looked a little harder.

The run was over and she had enjoyed it; but she wanted now to take as short a cut home as possible, and it was through this particular field that the most direct route undoubtedly lay. She was alone, but she knew every inch of the countryside, and but for this mischance of the plough she would have been well on her way. Being a sportswoman, she made the best of things, and did her utmost to soothe her mount's somewhat fiery temper.

"You shall have a clean jump at the end, Hector, old boy," she promised him. "We shall soon be out of it."

But in this matter also she was to receive a check; for when they came to the clean jump, it was to find a formidable fence of wooden paling confronting them, intervening directly in their line of march. It seemed that the energetic owner had been attending to his boundaries with a zeal that no huntsman would appreciate.

Doris bit her lip with a murmured "Too bad!"

There was nothing for it but to skirt the hedge in search of a gate. Hector was naturally even more indignant than she, and stamped and squealed as she turned him from the obstacle. He also wanted to get home, and he was tired of fighting his way through ploughed land that held him like a bog. To add to their discomfort it had begun to rain again, and there seemed every prospect of being speedily soaked to the skin.

Altogether the outlook was depressing; but someone was whistling cheerily on the farther side of the field, and Doris took heart. It was a long way to the gate, however, and when she reached it at length it was to find another disappointment in store. The gate was padlocked.

She looked round in desperation. Her only chance of escape was apparently to return by the way she had come by means of a gap which had not yet been repaired, and which would lead her in directly the opposite direction to that which she desired to take.

The rain was coming down in a sharp shower, and Hector was becoming more and more restive. She halted him by the gate and looked over. Beyond lay a field from which she knew the road to be easily accessible. She hated to turn her back upon it.

Behind her over a rise came the plough, drawn by two stout horses, driven by a sturdy figure that loomed gigantic against the sky. Glancing back, Doris saw this figure, and an odd little spirit of dare-devilry entered into her. She did not want to come face to face with the ploughman, neither did she want to beat a retreat before the five-barred gate that opposed her progress.

She spoke to Hector reassuringly and backed him several paces. He was quick to grasp her desire and eager to fall in with it. She felt him bracing himself under her, and she laughed in sheer delight as she set him at the gate.

He went at it with a will over the broken ground, rose as she lifted him, and made a gallant effort to clear the obstacle. But he was too heavily handicapped. He slipped as he rose to the leap. He blundered badly against the top bar of the gate, finally stumbled over and fell on the other side, pitching his rider headlong into a slough of trampled mud.

He was up in a moment and careering across the field, but Doris was not so nimble. It was by no means her first tumble, nor had it been wholly unexpected; but she had fallen with considerable violence, and it took her a second or two to collect her wits. Then, like Hector, she sprang up—only to reel back through the slippery mud and catch at the splintered gate for support, there to cling sick and dizzy, with eyes fast shut, while the whole world rocked around her in chaos indescribable.

A full minute must have passed thus, then very suddenly out of the confusion came a voice. Vaguely she recognized it, but she was too occupied in the struggle to keep her senses to pay much attention to what it said.

"I mustn't faint!" she gasped desperately through her set teeth. "I mustn't faint!"

A steady arm encircled her, holding her up.

"You'll be all right in half a minute," said the voice, close to her now. "You came down rather hard."

She fought with herself and opened her eyes. Her head was swimming still, but she compelled herself to look.

Jeff Ironside was beside her, one foot lodged upon the lowest bar of the gate while he propped her against his bent knee.

He looked down at her with a certain sternness of demeanour that was characteristic of him. "Take your time," he said. "It was a nasty knock-out."

"I—I'm all right," she told him breathlessly. "Where—where is Hector?"

"If you mean your animal," he said in the slow, grim way which she began to remember as his, "he is probably well on his way home by now. He'll be all right," he added. "The gate from this field into the road is open."

"Oh!" The faintness was overcoming her again as she tried to stand. She clutched and held his arm. "I'm sorry," she whispered. "I—never felt so stupid before."

"Don't be in a hurry!" he said. "You can't help it."

She sank back against his support again and so remained for a few seconds. He stood like a rock till she opened her eyes once more.

She found his own upon her, but he dropped them instantly. "You are not hurt anywhere, are you?" he said.

She shook her head. "No, it's nothing. I've wrenched my shoulder a little, but it isn't much."

"Which shoulder?"

"The right. No, really it isn't serious." She winced as he touched it with his hand nevertheless.

"Sure?" he said.

He began to feel it very carefully, and she winced again with indrawn breath.

"It's only bruised," she said.

"It's painful, anyhow," he remarked bluntly. "Well, you must be wet to the skin. You had better come with me to the mill and get dry."

Doris flushed a little. "Oh, thank you, but really—I don't want to—to trespass on your kindness. I can quite well walk home—from here."

"You can't," he said flatly. "Anyhow, you are not going to try. You had better let me carry you."

But Doris drew back at that with swift decision. "Oh no! I am quite well now—I can walk."

She stood up and he took his foot from the gate. She glanced at the top bar thereof that hung in splinters.

"I'm so sorry," she murmured apologetically.

He also looked at his damaged property. "Yes, it was a pity you attempted it," he said.

"I shall know better next time," she said with a wry smile. "Will it cost much?"

"Well, it can't be mended for nothing," said Jeff Ironside. "Things never are."

Doris considered him for a moment. He was certainly a fine animal, as Hugh Chesyl had said, well made and well put together. She liked the freedom of his pose, the strength of the great bull neck. At close quarters he certainly did not look like an ordinary labourer. He had an air of command that his rough clothes could not hide. There was nothing of the clod-hopper about him albeit he followed the plough. He was obviously a son of the soil, and he would wrest his living therefrom, but he would do it with brain as well as hands. He had a wide forehead above his somewhat sombre eyes.

"I am very sorry," she said again.

"I am sorry for you," he said. "Wouldn't it be as well to get out of this rain? It's only a step to the mill."

She turned with docility and looked towards the two horses standing patiently where he had left them on the brown slope of the hill.

"Not that way," he said. "Come across this field to the road. It is no distance from there."

Doris began to gather up her skirt. It was wet through and caked with mud. She caught her breath again as she did it. The pain in her shoulder was becoming intense.

And then, to her amazement, Jeff Ironside suddenly stooped and put his arms about her. Almost before she realized his intention, and while she was still gasping her astonishment, he had lifted her and begun to move with long, easy strides over the sodden turf.

"Oh," she said, "you—you—really you shouldn't!"

"It's the only thing to do," he returned.

And somehow—perhaps because he spoke with such finality—she did not feel inclined to dispute the point. She submitted with a confused murmur of thanks.

CHAPTER III

THE APOLOGY

On an old oaken settle, cushioned like a church-pew, before a generous, open fire, Doris began to forget her woes. She looked about her with interest the while she endeavoured to sip a cup of steaming milk treated with brandy that Jeff Ironside had brought her.

An old, old woman hobbled about the oak-raftered kitchen behind her while Jeff himself knelt before her and unlaced her mud-caked boots. She would have protested against his doing this had protest been of the smallest avail, but when she attempted it he only smiled a faint, grim smile and continued his task.

As he finally drew them off she thanked him in a small, shy voice. "You are very kind—much kinder than I deserve," she said. "Do you know I've often thought that I ought to have come to apologize for—for ordering you off your own ground that day in the summer?"

He looked up at her as he knelt, and for the first time she heard him laugh. There was something almost boyish in his laugh. It transformed him utterly, and it had a marvellous effect upon her.

She laughed also and was instantly at her ease. She suddenly discovered that he was young in spite of his ruggedness, and she warmed to him in consequence.

"But I really was sorry," she protested. "And I knew I ought to have told you so before. But, somehow"—she flushed under his eyes—"I hadn't the courage. Besides, I didn't know you."

"It wasn't a very serious offence, was it?" he asked.

"I should have been furious in your place," she said.

"It takes more than that to make me angry," said Jeff Ironside.

She put out her hand to him impulsively, the flush still in her cheeks.

"I am still perfectly furious with myself," she told him, "whenever I think about it."

His hand enclosed hers in an all-enveloping grasp. "Then I shouldn't think about it any more if I were you," he said.

"Very well, I won't," said Doris; adding with her own quaint air of graciousness, "and thank you for being so friendly about it."

He released her hand somewhat abruptly and got to his feet. "How is your shoulder now? Any better?"

"Oh, yes, it's better," she assured him. "Only rather stiff. Now, won't you sit down and have your breakfast? Please don't bother about me any more; I've wasted quite enough of your time."

He turned towards the table. "You must have some too. And then, when you're ready, I will drive you home."

"Oh, but that will waste your time still more," she protested. "I'm sure I can walk."

"I'm sure you won't try," he rejoined with blunt deliberation. "I hope you don't mind eating in the kitchen, Miss Elliot. I would have had a fire in the parlour if I had expected you."

"But, of course, I don't mind," she said. "And it's quite the finest old kitchen I've ever seen."

He turned to the old woman who still hovered in the background. "All right, Granny. Sit down and have your own."

"I'll wait on the lady first, Master Jeff," she returned, smiling upon him.

"No. I'm going to wait on the lady," said Jeff. "You sit down."

He had his way. It occurred to Doris that he usually did so. And presently he was waiting upon her as she lay against the cushions, as though she had been a princess in distress.

Their intimacy progressed steadily during the meal, and very soon Doris's shyness had wholly worn away. She could not quite decide if Jeff were shy or not. He was obviously quiet by nature. But his grimness certainly disappeared, and more than once she found herself wondering at his consideration and thought for her.

He went out after breakfast to put in the horse, and at once his old housekeeper expanded into ardent praise of him.

"He works as hard as ten men," she said. "That's how it is he gets on. I often think to myself that he works harder than he ought. It's all work and no play with him. But there, it's no good my talking. He only laughs at me, though I brought him up from his cradle. And a fine baby he was to be sure. His poor mother— she came of gentlefolk, ran away from home she did to marry Farmer Ironside—she died three days after he was born, which was a pity, for the old master was just wrapped up in her, and was never the same again. Well, as I was saying, his poor mother, she'd set her heart on his being given the education of a gentleman; which he was, but he always clung to the land did

Master Jeff. He was sent to Fordstead Grammar School along with the gentry, and a fine figure he cut there. But then his father died, and he had to settle down to farming at seventeen, and he's been farming ever since. He's very well-to-do is Master Jeff, thanks to his own energy and perseverance; for farming isn't what it was. But it's time he took a rest and looked about him. He's thirty come Michaelmas, and he ought to be settling down. As I say to him: 'Granny Grimshaw won't be here for always, and you won't like any other kind of housekeeper save and unless she's a wife as well.' He always laughs at me," said Granny Grimshaw, shaking her head. "But it's true as the sun's above us. Master Jeff ought to be stirring himself to find a wife. But he'll go to the gentry for one, same as his father did before him. He won't be satisfied with any of them saucy country lasses. He don't ever mix with them. He'll look high will Master Jeff if the time ever comes that he looks at all. He's a gentleman himself right through to the backbone, and he'll marry a lady."

By the time Jeff returned to announce that the rain had ceased and the cart was waiting, there were not many of his private affairs of the knowledge of which Doris had not been placed in possession.

She was smiling a little to herself over the old woman's garrulous confidences when he entered, and it was evident that he caught the smile, for he looked from her to his housekeeper with a touch of sharpness.

Granny Grimshaw hastened to efface herself with apologetic promptitude, and retired to the scullery to wash up.

Doris turned at once to her host. "Will you take me over the mill some day?" she asked.

He looked momentarily surprised at the suggestion, and then in a second he smiled. "Of course. When will you come?"

"On Sunday?" she ventured.

"It won't be working then."

"No. But other days you are busy."

Jeff dropped upon his knees again in front of her, and turned his attention to brushing the worst of the mud from her skirt. He attacked it with extreme vigour, his smooth lips firmly shut.

At the end of nearly a minute he paused. "I shan't be too busy for that any day," he said.

"Not really?" Doris sounded a little doubtful.

He looked at her, and somehow his brown eyes made her lower her own. They held a mastery, a confidence, that embarrassed her subtly and quite inexplicably.

"Come any time," he said, "except market-day. Mrs. Grimshaw will always know where I am to be found, and will send me word."

She nodded. "I shall come one morning then. I will ride round, shall I?"

He returned to his task, faintly smiling. "Don't take any five-barred gates on your way!" he said.

"No, I shan't do that again," she promised. "Five-barred gates have their drawbacks."

"As well as their advantages," said Jeff Ironside enigmatically.

CHAPTER IV

CORN

"Master Jeff!" The kitchen door opened with a nervous creak and a wrinkled brown face, encircled by the frills of a muslin nightcap, peered cautiously in. "Are you asleep, my dear?" asked Granny Grimshaw with tender solicitude.

He was sitting at the table with his elbows upon it and his head in his hands. She saw the smoke curling upwards from his pipe, and rightly deduced from this that he was not asleep.

She came forward, candle in hand. "Master Jeff, you'll pardon me, I'm sure. But it's getting so late—nigh upon twelve o'clock. You won't be getting anything of a night's rest if you don't go to bed."

Jeff raised his head. His eyes, sombre with thought, met hers. "Is it late?" he said abstractedly.

"And you such an early riser," said Granny Grimshaw.

She went across to the fire and began to rake it out, he watching her in silence, still with that sombre look in his dark eyes.

Very suddenly Granny Grimshaw turned and, poker in hand, confronted him. She was wearing a large Paisley shawl over her pink flannel nightdress, but the figure she presented, though quaint, was not unimposing.

"Master Jeff," she said, "don't you be too modest and retiring, my dear. You're just as good as the best of 'em."

A slow, rather hard smile drew the corners of the man's

mouth. "They don't think so," he observed.

"They mayn't," said Granny Grimshaw severely. "But that don't alter what is. You're a good man, and, what's more, a man of substance, which is better than can be said for old Colonel Elliot, with one foot in the grave, so to speak, and up to his eyes in debt. He owes money all over the place, I'm told, and the place is mortgaged for three times its proper value. His wife has a little of her own, so they say; but this poor young lady as was here this morning, she'll be thrown on the world without a penny to her name. A winsome young lady, too, Master Jeff. And she don't look as if she were made to stand many hard knocks. She may belong to the county, as they say, but her heart's in the right place. She'd make a bonny mistress in this old place, and it wants a mistress badly enough. Old Granny Grimshaw has done her best, my dear, and always will. But she isn't the woman she was." An odd, wheedling note crept into the old woman's voice. "She'll be wanting to sit in the chimney-corner soon, Master Jeff, and just mind the little ones. You wouldn't refuse her that?"

Jeff rose abruptly and went across to the fire to knock the ashes from his pipe. Having done so, he remained bent for several seconds, as though he were trying to read his fortune in the dying embers. Then very slowly he straightened himself and spoke.

"I think you forget," he said, "that Colonel Elliot was the son of an earl."

But Granny Grimshaw remained unabashed and wholly unimpressed. She laid down the poker with decision. "I was never one to sneer at good birth," she said. "But I hold that you come of a breed as old and as good as any in the land. Your father was a yeoman of the good old-fashioned sort; and your mother—well, everyone hereabouts knows that she was a lady born and bred. I don't see what titles have to do with breeding," said Granny Grimshaw stoutly. "Not that I despise the aristocracy. Dear me, no! But when all is said and done, no man can be better than a gentleman, and no woman can look higher. And there are gentlemen in every walk of life just the same as there are the other sort. And you, Master Jeff, you're one of the gentlemen."

Jeff laughed a somewhat grim laugh, and turned to put out the lamp.

"You're a very nice old woman, Granny," he said. "But you are not an impartial judge."

"Ah, my dearie," said Granny Grimshaw, "but I know what women's hearts are made of."

A somewhat irrelevant retort, which nevertheless closed the discussion.

They went upstairs together, and parted on the landing.

"And you'll go to bed now, won't you?" urged Granny Grimshaw.

"All right," said Jeff.

But once in his own room he went to the low lattice-window that overlooked the mill-stream, and stood before it looking gravely forth over the still water. It was a night of many stars. Beyond the stream there stretched a dream-valley across which the river mists were trailing. The tall trees in the meadows stood up with a ghostly magnificence against them. The whole scene was one of wondrous peace, and all, as far as he could see, was his. But the man's eyes brooded over his acres with a dumb dissatisfaction, and when he turned from the window at last it was with a gesture of hopelessness.

"God help me for a fool!" he muttered between his teeth. "If I went near her, they would kick me out by the back door."

He began to undress with savage energy, and finally flung himself down on the old four-poster in which his father had lain before him, lying there motionless, with fixed and sleepless eyes, while the hours went by over his head.

Once—it was just before daybreak—he rose and went again to the open window that overlooked his prosperous valley. A change had come over the face of it. The mists were lifting, lifting. He saw the dark forms of cattle standing here and there. The river wound, silent and mysterious, away into the dim, quiet distance. A church clock struck, its tone vague and remote as a voice from another world. And as if in answer to its solemn call a lark soared upwards from the meadow by the mill-stream with a burst of song.

The east was surely lightening. The night was gone. Jeff leaned his burning temple against the window-frame with a feeling akin to physical sickness. He was tired—dead tired; but he knew that he could not sleep now. The world was waking. From the farmyard round the corner of the house there came the flap of wings and the old rooster's blatant greeting to the dawn.

In another half-hour the whole place would be stirring. He had wasted a whole night's rest.

Fiercely he straightened himself. Surely his brain must be

going! Why, he had only spoken to her twice. And then, like a spirit that mocked, the words ran through his brain: "Who ever loved that loved not at first sight?"

So this was love, was it? This—was love!

With clenched hands he stood looking out to the dawning, while the wild fever leaped and seethed in his veins. He called up before his inner vision the light, dainty figure, the level, grey eyes, fearless, yet in a fashion shy, the glow of the sun-tanned skin, the soft, thick hair, brown in the shadow, gold in the sun.

Straight before him, low in the sky, hung the morning star. It almost looked as if it were drifting earthwards with all its purity, all its glistening sweetness, drifting straight to the heart of the world. He fixed his eyes upon it, drawn by its beauty almost in spite of himself. It was the only star in the sky, and it almost seemed as if it had a message for him.

But the day was dawning, the star fading, and the message hard to read. Why had she refused to marry Chesyl? he asked himself. The man was lukewarm in speech and action; but that surely was but the way of the world to which he belonged. No excess of emotion was ever encouraged there. Doubtless behind that amiable mask there beat the same devouring longing that throbbed in his own racing pulses. Surely Doris knew this! Surely she understood her own kind!

He recalled those words of hers that he had overheard, the slow utterance of them as of some pronouncement of doom. "If I can't have corn, I won't have husks. I will die of starvation sooner."

He had caught the pain in those words. Had Hugh Chesyl failed to do so? If so, Hugh Chesyl was a fool. He had never thought very highly of him, though he supposed him to be clever after his own indolent fashion.

Chesyl was the old squire's nephew and heir—a highly suitable *parti* for any girl. Yet Doris had refused him, not wholly without ignominy. A gentleman, too! Jeff's mouth twisted. The thought came to him, and ripened to steady conviction, that had Chesyl taken the trouble to woo, he must in time have won. The girl was miserable enough to admit the fact of her misery, and he offered her marriage with him as a friendly means of escape. On other ground he could have won her. On this ground he was probably the least likely man to win. She asked for corn, and he offered husks. What wonder that she preferred starvation!

His hands were still clenched as he turned from the window. Oh, to have been in Hugh Chesyl's place! She would have had no complaint then to make as to the quality of his offering. He would never have suffered her to go hungry. And yet the feeling that Hugh Chesyl loved her lingered still in his soul. Ah, what a fool! What a fool!

It was nearly three hours later that Jim Dawlish the miller answered Jeff Ironside's gruff morning greeting with an eager, "Have you heard the news, sir?"

Dawlish was of a cheery, expansive disposition, and not much of the village gossip ever escaped him or remained with him.

"What news?" demanded Jeff.

"Why, about the old Colonel up at the Place, to be sure," said Dawlish, advancing his floury person towards the doorway in which stood the master's square, strong figure.

"Colonel Elliot?" queried Jeff sharply. "What about him?"

Dawlish wagged a knowing head. "Ah, you may well ask that, sir. He died—early this morning—quite unexpected. Had a fit or some'at. They say it's an open question whether there'll be enough money to bury him. He has creditors all over the county."

"Good heavens!" said Jeff. He drew back swiftly into the open air as if he found the atmosphere of the mill oppressive. "Are you quite sure it's true?" he questioned. "How did you hear?"

"It's true enough," said the miller, with keen enjoyment. "I heard it from the police-sergeant. He says it was so sudden that there'll have to be an inquest. I'm sorry for the widow and orphans though. It'll fall a bit hard on them."

"Good heavens!" said Jeff again. "Good heavens!"

And then very abruptly he turned and left the mill.

"What's the matter with the boss?" asked the miller's underling. "Did the Colonel owe him money too?"

"That's about the ticket," said Jim Dawlish cheerily. "That comes of lending, that does. It just shows the truth of the old saying, 'Stick to your money and your money'll stick to you.' There never was a truer word."

"Wonder if he's lost much?" said the underling speculatively.

Whereupon Jim Dawlish waxed suddenly severe. He never tolerated idle gossip among his inferiors. "And that's no concern of yours, Charlie Bates," he said. "You get on with your work and don't bother your pudden head about what ain't in no way your business. Mr. Ironside is about the soundest man within fifty miles, and don't you forget it!"

"He wasn't best pleased to hear about the poor old Colonel though for all that," said Charlie Bates tenaciously. "And I'd give something to know what'll come of it."

If he had known, neither he nor Jim Dawlish would have got through much work that morning.

CHAPTER V

A BARGAIN

It was nearly a fortnight after Colonel Elliot's death that Jeff Ironside went to the stable somewhat suddenly one morning, saddled his mare, and, without a word to anyone, rode away.

Granny Grimshaw was the only witness of his departure, and she turned from the kitchen window with a secret smile and nod.

It was an autumn morning of mist and sunshine. The beech trees shone golden overhead, and the robins trilled loudly from the clematis-draped hedges. Jeff rode briskly, with too set a purpose to bestow any attention upon these things. He took a short cut across his own land and entered the grounds belonging to the Place by a side drive seldom used.

Thence he rode direct to the front door of the great Georgian house and boldly demanded admittance.

The footman who opened to him looked him up and down interrogatively. "Miss Elliot is at home, but I don't know if she will see anyone," he said uncompromisingly.

"Ask her!" said Jeff tersely. "My name is Ironside."

While the man was gone he took the mare to a yew tree that shadowed the drive at a few yards' distance and tied her to it. There was an air of grim resolution about all his actions. This accomplished, he returned to the great front door.

As he reached it there came the sound of light, hastening feet within, and in a moment the half-open door was thrown back. Doris herself, very slim and pale, but withal very queenly in her deep mourning, came forth with outstretched hand to greet him.

"But why did they leave you here?" she said. "Please come in!"

He followed her in with scarcely a word.

She led him down a long oak passage to a room that was plainly the library, and there in her quick, gracious way she turned and faced him.

"I am very pleased to see you, Mr. Ironside. I was going to write to you to thank you again for all your kindness, but lately—there has been so much to think about—so much to do. I know you will understand. Do sit down!"

But Jeff remained squarely on his feet. "I hope you have quite recovered from your fall?" he said.

"Quite, thank you." She smiled faintly. "It seems such an age ago. Hector came home quite safely too." She broke off short, paused as if seeking for words, then said rather abruptly, "I shall never go hunting again."

"You mean not this year?" suggested Jeff.

She looked at him, and he saw that her smile Was piteous. "No, I mean never. Everything is to be sold. Haven't you heard?"

He nodded. "Yes, I had heard. I hoped it wasn't true."

"Yes, it is true." Her two hands fastened very tightly upon the back of a chair. There was something indescribably pathetic in the action. She seemed on the verge of saying more, but in the end she did not say it. She just stood looking at him with the wide grey eyes that tried so hard not to be tragic.

Jeff stood looking back with great sturdiness and not much apparent feeling. He offered no word of condolence or sympathy. Only after a very decided pause he said, "I wonder what you will do?"

"I am going to London," she said.

"Soon?" Jeff's voice was curt, almost gruff.

"Yes, very soon." She hesitated momentarily, then went on rapidly, as if it were a relief to tell someone. "My father's life was insured. It has left my stepmother enough to live on; but, of course, not here. The place is mortgaged up to the hilt. I have nothing at all. I have got to make my own living."

"You?" said Jeff.

She smiled again faintly, "Yes, I. What is there in that? Lots of women work for their living."

"You are not going to work for yours," he said.

She thrust the chair from her with a quick little movement of the hands. "I would begin tomorrow—if I only knew how. But I don't—yet. I've got to look about me for a little. I am going first to a cousin at Kensington."

"Who doesn't want you," said Jeff.

She looked at him in sharp surprise. "Who—who told you that?"

"You did," he said doggedly. "At least, you told Mr. Chesyl—in my presence."

"Ah, I remember!" She uttered a tremulous little laugh. "That was the day I caught you eavesdropping and ordered you off your own ground."

"It was," said Jeff. "I heard several things that day, and I guessed—other things." He paused, still looking straight at her. "Miss Elliot," he said, "wouldn't it be easier for you to marry than to work for your living?"

The pretty brows went up in astonishment. "Oh!" she said, in quick confusion. "You heard that too?"

"Wouldn't it be easier?" persisted Jeff in his slow, stubborn way.

She shook her head swiftly and vehemently. "I shall never marry Mr. Chesyl," she said with determination.

"Where is he?" asked Jeff.

The soft colour rose in her face at the question. She looked away from him for the first time. "I don't quite know where he is. I believe he is up north somewhere—in Scotland."

"He knows what has been happening here?" questioned Jeff.

She made a slight movement as of protest. "No doubt," she said in a low voice.

Jeff's square jaw hardened. Abruptly he thrust Chesyl out of the conversation. "It doesn't matter," he said. "That isn't what I came to talk about. May I tell you just what I have come for? Will you give me a patient hearing?"

She turned to him again in renewed surprise. "Of course," she said.

His dark eyes were upon her. "It may not please you," he said slowly, "though I ask you to believe that it is not my intention to give you offence."

"But, of course, I know you would not," she said.

Jeff's fingers clenched upon his riding-switch. He spoke with difficulty, but not without a certain native dignity that made him impressive. "I have come," he said, "just to say to you that if it is possible that no one in your own world is wanting you, I am wanting you. All that I have is absolutely at your disposal. I heard you say—that day—that you would like to be a farmer's wife. Well—if you really meant it—you have your opportunity."

"Mr. Ironside!" She was gazing at him in wide-eyed amazement.

A dark flush rose in his swarthy face under her eyes, "I had to say it," he said with heavy deliberation, "though I know I'm only hammering nails into my own coffin. I had to take my only chance of telling you. Of course, I know you won't listen. I'm not of your sort—respectable enough, but not quite—not quite—" He broke off grimly, and for an instant his teeth showed clenched upon his lower lip. "But if by any chance, when everything else has failed," resolutely he went on, "you could bring yourself to think of me—in that way, I shall always be ready, quite ready, for you. That's what I came to say."

He straightened himself upon the words, and made as if he would turn and leave her. But Doris was too quick for him. She moved like a flash. She came between him and the door. "Please—please," she said, "you mustn't go yet!"

He stopped instantly and she stood before him breathing quickly, her hand upon the door.

She did not speak again very quickly; she was plainly trying to master considerable agitation.

Jeff waited immovably with eyes unvaryingly upon her. "I don't want to hurry you," he said at last. "I know, of course, what your answer will be. But I can wait for it."

That faint, fugitive smile of hers went over her face. She took her hand from the door.

"You—you haven't been very—explicit, have you?" she said. "Are you—are you being just kind to me, Mr. Ironside, like—like Hugh Chesyl?"

Her voice quivered as she asked the question, but her eyes met his with direct steadfastness.

He lowered his own very suddenly. "No," he said. "I wouldn't insult you by being kind. I shouldn't ask you to marry me if I didn't love you with all my heart and soul."

The words came quickly, with something of a burning quality. She made a slight movement as if she were taken by surprise.

After a moment she spoke. "There are two kinds of love," she said. "There's the big, unselfish kind—the real thing; and there's the other—the kind that demands everything, and even then, perhaps, is never satisfied. You hardly know me well enough to—to care for me in the first big way, do you? You don't even know if I'm worth it."

"I beg your pardon," said Jeff Ironside. "I think I do know you well enough for that. Anyhow, if you could bring yourself to marry me, I should be satisfied. The right to take care of you—make you comfortable—wait on you—that's all I'm asking. That would be enough for me—more than I've dared to hope for."

"That would make you happy?" she asked.

He kept his eyes lowered. "It would be—enough," he repeated.

She uttered a sudden quick sigh. "But wouldn't you rather marry a woman who was in love with you in just the ordinary way?" she said.

"No," said Jeff curtly.

"It would be much better for you," she protested.

He smiled a grim smile. "I am the best judge of that," he said.

She held out her hand to him. "Mr. Ironside, tell me honestly, wouldn't you despise me if I married you in that way—taking all and giving nothing?"

He crushed her hand in his. The red blood rose to his forehead. He looked at her for a moment—only a moment—and instantly looked away again.

"No," he said, "I shouldn't."

"I should despise myself," said Doris.

"I don't know why you should," he said.

She smiled again with lips that quivered. "No, you don't understand. You're too big for me altogether. I can't say 'Yes,' but I feel very highly honoured all the same. You'll believe that, won't you?"

"Why can't you say 'Yes'?" asked Jeff.

She hesitated momentarily. "You see, I'm afraid I don't care for you—like that," she said.

"Does that matter?" said Jeff.

She looked at him, her hand still in his. "Don't you think so?"

"No, I don't," he said, "unless you think you couldn't be happy."

"I was thinking of you," she said gently.

"Of me?" He looked surprised for an instant, and again his eyes met hers in a quick glance. "If you're going to think of me," he said, "you'll do it. I have told you, you needn't be afraid of my expecting too much."

But she shook her head. "I should be much more afraid of taking too much from you," she said. "The little I could offer would never satisfy you."

"Yes it would," he insisted. "I'm only asking to stand between you and trouble. It's all I want in life."

Again his eyes were upon her, dark and resolute. His hand held hers in a steady grip. For the first time her own resolution began to falter.

"Let me write to you, Mr. Ironside," she said at last, with a vague idea of softening a refusal that had become inexplicably hard.

"Write and say 'No'?" said Jeff.

She smiled a little, but her eyes filled with sudden tears. "You make it very hard for me to say 'No,'" she said.

"I would like to make it impossible," he said.

"Even when I have told you that I can't—that I don't—love you in the ordinary way?" she said almost pleadingly.

"I don't want to be loved in the ordinary way," he answered doggedly.

"I should be a perpetual disappointment to you," she said.

"I would rather have even that than—nothing," said Jeff.

One of the tears ran over and fell upon their clasped hands. "In fact, you want me at any price," she said.

"At any price," said Jeff.

She bent her head and choked back a sob. "And no one else wants me at all," she whispered.

He stooped towards her. Perhaps for her peace of mind it was as well that she did not see the sudden fire that blazed in his deep-set eyes as he did so.

"So you'll change your mind," he said, after a moment, to the bowed head. "You'll have me—you will?"

She caught back another sob and said nothing.

He straightened himself sharply. "Miss Elliot, if it's going to make you miserable, you had better send me away. I'll go—if it's for that."

He would have released her hand, but it tightened very suddenly upon his. "No, don't go—don't go!" she said.

"But you're crying," muttered Jeff uneasily.

She gave a big gulp and raised her head. The tears were running down her cheeks, but she smiled at him bravely notwithstanding. "I believe I should cry—much more—if you were to go now," she told him, with a quaint effort at humour.

Jeff Ironside put a strong grip upon himself. His heart was thumping like the strokes of a heavy hammer. "Then you'll have me?" he said.

She put her other hand, with a very winning gesture of

confidence, into his. "I don't see how I can help it," she said. "You've knocked down all my obstacles. But you do understand, don't you? You won't—won't—"

"Abuse your trust? No, never!" said Jeff Ironside. "I will die by my own hand sooner."

"Ah, I can't help liking you," Doris said impulsively, as if in explanation or excuse. "You're so big."

"Thank you," Jeff said very earnestly. "And you won't cry any more?"

She uttered a whimsical little laugh. "But I wasn't crying for myself," she said, as she dried her eyes. "I was crying for you."

"Well, you mustn't," said Jeff. "You have given me all I want—much more than I dared to hope for." He paused a moment, then abruptly, "You won't think better of it when I'm gone, will you?" he said. "You won't write and say you have changed your mind?"

She gave him her hand again with an air of comradeship. "It's a bargain, Mr. Ironside," she said, with gentle dignity. "A very one-sided one, I fear, but still—a bargain."

"I beg your pardon," murmured Jeff.

CHAPTER VI

THE WEDDING PRESENT

The marriage of Jeff Ironside to Colonel Elliot's daughter created a sensation in the neighbourhood even greater than that which followed the Colonel's death. But the ceremony itself was strictly private. It took place so quietly and so suddenly very early on a misty October morning that it was over before most people knew anything about it. Jim Dawlish knew, and was present with old Granny Grimshaw; but, save for the family lawyer who gave away the bride and the aged rector who married them, no one else was in the secret.

Mrs. Elliot knew, but she and her stepdaughter had never been in sympathy, and she had already left the place and gone to town.

Very small and pathetic looked the bride in her deep mourning on that dim autumn morning, but she played her part with queenly dignity, unfaltering, undismayed. If she had acted upon impulse she was fully prepared to face the consequences.

As for Jeff, he was gruff almost to rudeness, so desperate was the turmoil of his soul. Not one word did he address to his bride from the moment of entering the church to that of leaving it save such as were contained in the marriage service. And even when they passed out together into the grey churchyard he remained grimly silent till she turned with a little smile and addressed him.

"Good-morning, Jeff!" she said, and her slender, ungloved hand, very cold but superbly confident, found its way into his.

He looked down at her then and found his voice, the while his fingers closed protectingly upon hers. "You're cold," he said. "They ought to have warmed the church."

She turned her face up to the sky. "The sun will be through soon. Will you take me home across the fields?"

"Too wet," said Jeff.

"Not if we keep to the path," she said. "I must just say good-bye to Mr. Webster first."

Mr. Webster was the family lawyer. He came up with stilted phrases of felicitation which sent Jeff instantly back into his impenetrable shell of silence. Doris made reply on his behalf and her own with a dainty graciousness that covered all difficulties, and finally extricated herself and Jeff from the situation with a dexterity that left him spellbound.

She had her way. They went by way of the fields, he and she alone through the lifting mist, while Granny Grimshaw and Jim Dawlish marched solemnly back to the mill by the road.

"It's a very good morning's work," asserted Granny Grimshaw with much satisfaction. "I always felt that Master Jeff would never marry any but a lady."

"I'd rather him than me," returned Jim Dawlish obscurely.

Which remark Granny Grimshaw treated as unworthy of notice.

As Jeff Ironside and his bride neared the last stile the sun came through and shone upon all things.

"I'm glad we came this way," she said.

Jeff said nothing. He never spoke unless he had something to say.

They reached the stile. He strode over and reached back a hand to her. She took it, mounted and stepped over, then sat down unexpectedly on the top bar with the hand in hers.

"Jeff!" she said.

He looked up at her. Her voice was small and shy, her cheeks very delicately flushed.

"What is it?" said Jeff.

She looked down at the brown hand she held, all roughened and hardened by toil, and hesitated.

"Well?" said Jeff.

She turned her eyes upon his face. "Are you going back to work today, just as if—as if nothing had happened?" she asked.

He looked straight back at her. "You don't want me, do you?" he said.

She nodded. "Shall we go for a picnic?" she said.

"A picnic!" He seemed surprised at the suggestion.

She laughed a little. "Do you never go for picnics? I do—all by myself sometimes. It's rather fun, you know."

"By yourself?" said Jeff.

She rose from her perch. "It's more fun with someone certainly," she said.

Jeff's face reflected her smile for an instant. "All right," he said. "I'll take a holiday for once. But come home now and have some breakfast."

She stepped down beside him. "It's nice of you to give me the very first thing I ask for," she said. "Will you do something else for me?"

"Yes," said Jeff.

"Then will you call me Dot?" she said. "It was the pet name my mother gave me. No one has used it since she died."

"Dot," repeated Jeff. "You really want me to call you that?"

"But, of course," she said, smiling, "you haven't called me anything yet. Please begin at once! It really isn't difficult."

"Very well, Dot," he said. "And where are we going for our picnic?"

"Oh, not very far," she said. "Somewhere within a quite easy walk."

"Can't we ride?" suggested Jeff.

"Ride?" She looked at him in surprise.

"I have a horse who would carry you," he said.

"Have you—have you, really?" Quick pleasure came into her eyes. "Oh, Jeff, how kind of you!"

"No, it isn't," said Jeff bluntly. "I want you to be happy."

She laughed her quick, light laugh. "So you're going to spoil me?" she said.

They reached the pretty Mill House above the stream and found breakfast awaiting them in the oak-panelled parlour that overlooked a sunny orchard.

"How absolutely sweet!" said Doris.

He came and stood beside her at the window, looking silently forth.

She glanced at him half-shyly. "Aren't you very fond of it all?"

"Yes," he said.

"And I think I am going to be," said Doris.

"I hope you will," said Jeff.

She turned from him to Granny Grimshaw who entered at the moment with a hot dish.

"I don't think we ought to have been married so early," she said. "You must be quite tired out. Now, please, Mrs. Grimshaw, do sit down and let me wait on you for a change!"

Granny Grimshaw smiled at the bare suggestion.

"No, no, Mrs. Ironside, my dear. This is for you and Master Jeff. I've got mine in the kitchen."

"I never heard such a thing!" declared Doris. "Jeff, surely you are not going to allow that!"

Jeff came from the window. "Of course you must join us, Granny," he said.

But Granny Grimshaw was obdurate on that point. "My place is in the kitchen," she said firmly. "And there I must bide. But I am ready to show you the way to your room, my dear, whenever you want to go."

Doris bent forward impulsively and kissed her. "You are much, much too kind to me, you and Jeff," she said.

But as soon as she was alone with Jeff her shyness returned. She could not feel as much at ease with him in the house as in the open air. She did not admit it even to herself, but deep in her heart she had begun to be a little afraid.

Till then she had gone blindly forward, taking in desperation the only course that seemed to offer her escape from a position that had become wholly intolerable. But now for the first time misgivings arose within her. She remembered how slight was her knowledge of the man to whom she had thus impetuously entrusted her future; and, remembering, something of her ready confidence went from her. She fell silent also.

"You are not eating anything," said Jeff. She started at his voice and looked up.

"No, I'm not hungry," she said. "I shall eat all the more presently when we get out into the open."

He said no more, but finished his own breakfast with businesslike promptitude.

"Mrs. Grimshaw will take you upstairs," he said then, and went to the door to call her.

"Where will you be?" Doris asked him shyly, as he stood back for her to pass.

"I am going round to the stable," he said.

"May I come to you there?" she suggested.

He assented gravely: "Do!"

Granny Grimshaw was in her most garrulous mood. She took Doris up the old steep stairs and into the low-ceiled room with the lattice window that looked over the river meadows.

"It's the best room in the house," she told her. "Master Jeff was born in it, and he's slept here for the past ten years. You won't be lonely, my dear. My room is just across the passage, and he has gone to the room at the end which he always had as a boy."

"This is a lovely room," said Doris.

She stood where Jeff had stood before the open window and looked across the valley.

"I hope you will be very happy here, my dear," said Granny Grimshaw behind her.

Doris turned round to her impetuously. "Dear Mrs. Grimshaw, I don't like Jeff to give up the best room to me," she said. "Isn't there another one that I could have?"

She glanced towards a door that led out of the room in which they were.

"Yes, go in, my dear!" said Granny Grimshaw with a chuckle. "It's all for you."

Doris opened the door with a quick flush on her cheeks.

"Master Jeff thought you would like a little sitting-room of your own," said the old woman behind her.

"Oh, he shouldn't. He shouldn't!" Doris said.

She stood on the threshold of a sunny room that overlooked the garden with its hedge of lavender and beyond it the orchard with its wealth of ripe apples shining in the sun. The room had been evidently furnished for her especial use. There was a couch in one corner, a cottage piano in another, and a writing-table near the window.

"The old master bought those things for his bride," said Granny Grimshaw. "They are just as good as new yet, and Master Jeff has had the piano put in order for you. I expect you know how to play the piano, my dear?"

Doris went forward into the room. The tears were not far from her eyes. "He is too good to me. He is much too good," she said.

"Ah, my dear, and you'll be good to him too, won't you?" said Granny Grimshaw coaxingly.

"I'll do my best," said Doris quietly.

She went down to Jeff in the stable-yard a little later with a heart brimming with gratitude, but that strange, new shyness was with her also. She did not know how to give him her thanks.

He was waiting for her, and escorted her across to the stable. "You will like to see your mount," he said, cutting her short almost before she had begun.

She followed him into the stable. Jeff's own mare poked an inquiring nose over the door of her loose-box. Doris stopped to fondle her. Jeff plunged a hand into his pocket and brought out some sugar.

From the stall next to them came a low whinny. Doris, in the act of feeding the mare, looked up sharply. The next moment with a little cry she had sprung forward and was in the stall with her arms around the neck of its occupant—a big bay, who nozzled against her shoulder with evident pleasure.

"Oh, Hector! Hector!" she cried. "However did you come here?"

"I bought him," said Jeff, "as a wedding present."

"For me? Oh, Jeff!" She left Hector and came to him with both hands outstretched. "Oh, Jeff, I don't know how to thank you. You are so much too good. What can I say?"

He took the hands and gripped them. His dark eyes looked straight and hard into hers, and a little tremor went through her. She lowered her own instinctively, and in the same instant he let her go. He did not utter a word, and she turned from him in silence with a face on fire.

She made no further effort to express her gratitude.

CHAPTER VII

THE END OF THE PICNIC

Those odd silences of Jeff's fell very often throughout the day, and they lay upon Doris's spirit like a physical weight. They rode through autumn woodlands, and picnicked on the side of a hill. The day was warm and sunny, and the whole world shone as through a pearly veil. There were blackberries in abundance, large and ripe, and Doris wandered about picking them during the afternoon while Jeff lounged against a tree and smoked.

He did not offer to join her, but she had a feeling that his eyes followed her wherever she went, and a great restlessness kept her moving. She could not feel at her ease in his vicinity. She wanted very urgently to secure his friendship. She had counted upon that day in his society to do so. But it seemed to be his resolve to hold aloof. He seemed disinclined to commit himself to anything approaching intimacy, and that attitude of his filled her with misgiving. Had he begun to repent of the one-sided bargain, she asked herself? Or could it be that he also was oppressed by shyness? She longed intensely to know.

The sun was sinking low in the sky when at length reluctantly she went back to him. "It's getting late," she said. "Don't you think we ought to go home?"

He was standing in the level sun-rays gazing sombrely down into the valley from which already the mists were beginning to rise.

He turned at her voice, and she knew he looked at her, though she did not meet his eyes. For a moment or two he stood, not speaking, but as though on the verge of speech; and her heart quickened to a nervous throbbing.

Then unexpectedly he turned upon his heel. "Yes. Wait here, won't you, while I go and fetch the animals?"

He went, and a sharp sense of relief shot through her. She was sure that he had something on his mind; but inexplicably she was thankful that he had not uttered it.

The sun was dropping out of sight behind the opposite hill, and she was conscious of a growing chill in the atmosphere. A cockchafer whirred past her and buried itself in a tuft of grass hard by. In the wood behind her a robin trilled a high sweet song. From the farther side of the valley came a trail of smoke from a cottage bonfire, and the scent of it hung heavy in the evening air.

All these things she knew and loved, and they were to be hers for the rest of her life; yet her heart was heavy within her. She turned and looked after Jeff with a wistful drooping of the lips.

He had passed out of sight behind some trees, but as she turned she heard a footfall in the wood close at hand, and almost simultaneously a man emerged carrying a gun.

He stopped at sight of her, and on the instant Doris made a swift movement of recognition.

"Why Hugh!" she said.

He came straight to her, with hand outstretched. "My dear, dear girl!" he said.

Her hand lay in his, held in a clasp such as Hugh Chesyl had never before given her, and then all in a moment she withdrew it.

"Why, where have you come from?" she said, with a little nervous laugh.

His eyes looked straight down to hers. "I've been yachting," he said, "along Argyll and Skye. I didn't know till the day before yesterday about the poor old Colonel. I came straight back directly I knew, got here this morning, but heard that you had gone to town. I was going to follow you straightway, but the squire wouldn't hear of it. You know what he is. So I had to compromise and spend one night with him. By Jove! it's a bit of luck finding you here. I'm pleased, Doris, jolly pleased. I've been worried to death about you—never moved so fast in my life."

"Haven't you?" said Doris; she was still smiling a small, tired smile. "But why? I don't see."

"Don't you?" said Hugh. "How shall I explain? You have got such a rooted impression of me as a slacker that I am half afraid of taking your breath away."

She laughed again, not very steadily. "Oh, are you turning over a new leaf? I am delighted to hear it."

He smiled also, his eyes upon hers. "Well, I am, in a way. It's come to me lately that I've been an utter ass all this time. I expect you've been thinking the same, haven't you?"

"No, I don't think so," said Doris.

"No? That's nice of you," said Hugh. "But it's the truth nevertheless. I haven't studied the art of expressing myself properly. I can't do it even yet. But it occurred to me—it just occurred to me—that perhaps I'd never succeeded in making you understand how awfully badly I want to marry you. I think I never told you so. I always somehow took it for granted that you knew. But now—especially now, Doris, when you're in trouble—I want you more than ever. Even if you can't love me as I love you—"

He stopped, for she had flung out her hands with an almost agonized gesture, and her eyes implored him though she spoke no word.

"Won't you listen to me just this once—just this once?" he pleaded. "My dear, I love you so. I love you enough for both if you'll only marry me, and give me the chance of making you happy."

An unwonted note of feeling sounded in his voice. He stretched out his hand to her.

"Doris, darling, won't you change your mind? I'm miserable without you."

And then very suddenly Doris found her voice. She spoke with breathless entreaty. "Hugh, don't—don't! I can't listen to you. I married Jeff Ironside this morning."

His hand fell. He stared at her as if he thought her mad. "You—married—Jeff Ironside! I don't believe it!"

She clenched her hands tightly to still her agitation. "But it's true," she said.

"Doris!" he said.

She nodded vehemently, keeping her eyes on his. "It's true," she said again.

He straightened himself up with the instinctive movement of a man bracing himself to meet a sudden strain. "But why? How? I didn't even know you knew the man."

She nodded again. "He helped me once when I was out cubbing, and I went to his house. After that—when he heard that I had nothing to live on—he came and asked me if I would marry him. And I was very miserable because nobody wanted me. So I said 'Yes.'"

Her voice sank. Her lips were quivering.

"I wanted you," Hugh said.

She was silent.

He bent slowly towards her, looking into her eyes. "My dear, didn't you really know—didn't you understand?"

She shook her head; her eyes were suddenly full of tears. "No, Hugh."

He held out his hand again and took hers. "Don't cry, Doris! You haven't lost much. I shall get over it somehow. I know you never cared for me."

She bent her head with some murmured words he could not catch.

He leaned nearer. "What, dear, what? You never did, did you?"

He waited for her answer, and at last through tears it came. "I've been struggling so hard, so hard, to keep myself from caring."

He was silent a moment, and again it was as if he were collecting his strength for that which had to be endured. Then slowly: "You thought I wasn't in earnest?" he said. "You thought I didn't care enough?"

She did not answer him in words; her silence was enough.

"God forgive me!" whispered Hugh.<N>.<N>.<N>.

There came the thud of horses' hoofs upon the grass, and his hand relinquished hers. He turned to see Jeff Ironside barely ten paces away, leading the two animals. Very pale but wholly collected, Hugh moved to meet him.

"I have just been hearing about your marriage, Ironside," he said. "May I congratulate you?"

Jeff's eyes, with the red sunlight turning them to a ruddy brown, met his with absolute directness as he made brief response. "You are very kind."

"Doris and I are old friends," said Hugh.

"Yes, I know," said Jeff.

Spasmodically Doris turned and joined the two men. "We hope Mr. Chesyl will come and see us sometimes, don't we, Jeff?" she said.

"Certainly," said Jeff, "when he has nothing better to do."

She turned to Hugh with a bright little smile. Her tears were wholly gone, and he marvelled. "I hope that will be often, Hugh," she said.

"Thank you," Hugh said gravely. "Thank you very much." He added, after a moment, to Jeff: "I shall probably be down here a good deal now. The squire is beginning to feel his age. In fact, he wants me to make my home with him. I don't propose to do that entirely, but I can't leave him alone for long at a time."

"I see," said Jeff. He glanced towards Doris. "Shall we start back?" he said.

Hugh propped his gun against a tree, and stepped forward to mount her. "So you still have Hector," he said.

"Jeff's wedding present," she answered, still smiling.

Lightly she mounted, and for a single moment he felt her passing touch upon his shoulder. Then Hector moved away, stepping proudly. Jeff was already in the saddle.

"Good-bye!" said Doris, looking back to him. "Don't forget to come and see us!"

She was gone.

Hugh Chesyl turned with the sun-rays dazzling him, and groped for his gun.

He found it, shouldered it, and strode away down the woodland path. His face as he went was the face of a man suddenly awakened to the stress and the turmoil of life.

CHAPTER VIII

THE NEW LIFE

There was no doubt about it. Granny Grimshaw was not satisfied. Deeper furrows were beginning to appear in her already deeply furrowed face. She shook her head very often with pursed lips when she was alone. And this despite the fact that she and the young mistress of the Mill House were always upon excellent terms. No difficulties ever arose between them. Doris showed not the smallest disposition to usurp the old housekeeper's authority. Possibly Granny Grimshaw would have been better pleased if she had. She spent much of her time out-of-doors, and when in the house she was generally to be found in the little sitting-room that Jeff had fitted up for her.

She had her meals in the parlour with Jeff, and these were the sole occasions on which they were alone together. If Doris could have had her way, Granny Grimshaw would have been present at these also, but on this point the old woman showed herself determined, not to say obstinate. She maintained that her place was the kitchen, and that her presence was absolutely necessary there, a point of view which no argument of Doris's could persuade her to relinquish.

So she and Jeff breakfasted, dined, and supped in solitude, and though Doris became gradually accustomed to these somewhat silent meals, she never enjoyed them. Of difficult moments there were actually very few. They mutually avoided any but the most general subjects for conversation. But of intimacy between them there was none. Jeff had apparently drawn a very distinct boundary-line which he never permitted himself to cross. He never intruded upon her. He never encroached upon the friendship she shyly proffered. Once when she somewhat hesitatingly suggested that he should come to her sitting-room for a little after supper he refused, not churlishly, but very decidedly.

"I like to have my pipe and go to bed," he said.

"But you can bring your pipe, too," she said.

"No, thanks," said Jeff. "I always smoke in the kitchen or on the step."

She said no more, but went up to her room, and presently Jeff, moodily puffing at his briar in the porch, heard the notes of her piano overhead. She played softly for some little time, and Jeff's pipe went out before it was finished—a most rare occurrence with him.

Only when the piano ceased did he awake to the fact, and then half-savagely he knocked out its half-consumed contents and turned inwards.

He found Granny Grimshaw standing in the passage in a listening attitude, and paused to bid her good-night.

"Be you going to bed, Master Jeff?" she said. "My dear, did you ever hear the like? She plays like an angel."

He smiled somewhat grimly, without replying.

The old woman came very close to him. "Master Jeff, why don't you go and make love to her? Don't you know she's waiting for you?"

"Is she?" said Jeff, but he said it in the tone of one who does not require an answer, and with the words very abruptly he passed her by.

Granny Grimshaw shook her head and sighed, "Ah, dear!" after his retreating form.

It was a few days after this that a letter came for Doris, one morning, bearing the Squire's crest. Her husband handed it to her at the breakfast-table, and she received it with a flush. After a moment, seeing him occupied with a newspaper, she opened it.

"Dear Doris," it said. "You asked me to come and see you, but I have not done so as I was not sure if, after all, you meant me to take the invitation literally. We have been friends for so long that I feel constrained to speak openly. For myself, I only ask to go on being your friend, and to serve you in any way possible. But perhaps I can serve you best by keeping away from you. If so, then I will do even that.—Yours ever,

"Hugh."

Something within moved Doris to raise her eyes suddenly, and instantly she encountered Jeff's fixed upon her. The flush in her cheeks deepened burningly. With an effort she spoke:

"Hugh Chesyl wants to know if he may come to see us."

"I thought you asked him," said Jeff.

A little quiver of resentment went through her; she could not have said wherefore. "He was not sure if I meant it," she said.

There was an instant's silence; then Jeff did an extraordinary thing. He stretched out his hand across the table, keeping his eyes on hers.

"Let me have his letter to answer!" he said.

She made a sharp instinctive movement of withdrawal. "Oh, no!" she said. "No!"

Jeff said nothing; but his face hardened somewhat, and his hand remained outstretched.

Doris's grey eyes gleamed. "No, Jeff!" she repeated, more calmly, and with the words she slipped Hugh's envelope into the bosom of her dress. "I can't give you my letters to answer indeed."

Jeff withdrew his hand, and began to eat his breakfast in utter silence.

Doris played with hers until the silence became intolerable, and then, very suddenly and very winningly, she leaned towards him.

"Dear Jeff, surely you are not vexed!" she said.

He looked at her again, and in spite of herself she felt her heart quicken.

"Are you, Jeff?" she said, and held out her hand to him.

For a moment he sat motionless, then abruptly he grasped the hand.

"May I say what I think?" he asked her bluntly.

"Of course," she said.

"Then I think from all points of view that you had better leave Chesyl alone," he said.

"What do you mean?" Quickly she asked the question; the colour flamed in her face once more. "Tell my why you think that!" she said.

"I would rather not," said Jeff.

"But that is not fair of you, Jeff," she protested.

He released her hand slowly. "I am sorry," he said. "If I were more to you, I would say more. As it is—well, I would rather not."

She rose impetuously. "You are very—difficult," she said.

To which he made answer with that silence which was to her more difficult than speech.

Yet later, when she was alone, her sense of justice made her admit that he had not been altogether unreasonable. She recalled the fact that he had overheard that leisurely proposal of marriage that Hugh had made her in the cornfield on the occasion of their first meeting, and her face burned afresh as she remembered certain other items of that same conversation that he must also have overheard. No, on the whole it was not surprising that he did not greatly care for Hugh—poor Hugh, who loved her and had so narrowly missed winning her for himself. She wondered if Hugh were really very miserable. She herself had passed through so many stages of misery since her wedding-day. But she had sufficient knowledge of herself to realize that it was the loneliness and lack of sympathy that weighed upon her most.

Her feeling for Hugh was still an undeveloped quantity, though the certainty of his love for her had quickened it to keener life. She was not even yet absolutely certain that he could have satisfied her. It was true that he had been deeply stirred for the moment, but how deeply and how lastingly she had no means of gauging. Knowing the indolence of his nature, she was inclined to mistrust the permanence of his feeling. And so resolutely had she restrained her own feeling for him during the whole length of their acquaintance that she was able still to keep it within bounds. She knew that the sympathy between them was fundamental in character, but she had often suspected—in her calmer moments she suspected still—that it was of the kind that engenders friendship rather than passion.

But even so, his friendship was essentially precious to her, all the more so for the daily loneliness of spirit that she found herself compelled to endure. For—with this one exception—she was practically friendless. She had known that in marrying Jeff Ironside she was relinquishing her own circle entirely. But she had imagined that there would be compensations. Moreover, so far as society was concerned, she had not had any choice. It had been this or exile. And she had chosen this.

Wherefore? Simply and solely because Jeff, of all she knew, had wanted her.

Again that curious little tremor went through her. Had he wanted her so very badly after all? Not once since their wedding-day had he made any friendly overture or responded to any overture of hers. They were as completely strangers now as they had been on the day he had proposed to her.

A sharp little sigh came from her. She had not thought somehow that Jeff would be so difficult. He had told her that he loved her. She had counted on that for the foundation of their friendship, but no structure had she succeeded in raising thereon. He asked nothing of her, and, save for material comforts, he bestowed nothing in return. True, it was what she had bargained for. But yet it did not satisfy her. She was not at her ease with him, and she began to think she never would be.

As to Hugh, she hardly knew how to proceed; but she finally wrote him a friendly note, concurring with his suggestion that they should not meet again for a little while—"only for a little while, Hugh," she added, almost in spite of herself, "for I can't afford to lose a friend like you."

And she did not guess how the heart-cry of her loneliness echoed through the words.

CHAPTER IX

THE WAY TO BE HAPPY

It was not until the week before Christmas that Doris saw Hugh again. They met in the hunting-field. It was the first hunt she had attended since her marriage, and she went to it alone.

The meet was some distance away, and she arrived after the start, joining the ranks of the riders as they waited outside a copse which the hounds were drawing.

The day was chill and grey. She did not altogether know why she went, save that the loneliness at the Mill House seemed to become daily harder to bear, and the longing to escape it, if only for a few hours, was not to be denied.

She was scarcely in a sporting mood, and the sight of old acquaintances, though they greeted her kindly enough, did not tend to raise her spirits.

The terrible conviction had begun to grow upon her of late that she had committed a great mistake that no effort of hers could ever remedy, and the thought of it weighed her down perpetually night and day.

But the sight of Hugh as he came to her along the edge of the wood was a welcome one. She greeted him almost with eagerness, and the friendly grasp of his hand sent warmth to her lonely young heart.

"I am very glad to see you following the hounds," Hugh said. "Are you alone?"

"Quite alone," she said, feeling a lump rise in her throat.

"Then you'll let me take care of you," he said, with a friendly smile.

And she could but smile and thank him.

It was not a particularly satisfactory day from a fox-hunting point of view. The weather did not improve, and the scent was misleading. They found and lost, found and lost again, and a cold drizzle setting in with the afternoon effectually cooled the ardour of even the most enthusiastic.

Yet Doris enjoyed herself. She and Hugh ate their lunch together under some dripping trees, and they managed to make merry over it in spite of the fact that both were fairly wet through. He made her share the sherry in his flask, laughing down all protests, treating her with the absolute ease that had always characterized their friendship. It was such a day as Doris had often spent in his company, and the return to the old genial atmosphere was like the sweetness of a spring day in the midst of winter.

It was he who at length suggested the advisability of returning home. "I'm sure you ought to get back and change," he said. "It'll be getting dark in another hour."

Her face fell, "I have enjoyed it," she said regretfully.

"You'll come again," said Hugh. "They are meeting at Kendal's Corner on Christmas Eve. I shall look out for you."

She smiled. "Very well, I'll be there. Thank you for giving me such a good time, Hugh."

"My dear girl!" said Hugh.

They rode back together through a driving drizzle, and, as Hugh had predicted, the early dusk had fallen before they reached the mill. The roar of the water sounded indescribably desolate as they drew near, and Doris gave a sharp, involuntary shiver.

It was then that Hugh drew close to her and stretched out a hand in the growing darkness. "Doris!" he said softly.

She put her own into it swiftly, impulsively. "Oh, Hugh!" she said with a sob.

"Don't!" said Hugh gently. "Stick to it, dear! I think you won't be sorry in the end. I believe he's a good chap. Give him all you can! It's the only way to be happy."

Her fingers tightened convulsively upon his. She spoke no word.

"Don't, dear!" he said again very earnestly. "It's such a mistake. Honestly, I don't think you've anything to be sorry for. So don't let yourself be faint-hearted! I know he's not a bad sort."

"He's very good," whispered Doris.

"Yes, that's just it," said Hugh. "So don't be afraid of giving!

You'll never regret it. No one could help loving you, Doris. Remember that, dear, when you're feeling down! You're just the sweetest woman in the world, and the man who couldn't worship you would be a hopeless fool."

They were passing over the bridge that spanned the stream. The road was narrow, and their horses moved side by side. They went over it with hands locked.

They were nearing the house when Doris reined in. "Good-bye, dear Hugh!" she said. "You're the truest friend any woman ever had."

He reined in also. They stood in the deep shadow of some trees close to the gate that led into the Mill House garden. The roar of the water was all about them. They seemed to be isolated from all the world. And so Hugh Chesyl, being moved beyond his wont, lifted the hand that lay so confidingly in his, and kissed it with all reverence.

"I want you to be happy," he said.

A moment later they parted without further words on either side, he to retrace his steps across the bridge, she to turn wearily in at the iron gate under the dripping trees that led to the Mill House porch.

She heard a man's step in front of her as she went, and at the porch she found her husband.

"Oh, Jeff!" she said, slightly startled. "I didn't know it was you."

"I've been looking out for you for some time," he said. "You must be very wet."

"Yes, it's rained nearly all day, hasn't it? We didn't have much sport, but I enjoyed it." Doris slid down into the hands he held up to her. "Why, you are wet too," she said. "Hadn't you better change?"

"I'll take the horse round first," he said. "Won't you go in?"

She went in with a feeling of deep depression. Jeff's armour of reserve seemed impenetrable. With lagging feet she climbed the stairs and entered her sitting-room.

A bright fire was burning there, and the lamp was alight. A little thrill of purely physical pleasure went through her at the sight. She paused to take off her hat, then went forward and stooped to warm her hands at the blaze.

She was certainly very tired. The armchair by the hearth was invitingly near. She sank into it with a sigh and closed her eyes.

It must have been ten minutes later that the door, which she had left ajar, was pushed open, and Jeff stood on the threshold.

He was carrying a steaming cup of milk. A moment he paused as if on the verge of asking admittance; then as his eyes fell upon the slight young figure sunk in the chair, he closed his lips and came forward in silence.

A few seconds later, Doris opened her eyes with a start at the touch of his hand on her shoulder.

She sat up sharply. "Oh, Jeff, how you startled me!"

It was the first time she had ever seen him in her little sitting-room, though she had more than once invited him thither. His presence at that moment was for some reason peculiarly disconcerting.

"I am sorry," he said, in his slow way. "The door was half open, and I saw you were asleep. I don't think you are wise to sit down in your wet clothes. I have brought you some milk and brandy."

"Oh, but I never take brandy," she said, collecting herself with a little smile and rising. "It's very kind of you, Jeff. But I can't drink it, really. It would go straight to my head."

"You must drink it," said Jeff.

He presented it to her with the words, but Doris backed away half-laughing.

"No, really, Jeff! I'll go and have a hot bath. That will do quite as well."

"You must drink this first," said Jeff.

There was a dogged note in his voice, and at sound of it Doris's brows went up, and her smile passed.

"I mean it," said Jeff, setting cup and saucer on the table before her. "I can't run the risk of having you laid up. Drink it now, before it gets cold!"

A little gleam of mutiny shone in Doris's eyes. "My dear Jeff," she said very decidedly. "I have told you already that I do not drink brandy. I am going to have a hot bath and change, and after that I will have some tea. But I draw the line at hot grog. So, please, take it away! Give it to Granny Grimshaw! It would do her more good."

She smiled again suddenly and winningly with the words. After all it was absurd to be vexed over such a trifle.

But, to her amazement, Jeff's face hardened. He stepped to her, and, as if she had been a child, took her by the shoulders, and put her down into a chair by the table.

"Doris," he said, and his voice sounded deep and stern above her head, "I may not get much out of my bargain, but I think I may claim obedience at least. There is not enough brandy there to hurt you, and I wish you to take it."

She stiffened at his action, as if she would actively resist; but she only became rigid under his hands.

There followed a tense and painful silence. Then without a word Doris took the cup and raised it unsteadily to her lips. In the same moment Jeff took his hands from her shoulders, straightened himself, and in silence left the room.

CHAPTER X

CHRISTMAS EVE

It was only a small episode, but it made an impression upon Doris that she was slow to forget. It was not that she resented the assertion of authority. She had the fairness to admit his right, but in a very subtle fashion it hurt her. It made her feel more than ever the hollowness of the bargain, to which he had made such grim allusion. It added, moreover, to her uneasiness, making her suspect that he was fully as dissatisfied as she. Yet, in face of the stony front he presented she could not continue to proffer her friendship. He seemed to have no use for it. He seemed, in fact, to avoid her, and the old shyness that had oppressed her in the beginning returned upon her fourfold. She admitted to herself that she was becoming afraid of the man. The very sound of his voice made her heart beat thick and hard, and each succeeding day witnessed a diminishing of her confidence.

Under these circumstances she withdrew more and more into her solitude, and it was with something like dismay that she received the news from Granny Grimshaw at the beginning of Christmas week that it was Jeff's custom to entertain two or three of his farmer friends at supper on Christmas Eve.

"Only the menkind, my dear," said Granny Grimshaw consolingly. "And they're easy enough to amuse, as all the world knows. Give 'em a good feed, and they won't give any trouble. It's quite a job to get ready for 'em, that it is, but it's the only bit of entertaining he does all the year round, so I don't grudge it."

"You must let me help you," Doris said.

And help she did, protest notwithstanding, so that Jeff, returning from his work in the middle of the day, was surprised to find her flushed and animated in the kitchen, clad in one of Granny Grimshaw's aprons, rolling out pastry with the ready deftness of a practised pastry-cook.

There was no dismay in her greeting of him, and only she knew of that sudden quickening of the heart that invariably followed his appearance.

"You didn't tell me about your Christmas party, Jeff," she said. "Granny and I are going to give you a big spread. I hope you will invite me to the feast."

Jeff's dark face flushed a little as he made reply. "I'm afraid you wouldn't enjoy it much."

"But you haven't introduced me to any of your friends yet," she protested. "I should like to meet them."

"I'm not so sure of that," said Jeff.

She looked up at him for a moment. "Don't you think that's rather a mistake?" she said.

"Why?" said Jeff.

With something of an effort she explained. "To take it for granted that I shall look down on them. I don't want to look down on them, Jeff."

"It isn't that," said Jeff curtly. "But they're not your sort. They don't talk your language. I'm not sure that I want you to meet them."

"But you can't keep me away from everyone, can you?" she said gently.

He did not answer her, and she returned to her pastry-making in silence.

But evidently her words had made some impression, for that evening when she rose from the supper table to bid him a formal good-night, he very abruptly reverted to the subject.

"If you really think you can stand the racket on Christmas Eve, I hope you will join the party. There will be only four or five besides myself. I have never invited the womenkind."

"Perhaps by next Christmas I shall have got to know them a little," said Doris, "and then we can invite them too. Thank you for asking me, Jeff. I'll come."

But yet she viewed the prospect with considerable misgiving, and would have thankfully foregone the ordeal, if she had not felt constrained to face it.

The preparations went forward under Granny Grimshaw's guidance without a hitch, but they were kept busy up to the last moment, and on the day before Christmas Eve Doris scribbled a hasty note to Hugh Chesyl, excusing herself from attending the meet.

It was the only thing to be done, for she could not let him expect her in vain, but she regretted it later when at the breakfast-table the following day her husband silently handed to her Hugh's reply.

Hugh had written to convey his good wishes for Christmas, and this she explained to Jeff; but he received her explanation in utter silence, and she forthwith abandoned the subject. A smouldering resentment began to burn within her. What right had he to treat Hugh's friendship with her as a thing to be ashamed of? She longed to ask him, but would not risk an open rupture. She knew that if she gave her indignation rein she would not be able to control it.

So the matter passed, and she slipped Hugh's note into her bosom with a sense of outraged pride that went with her throughout the day. It was still present with her like an evil spirit when she went to her room to dress.

She had not much time at her disposal, and she slipped into her black evening gown with a passing wonder as to how Jeff's friends would be attired. Descending again, she found Jim Dawlish fixing a piece of mistletoe over the parlour door, and smiled at his occupation.

He smiled at her in a fashion that sent the blood suddenly and hotly to her face, and she passed on to the kitchen, erect and quivering with anger.

"Lor', my dearie, what a pretty picture you be, to be sure!" was Granny Grimshaw's greeting, and again a tremor of misgiving went through the girl's heart. Had she made herself too pretty for the occasion?

She mustered spirit, however, to laugh at the compliment, and busied herself with the final arrangements.

Jeff appeared a few minutes later, clad in black but not in evening dress. His eyes dwelt upon his wife for a moment or two before he addressed her.

"Do you mind being in the parlour when they come in?"

She looked up at him with a smile which she knew to be forced. "Are you sure I shan't be one too many, Jeff?"

"Quite," said Jeff.

There was no appealing against that, and she accompanied him without further words.

Jim Dawlish was standing by the parlour door, admiring his handiwork. He nudged Jeff as he went by, and was rewarded by Jeff's heaviest scowl.

A minute later, to Doris's mingled relief and dread, came the sounds of the first arrival.

This proved to be a Mr. Griggs and his son, a horsey young man, whom she vaguely knew by sight, having encountered him when following the hounds. Mr. Griggs was a jolly old farmer, with a somewhat convivial countenance. He shook her warmly by the hand, and asked her how she liked being married.

Doris was endeavouring to reply to this difficult question as airily as possible, when three more of Jeff's friends made their appearance, and were brought up by Jeff in a group for introduction, thereby relieving her of the obligation.

The party was now complete, and they all sat down to supper in varying degrees of shyness. Doris worked hard to play her part as hostess, but it was certainly no light task. Two of the last-comers were brothers of the name of Chubb, and from neither of these could she extract more than one word at a time. The third, Farmer Locke, was of the aggressive, bulldog type, and he very speedily asserted himself. He seemed, indeed, somewhat inclined to browbeat her, loudly arguing her slightest remark after a fashion which she found decidedly exasperating, but presently discovered to be his invariable habit with everyone. He flatly contradicted even Jeff, but she was pleased to hear Jeff bluntly hold his own, and secretly admired him for the achievement.

On the whole, the meal was not quite so much of an ordeal as she had anticipated, and she was just beginning to congratulate herself upon this fact when she discovered that young Griggs was ogling her with most unmistakable familiarity whenever she glanced his way. She at once cut him pointedly and with supreme disdain, only to find his father, who was seated on her right, doing exactly the same thing.

Furious indignation entered her sore soul at this second discovery, and from the smiling, genial hostess she froze into a marble statue of aloofness. But tongues were loosened somewhat by that time, and her change of attitude did not apparently affect the guests.

Mr. Locke continued his aggressive course, and the brothers Chubb were emboldened to take it by turns to oppose him, while old Griggs drank deeply and smacked his lips, and young Griggs told Jeff anecdotes in an undertone which he interspersed with bold glances in the direction of his stony-faced young hostess.

The appearance of Jim Dawlish carrying a steaming bowl of

punch seemed to Doris at length the signal for departure, and she rose from the table.

Jeff instantly rose at the farther end, and she divined that he had no wish to detain her. Mr. Griggs the elder, on the other hand, was loud in protest.

"We haven't drunk your health yet, missis," he said.

She forced herself to smile. "That is very kind of you. I am sure Jeff will return thanks for me."

She made it evident that she had no intention of remaining, protest notwithstanding, so Mr. Griggs arose and turned to open the door, still loudly deploring her departure. Young Griggs was already there, however. He leered at her as she approached him, and it occurred to her that he was not very steady on his legs. She prepared him an icy bow, which she was in the very act of executing when he made a sudden lurch forward, and caught her round the waist. She heard him laugh with coarse mirth, and had a glimpse of the bunch of mistletoe dangling above their heads ere she fiercely pushed him from her into the passage.

The next instant Jeff was beside her, and she turned and clung to him in desperation.

"Jeff, don't let him!" she cried.

Jeff stretched out an arm to keep the young man back. A roar of laughter rose from the remaining guests.

"Kiss her yourself then, Jeff!" cried old Griggs, hammering on the table. "You've got her under the mistletoe."

"He daren't!" said Jim Dawlish, with a wink.

"Afraid to kiss his own wife!" gibed Locke, and the Chubb brothers laughed in uproarious appreciation of the sally.

It was then that Doris became aware of a change in Jeff. The arm he had stretched out for her protection suddenly encircled her. He bent his face to hers.

"They shan't say that!" he muttered under his breath.

She divined his intention in an instant, and a wild flame of anger shot up within her. This was how he treated her confidence! She made a swift effort to wrench herself from him, then, feeling his arm tighten to frustrate her, she struck him across the face in frantic indignation.

Again a roar of laughter arose behind them, and then very suddenly she forgot everyone in the world but Jeff, for it was as if at that blow of hers an evil spirit had taken swift possession of him. He gripped her hands with savage strength, forcing them behind her, and so holding her, with eyes that seared her soul, he kissed her passionately, violently, devouringly, on face and neck and throat, sparing her not a whit, till in an agony of helpless shame she sank powerless in his arms.

She heard again the jeering laughter in the room behind her, but between herself and Jeff there was a terrible silence, till abruptly he set her free, saying curtly, "You brought it on yourself. Now go!"

Her knees were shaking under her. She was burning from head to foot, as though she had been wrapped in flame. But with an effort she controlled herself.

She went in utter silence, feeling as if her heart were dead within her, mounted the stairs with growing weakness, found and fumbled at her own door, entered at last, and sank inert upon the floor.

CHAPTER XI

CHRISTMAS MORNING

Christmas morning broke with a sprinkle of snow, and an icy wind that blew from the north, promising a heavier fall ere the day was over.

Jeff was late in descending, and he saw that the door of Doris's room was open as he passed. He glanced in, saw that the room was empty, and entered to lay a packet that he carried on her dressing-table. As he did so, his eyes fell upon an envelope lying there, and that single glance revealed the fact that it was addressed to him.

He picked it up, and, turning, cast a searching look around the room. Across the end of the great four-poster bed hung the black lace gown she had worn the previous evening, but the bed itself was undisturbed. He saw in a moment that it had not been slept in. Sharply he turned to the envelope in his hand, and ripped it open. Something bright rolled out upon the floor. He stopped it with his foot. It was her wedding-ring.

An awful look showed for a moment in Jeff's eyes and passed. He stooped and picked up the ring; then, with a species of deadly composure more terrible than any agitation, he took out the letter that the envelope contained.

It was very short—the first letter that she had ever written to him.

"Dear Jeff," it ran, "after what happened last night, I do not think you will be surprised to hear that I feel I cannot stay any longer under your roof. I have tried to be friends with you, but you would not have it so, and now it has become quite impossible for me to go on. I am leaving for town by the first train I can catch. I am going to work for my living, and some day I shall hope to make good to you all that I know you have spent on my comfort.

"Please do not imagine I am going in anger. I blame myself more than I blame you. I never ought to have married you, knowing that I did not love you in the ordinary way. But this is the only course open to me now. So good-bye!

"Doris."

Jeff Ironside looked up from the letter, and out across the grey meadows. His face was pale, the square jaw absolutely rigid; but there was no anger in his eyes, only the iron of an implacable determination. For several seconds he watched the feathery snowflakes drifting over the fields; then, with absolute steadiness, he returned both letter and ring to the envelope, placed them in his pocket, and, turning, left the room.

Granny Grimshaw met him at the foot of the stairs. "Oh, Master Jeff," she said, "I am that worried. We can't find Mrs. Ironside."

Jeff paused an instant and turned his grim face to her. "It's all right, Granny. I know where she is," he said. "Keep the breakfast hot!"

And with that he was gone.

He drove out of the yard a few minutes later in his dog-cart, muffled in a great coat with the collar up to his ears.

At the station, Doris sat huddled in a corner of the little waiting-room counting the dreary minutes as she waited for her train. No one beside herself was going by it.

She had walked across the fields, and had made a *détour* to leave a note at the Manor for Hugh. She could not leave Hugh in ignorance of her action.

She glanced nervously at the watch on her wrist. Yes, Jeff probably knew by this time. How was he taking it? Was he very angry? But surely even he must see how impossible he had made her life with him.

Restlessly she arose and went to the window. It had begun to snow in earnest. The road was all blurred and grey with the falling flakes. She shivered again. Her feet were like ice. Very oddly her thoughts turned to that day in September when Jeff had knelt before her and drawn off her muddy boots before the great open fire. A great sigh welled up within her and her eyes filled with quick tears. If only he would have consented to be her friend. She was so lonely—so lonely!

There came the sound of wheels along the road, and she turned away. Evidently someone else was coming for the train. A little tremor of impatience went through her. Would the train never come?

The wheels stopped before the station door. Someone descended, and there followed the sound of a man's feet approaching her retreat. A hand was laid upon the door, and she braced herself to meet a possible acquaintance. It opened, and she glanced up.

"Oh, Jeff!" she said.

He shut the door behind him and came forward. His face was set in dogged, unyielding lines.

"I have come to take you back," he said.

She drew sharply away from him. This was the last thing she had expected.

Desperately she faced him. "I can't come with you, Jeff," she said. "My mind is quite made up. I am very sorry for everything, especially sorry that you have taken the trouble to follow me. But my decision is quite unalterable."

Her breath came fast as she ended. Her heart was throbbing in thick, heavy strokes. There was something so implacable in his attitude.

He did not speak at once, and she stood before him, striving with all her strength to still her agitation. Then quite calmly he stood back and motioned her to pass him. "Whatever you decide to do afterwards," he said, "you must come back with me now. We had better start at once before it gets worse."

A quiver of anger went through her; it was almost a sensation of hatred. She remained motionless. "I refuse," she said in a low voice, her grey eyes steadily raised to his.

She saw his black brows meet, but he gave no sign of impatience. "And I—insist," he said stubbornly.

She felt the blood receding from her face. It was to be open conflict, then. She collected all her resolution to oppose him, for to yield at that moment was out of the question.

It was then, while she stood summoning her forces, that there came to her ears the distant hum and throb of an approaching train. It was coming at last. A porter ran past the window that looked upon the platform, announcing its approach with a dismal yell. Doris straightened and turned to go.

Jeff turned also. An odd light sprang up in his gipsy eyes. He went straight to the door ere she could reach it, locked it, and withdrew the key.

That fired Doris. Her composure went in a single instant. "Jeff," she exclaimed, "how dare you?"

He turned to the dingy window overlooking the line. "You compel me," he said.

She sank back impotent against the table. He stood staring grimly forth, filling the window with his bulk.

Nearer came the train and nearer. Doris felt the hot blood drumming in her brain. Something that was very nearly akin to frenzy entered into her. She stood up with sudden, fierce resolution.

"Jeff," she said, "I will not be kept here against my will! Do you hear? I will not! Give me that key!"

He took no more notice of the command than if it had been the buzzing of a fly. His attention apparently was caught by something outside. He leaned forward, watching intently.

Something in his attitude checked her wrath at its height. It was as though a cold hand had been laid upon her heart. What was it he was looking at? She felt she must know. As the train thundered into the station she went to his side and looked forth also.

The next moment, with a shock that was physical, she saw the object of his interest. Hugh Chesyl, with a face of grave perturbation, was standing on the platform, searching this way and that. It was evident that he had but just arrived at the station, and in a flash she divined the reason of his coming. Quite obviously he was looking for her.

Sharply she withdrew herself from the window, and in the same moment Jeff also turned. Their eyes met, and Doris caught her breath.

For it was as if a sword had pierced her. In a single, blinding instant of revelation she read his thought, and sheer horror held her silent before him. She stood as one paralyzed.

He did not utter a word, simply stood and looked at her, with eyes grown devilish in their scrutiny. Then very suddenly and terribly he laughed, and flung round upon his heel.

In that instant Doris's powers returned to her, urged by appalling necessity. She sprang forward, reached the door, set her back against it, faced him with the wild courage of agonizing fear.

"Jeff! Jeff!" she panted. "What are you going to do?"

The train had come to a standstill. There was a commotion of voices and running feet. Jeff, still with that awful look in his eyes, stood still.

"You will miss your train," he said.

"What are you going to do?" she reiterated.

He smiled—a grim, dreadful smile. "I am going to see you off. You can go now. Your friend Chesyl can follow by the next train—when I have done with him."

He had the key in his hand. He stooped to insert it in the lock. But swiftly she caught his wrist. "Jeff, stop—stop!" she gasped; and, as he looked at her: "I'm not going away now!"

He wrung his hand free. "You had better go—for your own sake!" he said.

She flinched in spite of herself from the blazing menace of his eyes, but again necessity spurred her. She stretched out her arms, barring his way.

"I won't! I can't! Jeff—Jeff—for Heaven's sake—Jeff!" Her voice broke into wild entreaty. He had taken her roughly by the shoulders, pulling her from his path. He would have put her from him, but she snatched her opportunity and clung to him fast with all her quivering strength.

He stood still then, suddenly rigid. "I have warned you!" he said, in a voice so deep with passion that her heart quailed and ceased to beat.

"Let me go!"

But she only tightened her trembling hold. "You shan't go, Jeff! You shan't insult Hugh Chesyl! He is a gentleman!"

"Is he?" said Jeff, very bitterly.

She could feel his every muscle strung and taut, ready for uncontrolled violence. Yet still with her puny strength she held him, for she dared not let him go.

"Jeff, listen to me! You must listen! Hugh is my very good friend—no more than that. He has come here to say 'Good-bye.' I left a note for him on my way here, just to tell him I was going. He is my friend—only my friend."

"I don't believe you," said Jeff.

She shrank as if he had struck her, but her hands still clutched his coat. She attempted no further protestations, only stood with her white face lifted and clear eyes fixed on his. The red fire that shone fiercely back on her was powerless to subdue her steady regard, though she felt as though it scorched her through and through.

From the platform came the shriek of the guard's whistle. The train was departing.

Doris heard it go with a sick sense of despair. She knew that her liberty went with it. As the last carriage passed she spoke again.

"I will go back with you now."

"If I will take you back," said Jeff.

Her hands clenched upon his coat. An awful weakness had begun to assail her. She fought against it desperately.

Someone tried the handle of the door, pulled at it and desisted. She caught her breath. Jeff's hand went out to open, but she shifted her grasp, and again gripped his wrist.

"Wait! Wait!" she whispered through her white lips.

This time he did not shake her off. He stood with his eyes on hers and waited.

The man on the other side of the door, evidently concluding that the waiting-room had not been opened that day, gave up the attempt and passed on. With straining ears Doris listened to his departing footsteps. A few seconds later she saw Jeff's eyes go to the farther window. Her own followed them. Hugh Chesyl, clad in a long grey ulster, was tramping away through the snow.

He passed from sight, and Doris relaxed her hold. Her face was white and spent. "Will you take me home?" she said faintly.

Slowly Jeff's eyes came back to her, dwelt upon her. He must have seen the exhaustion in her face, but his own showed no softening.

He spoke at last sternly, with grim mastery. "If I take you back it must be on a different footing. You tell me this man is no more to you than a friend. I am even less. Do you think I will be satisfied with that?"

"I have tried to make you my friend," she said.

"And you have failed," he said. "Shall I tell you why? Or can you guess?"

She was silent.

He clenched his hands hard against his sides. "You know what happened yesterday," he said. "It had nearly happened a hundred times before. I kept it back till it got too strong for me. You dangled your friendship before me till I was nearly mad with the want of you. You had better have offered me nothing at all than that."

"Oh, Jeff!" she said.

He went on, heedless of reproach. "It has come to this with me: friendship, if it comes at all, must come after. You tell me Chesyl is not your lover. Do you deny that he has ever made love to you?"

"Since he knew of my marriage—never!" she said.

"Yet you ride home with him in the dark hand in hand!" said Jeff.

The colour flamed in her face and as swiftly died. "Hugh Chesyl is not my lover," she said proudly.

"And you expect me to believe you?" he said.

"I do."

He gazed at her without pity. "You will secure my belief in you," he said, "only by coming to me as my wife."

A great shiver went through her. She stood silent.

"As my wife," he repeated looking straight into her face with eyes that compelled. She was trembling from head to foot. He waited a moment, then: "You would sooner run away with Hugh Chesyl?" he asked very bitterly.

Sheer pain drove her into speech. "Oh, Jeff," she cried passionately, "don't make me hate you!"

He started at that as an animal starts at the goad, and in an instant he took her suddenly and fiercely by the shoulders. "Hate me, then! Hate me!" he said, and kissed her again savagely on her white, panting lips as he had kissed her the night before, showing no mercy.

She did not resist him. Her strength was gone. She hung quivering in his arms till the storm of his passion had passed also. Then: "Let us go!" she whispered: "Let us go!"

He released her slowly and turned to open the door. Then, seeing that she moved unsteadily, he put his arm about her, supporting her. So, side by side and linked together, they went out into the driving snow.

CHAPTER XII

CHRISTMAS NIGHT

Doris was nearly fainting with cold and misery when they stopped at last before the Mill House door. All the previous night she had sat up listening with nerves on edge, and had finally taken her departure in the early morning without food.

When Jeff turned to help her down she looked at him helplessly, seeing him through a drifting mist that obscured all besides. He saw her weakness at a single glance, and, mounting the step, took her in his arms.

She sank down against his shoulder. "Oh, Jeff, I can't help it," she whispered, through lips that were stiff and blue with cold.

"All right. I know," he said, and for the first time in many days she heard a note of kindness in his voice.

He bore her straight through to the kitchen, and laid her down upon the old oak settle, just as he had done on that day in September when first he had brought her to his home.

Granny Grimshaw, full of tender solicitude, came hastening to her, but Jeff intervened.

"Hot milk and brandy—quick!" he ordered, and fell himself to chafing the icy fingers.

When Granny Grimshaw brought the cup, he took it from her, and held it for Doris to drink; and then, when she had swallowed a little and the blood was creeping back into her face, he took off her boots and chafed her feet also.

Granny Grimshaw put some bread into the milk while this was in progress and coaxed Doris to finish it. She asked no questions, simply treating her as she might have treated a lost child who had strayed away. There was a vast fund of wisdom in the old grey head that was so often shaken over the follies of youth.

And, finally, when Doris had a little recovered, she went with her to her room, and helped her to bed, where she tucked her up with her own hot-water bottle and left her.

From sheer exhaustion Doris slept, though her sleep was not a happy one. Long, tangled dreams wound in a ceaseless procession through her brain, and through them all she was persistently and fruitlessly striving to persuade Jeff to let her go.

In the late afternoon she awoke suddenly to the sound of men's voices in the room below her, and started up in nameless fear.

"Were you wanting anything, my dearie?" asked Granny Grimshaw, from a chair by the fire.

"Who is that talking?" she asked nervously.

"It's Master Jeff and a visitor," said the old woman. "Now, don't you bother your head about them! I'm going along to get you some tea."

She bustled away with the words, and Doris lay back, listening with every nerve stretched. Her husband's deep voice was unmistakable, but the other she could not distinguish. Only after a while there came the sounds of movement, the opening of a door.

When that happened she sprang swiftly from the bed to her own door, and softly opened it.

Two men stood in the hall below. Slipping out on to the landing, she leaned upon the banisters in the darkness and looked down. Even as she did so, a voice she knew well came up out of the gloom—a kindly, well-bred voice that spoke with a slight drawl.

"I shouldn't be downhearted, Ironside. Remember, no one is cornered so long as he can turn round and go back. It's the only thing to do when you know you've taken a wrong turning."

Doris caught her breath. Her fingers gripped the black oak rail. She listened in rigid expectancy for Jeff's answer. But no answer came.

In a moment Hugh's voice came again, still calm and friendly. "I'm going away directly. The Squire has been ordered to the South for the rest of the winter, and I've promised to go with him. I suppose we shall start some time next week. May I look in and say 'Good-bye'?"

There was a pause. The girl on the landing above waited tensely for Jeff's answer. It came at last slowly, in a tone that was not unfriendly, but which did not sound spontaneous. "You can do as you like, Chesyl. I have no objection."

"All right, then. Good-bye for the present! I hope when I do come I shall find that all's well. All will be well in the end, eh, Jeff?"

There was a touch of feeling in the question that made Doris aware that the speaker had gripped her husband's hand.

But again there was a pause before the answer came, heavily, it seemed reluctantly: "Yes, it'll be all right for her in the end. Good-bye!"

The front-door opened; they went out into the porch together. And Doris slipped back, to her room.

Those last words of her husband's rang strangely in her heart. Why had he put it like that?

Her thoughts went to Hugh—dear and faithful friend who had taken this step on her behalf. What had passed between him and her husband during that interview in the parlour? She longed to know.

But whatever it had been, Hugh had emerged victorious. He had destroyed those foul suspicions of Jeff's. He had conquered the man's enmity, overthrown his passionate jealousy, humbled him into admitting himself to be in the wrong. Very curiously that silent admission of Jeff's hurt her pride almost as if it had been made on her behalf. The thought of Jeff worsted by Hugh Chesyl, however deeply in the wrong he might be, was somehow very hard to bear. Her heart ached for the man. She did not want him to be humbled.

When Granny Grimshaw came up with her tea, she was half-dressed.

"I couldn't sleep any longer," she said. "It's dear of you to take such care of me. But I'm quite all right. Dear Granny, forgive me for giving you such a horrible Christmas Day!" She bent suddenly forward and kissed the wrinkled face.

"My dearie! My dearie!" said Granny Grimshaw.

And then, exactly how it happened neither of them ever knew, all in a moment Doris found herself folded close in the old woman's arms, sobbing her heart out on the motherly shoulder.

"You shouldn't cry, darling; you shouldn't cry," murmured Granny Grimshaw, softly patting the slim young form. "It would hurt Master Jeff more than anything to have you cry."

"No, no! He doesn't really care for me. I could bear it better if he did," whispered Doris.

"Not care for you, my dearie? Why, what ever can you be thinking of?" protested Granny Grimshaw. "He's eating his very heart out for you, and I verily believe he'd kill himself sooner than make you unhappy."

"Ah! You don't understand," sighed Doris. "He only wants—material things."

"Oh, my dear, my dear!" said Granny Grimshaw. "Did you suppose that the man ever lived who could love a woman without? We're human, dear, the very best of us, and there's no getting out of it. Besides, love is never satisfied with half measures."

She drew the girl down into the chair before the fire and fussed over her tenderly till she grew calmer. And then presently she slipped away.

Doris finished her tea slowly with her eyes on the red coals, then rose at length to continue her dressing. As she stood at the table twisting up her hair, her glance fell on a small packet that lay there.

With fingers that trembled a little she opened it. It contained a small object wrapped in a slip of paper. There was writing upon it, which she deciphered as she unrolled it. "For my wife, with all my love. Jeff." And in her hand there lay a slender gold ring, exquisitely dainty, set with pearls. A quick tremor went through Doris. She guessed that it had belonged to his mother.

Again she read the few simple words; they seemed to her to hold an appeal which the man himself could never have uttered, and her heart quivered in response as a finely tempered instrument vibrates to a sudden sound. Had she never understood him?

She finished her dressing with impulsive haste, and with Jeff's gift in her hand turned to leave the room.

Her heart throbbed violently as she descended.

What would his mood be when she found him? If he would only be kind to her! Ah, if only he would be kind! Granny Grimshaw was lighting the lamps in the hall and parlour.

"Everyone's out but me," she said. "Master Jeff and I generally keep house alone together on Christmas night. I don't know why he doesn't come in. He went out to see to the horses half an hour ago. He hasn't had his tea yet."

"I will give him his tea," Doris said.

"Very well," said Granny Grimshaw. "I'll leave the kettle on for you while I go up and dress."

Doris went into the parlour to wait. The lamp on the table was alight, the teacups ready, and a bright fire made the room cosy. She went to the window and drew aside the curtain.

The snow had ceased, and the sky was clear. Stars were beginning to pierce the darkness.

Slowly the minutes crawled by. She began to listen for his coming, to chafe at his delay. At last, grown nervous with suspense, she turned from the window and went into the hall. She opened the door and stepped out into the porch.

Still and starlit lay the path before her. The snow had been swept away. Impulse seized her. She felt she could wait no longer. She slipped back into the hall, took a coat of Jeff's from a peg, put it on, and so passed out into the open.

The way to the stable lay past the mill-stream. On noiseless feet she followed it. The water was deep and dark and silent. She shivered as she drew near. In the stable beyond, close to the mill, she saw a light. It was moving towards her. In a moment she discovered Jeff's face above it, and—was it something she actually saw in the face, or was it an illusion created by the swinging lantern?—her heart gave a sudden jerk of horror. For it was to her as if she looked upon the face of a dead man.

She stood still in the shadow of a weeping willow, arrested by that look, and watched him come slowly forth.

He moved heavily as one driven by Fate, pulling the stable door to after him. This he turned to lock, then stooped, still with that face as of a death-mask, and deliberately extinguished his lantern.

Doris's heart jerked again at the action, and every pulse began to clamour. Why did he put out the lantern before reaching the house?

The next moment she heard his footsteps, slow and heavy, coming towards her. The path wound along a bank a couple of feet above the millstream. He approached till in the darkness he had nearly reached her, then he stopped.

She thought he had discerned her, but the next moment she realized that he had not. He was facing the water; he seemed to be staring across it. And even as she watched he took another step straight towards it.

It was then that like a flashlight leaping from his brain to hers she realized what he was about to do. How the knowledge came to her she knew not, but it was hers past all disputing in that single second of blinding revelation. And just as that morning she had been inspired to act on sheer wild impulse, so now without an instant's pause she acted again. She sprang from her hiding-place with a strangled cry, and threw her arms about him.

"Jeff! Jeff! What are you doing here?"

He gave a great start that made her think of a frightened animal, and stood still. She felt his arms grow rigid at his sides, and knew that his hands were clenched.

"Jeff!" she cried again, clinging faster. "You—you're never thinking of—of that?"

Her utterance ended in a shudder as she sought with all her strength to drag him away from the icy water.

He resisted her doggedly, standing like a rock. "Whatever I'm thinking of doing is my affair," he said, shortly and sternly. "Go away and leave me alone!"

"I won't!" she cried back to him half-hysterically. "I won't! If—if you're going to do that, you'll take me with you!"

He turned round then and moved back to the path. "Who said I was going to do anything?" he demanded in a voice that sounded half-angry and half-ashamed.

She answered him with absolute candour. "I saw your face just now. I couldn't help knowing. Oh, Jeff, Jeff! is it as bad as that? Do you hate me so badly as that?"

He made a movement of the arms that was curiously passionate, but he did not attempt to take her into them. "I don't hate you," he said, in a voice that sounded half-choked. "I love you—so horribly"—there was a note of ferocity in the low-spoken words—"that I can never know any peace without you! And since with you it is otherwise, what remedy is there? You love Hugh Chesyl. You only want to be free to marry him. While I—"

He broke off in fierce impotence, and began to thrust her from him. But she held him fast.

"Jeff—Jeff, this is madness! Listen to me! You must listen! Hugh and I are friends, and we shall never be anything more. Jeff, let me be with you! Teach me to love you! You can if you will. Don't—don't ruin both our lives!"

She was pleading with him passionately, still holding him back. And, as she pleaded, she reached up her arms and slowly clasped his neck.

"Oh, Jeff, be good to me—be good to me just this once!" she prayed. "I've made such a hideous mistake, but don't punish me like this! I swear if you go, I shall go too! There'll be nothing left to live for. Jeff—Jeff, if you really love me, spare me this!"

The broken entreaty went into agonized sobbing, yet she kept her face upraised to his. Instinctively she knew that in that eleventh hour she must offer all she had.

Several moments throbbed away. She began to think that she had failed. And then very suddenly he moved, put his arm about her, led her away.

Not a word did he utter, but there was comfort in the holding of his arm. She went with him with the curious hushed sense of one who stands on the threshold of that which is sacred.

CHAPTER XIII

A FARMER'S WIFE

Two eyes, old but yet keen, peered forth into the wintry night, and a grey head nodded approvingly, as Jeff Ironside and his wife came in silence to their home. And then the bedroom blind came down, and Granny Grimshaw sat down cosily by her bit of wood fire to hold a strictly private little service of thanksgiving.

Downstairs into the raftered kitchen two people came, each holding each, both speechless, with a restraint that bound them as by a spell.

By nature the woman spoke first, her voice no more than a whisper. "Sit on the settle, won't you? I'm going to get your tea."

His arm fell from her. He sat down heavily, not looking at her. She stepped to the fire and took the empty teapot from the hob, then light-footed to the dresser for the tea.

He did not watch her. For a while he sat staring blindly straight before him. Then slowly he leaned forward, and dropped his head into his hands.

Not till the tea was made did she so much as glance towards him, so intent to all seeming was she upon her task. But when it was done, she looked at him sitting there bowed upon the settle, and very suddenly, very lightly, she came to his side.

"Jeff!" she said.

He neither moved nor spoke.

She laid a shy hand on his shoulder. "Jeff!" Her voice was pleading and rather breathless, as though she would ask him to bear with her. "I want to thank you so much—so very much—for your Christmas gift. See! I'm wearing it."

She slipped her hand down into his, so that he held it pressed against his cheek. He spoke no word, but against her fingers she felt a quiver.

She bent over him, growing bolder. "Jeff, I—I want you to give me back—my wedding-ring."

He did not stir or answer.

"Please!" she whispered. "Won't you?"

And then dumbly, keeping his face hidden, he drew her hand down to his breast-pocket.

"Is it there?" she whispered. "May I take it?"

Her fingers felt for and found what they sought. Her hand came up again, wearing the ring. And then, with a swift, impulsive movement she knelt before him, clasping his two wrists.

"Jeff—Jeff! will you—will you try to forgive me?"

There followed silence, but very strangely no misgiving assailed her. She strove with gentle insistence to draw the shielding hands away.

At first he resisted her, and then very suddenly he yielded. His hands went out to her, his head dropped forward upon her shoulder. A strangled sob shook him.

And Doris knelt up with all her woman's compassion leaping to his need, and clasped her warm arms about him, holding him to her heart.

That broke him, broke him utterly, so that for a while no words could pass between them. For Doris was crying too, even while she sought to comfort.

But at last, with a valiant effort, she checked her tears. "Jeff—darling, don't let us be so—so silly," she murmured, with one quivering hand laid upon his head. "We've got all we want—both of us. Let's forget it all! Let's begin again!"

He put his arms around her, not lifting his head.

"Can't we?" she said softly. "I'm ready."

He spoke at last below his breath. "You couldn't! You'll never forget what a brute I've been."

She turned her head quickly and laid her cheek against his forehead. "Shall I tell you just how much I am going to remember?"

He was silent, breathing deeply.

"Just this," she said. "That you love me—so much—that you can't do without me, and that you were willing—to give your life—for my happiness. That is what I am going to remember, Jeff, and it will be a very precious memory. And I want to tell you just one little thing before we go any farther. It's about Hugh. I don't love him in the way that you and I count love. I did very nearly for a little while. But that is over. I don't think—I never have quite thought—that he is altogether my sort, or I his. Jeff dear, you believe that?"

"Yes," said Jeff.

"Thank you," she said simply. "I want you to try and believe me always, because I do tell the truth. And now, Jeff, I've got to tell you that I'm dreadfully sorry for the way I've treated you. Yes, let me say it," as he made a quick movement of protest. "It's true. I've treated you abominably, mainly because I didn't understand. I do understand now. You—you've opened my eyes. Oh, Jeff, thank God they were opened even at the eleventh hour! What should I have done if—if—" She broke off with a shiver, and then nestled to him like a child, as though that were the end of the argument. "And now I'm going to be such a good wife to you," she whispered, "to make up for it all. I always wanted to be a farmer's wife, you know. But you must help me. Jeff, will you?"

"I would die for you," he said, his head still bent as though he could not wholly trust himself to look her in the face.

She gave a funny little tremulous laugh. "Yes, I know. But that wouldn't be a bit of good. You would only break my heart. You don't want to do that, do you?"

"Doris!" he said.

"Why won't you call me Dot?"

"Dot!" said Jeff very softly.

"That's better." Again her voice quivered upon a laugh. Her arms slackened from his shoulders, and instantly his fell away, setting her free. She rose to her feet, yet lingered a moment, bending slightly over him, her eyes very bright.

But Jeff did not move, and with a half-sigh she turned away. "Would you like to carry the teapot?" she said.

He got up.

"And you can hang up this coat of yours," she added. "I'll come in a moment."

She watched him go in his slow, strong fashion; then for a few still seconds she stood quite tense with hands tightly gripped together. What passed within her during those moments only her own heart ever knew, how much of longing, how much of regret, how much of earnest, quivering hope.

She followed him almost at once as she had promised.

The parlour door was open. She came to it in her light, impetuous way. She halted on the threshold.

"Jeff!" she said. "Come here!"

She reached out her hands to him—little, nervous hands full of purpose. She drew him close. She raised her lips to his. The mistletoe dangled above their heads.

"Will you kiss me, Jeff?" she whispered.

He stooped, half-hesitating.

Her arms stole about his neck. "You needn't—ever—be afraid to kiss your own wife, dear," she said. "I want your love just in the ordinary way—the ordinary way."

He held her to him. "Dot—Dot—forgive me!"

She shook her head with frank, fearless eyes raised to his. "It was a bad bargain, Jeff. Forget it!"

"And make another?" he suggested.

To which she answered with her quick smile. "Love makes no bargains, Jeff. Love just gives—and gives—and gives."

And as his lips met hers he knew the wondrous truth of what she said. For in that one long kiss she gave him all she had. And love conquered, just in the old, sweet, ordinary way.

The Place of Honour

Wherein a woman with a love of freedom, two soldiers in the Indian Army, and a snake-bite are most intimately concerned.

CHAPTER I

THE BRIDE

"And that is the major's bride? Ah, what a pity!"

The soft, Irish eyes of Mrs. Raleigh, the surgeon's wife, looked across the ball-room with a very real compassion in their grey depths.

"Pity?" said young Turner, the subaltern, who chanced to be at that moment in attendance upon her. "It's worse than that; it's a monstrous shame! She's only nineteen, you know; and he is twenty years older at least."

Mrs. Raleigh sighed.

"You have met her, Phil," she said. "I am going to get you to introduce me. Let us go across to her."

Mrs. Raleigh was greatly beloved by all subalterns. Her husband's bungalow was open to them day and night, and they took full advantage of the fact.

It was not that there was anything particularly brilliant about the surgeon's wife, but her ready sympathy made her a general favourite, and her kindness of heart was known to be equal to the severest strain.

Therefore, among the boys of the regiment she ruled supreme, and the expression of her lightest wish generally provoked a jealous scramble.

On the present occasion, however, young Turner did not display any special alacrity to serve her.

"There's such a crowd round her it's difficult to squeeze in edgeways," he said. "I shouldn't trouble to go across yet if I were you."

Mrs. Raleigh laughed a little and laid her hand on his arm.

"So you don't like hovering on the outskirts, Phil," she said.

He frowned, and then as suddenly smiled.

"I'm not the sort that cares to fool with a married woman," he declared. "There goes Devereux to swell the throng. I say, let's go and have a drink."

She laughed again as she rose to accompany him. Phil Turner was severely honest in all his ways, and, being a good woman, she liked him for it.

Nevertheless, though she yielded, her eyes still dwelt upon the girl in bridal white who sat like a queen among her courtiers. The dark head that was held so regally erect caught and chained the elder woman's fancy. And the vivid, careless beauty of the face was a thing to bear away in the heart and dream of in solitude. For the girl was lovely with that loveliness which even the most grudging must acknowledge. She shone in the crowd that surrounded her like a rare and brilliant flower in a garden of herbs.

Phil Turner's arm stirred with slight impatience under Mrs. Raleigh's hand, and she turned beside him.

"There is nothing like a really beautiful English girl in all the world," she said, with a smile and another glance in the bride's direction.

Young Turner grunted, and she gave his arm a slight shake.

"You don't deceive me," she said. "You admire her as much as I do. Now, be honest."

He looked at her for a moment moodily. Then——

"Yes," he said abruptly, "I do admire her. But, as for the major, I think he's the biggest fool on this side of the Indian Ocean, and that's saying a good deal."

Mrs. Raleigh shook her head as if she desired to disagree.

"Time alone will prove," she said.

CHAPTER II

EARLY BREEZES

"It's been lovely," said the bride. She leant back in the open carriage, gazing with wide, charmed eyes into the vivid Indian night. "And I'm not a bit tired," she added. "Are you?"

The man beside her did not instantly reply. He was a man of medium height, dark and lithe and amazingly strong. It was not his habit to speak much, but what little he said was usually very much to the point. It was his custom to mask his feelings so completely that very few had the smallest inkling as to his state of mind.

He was considered a hard man in his regiment, but he was known to be a splendid soldier, and chiefly for that reason he was respected rather than disliked. But the kindest critic could not have called him either popular or attractive. And the news of his marriage in England had fallen like a thunderbolt upon his Indian acquaintances, for he had long ago come to be regarded among them as the last man in the world to commit such a folly.

The full extent thereof had not been apparent till his return to his regiment, accompanied by his bride, and then as one man the whole mess had risen and condemned him in no measured terms, for the bride, with all her entrancing beauty, her vivacity, her charm, was certainly a startling contrast to the man who had wedded her—a contrast so sharp as to be almost painful to the onlookers.

She herself, however, seemed to be wholly unaware of any incongruity. Perhaps she had not seen enough of the world to feel it, or perhaps she was wilfully blind to the things she did not desire to see.

In any case her face, as she lay back in the carriage by her husband's side, expressed only the most complete contentment.

"Are you tired, Eustace?" she asked, as he did not hasten to reply to her first question.

"No," he answered, "not tired; but glad to be going back."

"You've been bored," she said quickly. "What a frightful pity! Why did you stay so long?"

Again he paused before replying, and she drummed on his knee with her fingers with slight impatience.

"I had a notion," he said, in his quiet, unhurried tones, "that my wife would have considered it rather hard lines to be dragged away while there was a single man left to dance with."

The bride snatched her hand from his knee with a swiftness of action that could hardly be mistaken. He might have been speaking in fun, but, even so, it was an ugly jest. More probably he had meant the sting that his words conveyed, for, owing to a delicate knee-cap that had once been splintered by a bullet and still at times gave him trouble, Major Tudor was a non-dancer. Whatever his meaning, the remark came upon her flushed triumph like the icy chill before the dawn, dispelling dreams.

"I am sorry," she said, with all the haste of youth, "that you sacrificed yourself to please me. I hope you will not do so again. Now that I am married, I do not need a chaperon. I could quite well return alone."

It was childishly spoken, but then she was a child, and the admiration she had enjoyed throughout the evening had slightly turned her head. He did not reply to her speech. Indeed, it was as if he had not heard it. And her indignation mounted. There was not another man of her acquaintance who would have treated her with a like lack of courtesy. Did he think, because he was her husband, that she belonged to him so completely that he could behave to her exactly as he saw fit? Perhaps. She did not know him very well; nor apparently did he know her. For during the brief six weeks of their married life she had been a little shy, a little constrained, in his presence. But her success had, as it were, unshackled her. Without hesitation she gave her feelings the rein.

"Do you consider that I am not to be trusted?" she asked him sharply.

"I beg your pardon?"

There was a note of surprised interrogation in his voice. She did not look at him, but she knew that his eyebrows were raised, and a faint—quite a faint—sense of misgiving stole over her.

"I asked if you thought me untrustworthy," she asked.

"Oh!"

He relapsed into silence again, and she became exasperated.

"Why don't you answer me?" she said, with quick impatience.

He turned his head deliberately and looked at her; and again she tingled with an apprehension which no previous word or action of his had ever justified.

"Unprofitable questions," he said coolly, "like ill-timed jests, are better left alone."

It was the first intentional snub he had ever administered to her, and she quivered under it, furious but impotent. All the evening's enjoyment had gone out of her. She was conscious only of a desire to strike back and wound him as he had wounded her.

She did not utter another word during the drive, and when they reached their bungalow—the daintiest and most luxurious in the station—she alighted without touching the hand he offered her.

Refreshments awaited them in the dining-room, and the bride swept in and helped herself, suffering her cloak to fall from her shoulders. He picked it up and threw it over a chair. His dark face was quite composed and inscrutable. He was not a handsome man, but there was something undeniably striking about him, a strength of personality that made him somehow formidable. The red and gold uniform he wore served to emphasise the breadth of shoulder, which his height did not justify. He was a splendid wrestler. There was not a man in the mess whom he could not throw.

Yet to those who knew him best, his strength seemed to lie less in what he did than in what he left undone. His restraint was the secret of his power.

Perhaps his young wife felt this, for notwithstanding her utmost effort she knew herself to be at a disadvantage. She set down her glass of sherbet unfinished and turned to the door. It was an abrupt move, but he was ready for it. Before she reached it, he was waiting with the handle in his grasp.

"Going to bed, Audrey?" he asked gravely, "Good-night!"

His manner did not betray that he was aware of her displeasure, yet somehow she was quite convinced that he knew. She paused for a second, and then, with her head held high, she was about to pass him without an answering word or glance. But to her amazement he stopped her, his hand upon her arm.

"Good-night!" he said again.

She faced him then in a blaze of passion, with white cheeks and flaming eyes. But as she met his look her heart gave a sudden thump of fright, and in a second her resistance had crumbled away. He did not speak another word, but his look compelled. Undeniably he was master.

Mutely she raised her face for his kiss, and he kissed her.

"Sleep well," he said.

And she went from him, subdued and humbled, to her room.

CHAPTER III

AMID THE RUINS

"Do let us get away somewhere and enjoy ourselves!"

Audrey spoke in a quick undertone to the man nearest to her. It was three weeks since her arrival at the Frontier station, and she had settled down to the life with the ease of a born Anglo-Indian. Her first vivid enjoyment of its gaieties was a thing of the past, but no one suspected the fact, her husband least of all. She had not, as a matter of fact, been much with him during those three weeks, for she had struck up a warm friendship with Mrs. Raleigh, and in common with all the younger spirits of the regiment she availed herself fully of the privileges of the latter's hospitality.

On the present occasion, however—that of a picnic by moonlight at the crumbling shrine of some long-forgotten holy man—Mrs. Raleigh was absent, and Audrey was bored. She had arrived in her husband's ralli-car, which he had driven himself, but she had speedily drifted away from his side.

There was an element of perversity in her which made her resent the feeling that he only accompanied her into society to watch over her, and, if necessary, to keep her in order. It was not a particularly worthy feeling, but certainly there was something about his attitude that fostered it.

She guessed, and rightly, that, but for her, he would not have troubled himself to attend these social gatherings, which he obviously enjoyed so little. So when, having deliberately and with mischievous intent given him the slip, she awoke suddenly to the fact that he had followed and was standing near her, Audrey became childishly exasperated and seized the first means of escape that offered.

The man she addressed was one of the least enthusiastic of her admirers, but this did not trouble her at all. She had been a spoilt child all her life, and she was accustomed to make use of others without stopping to ascertain their inclinations.

Phil Turner, however, was by no means unwilling to be made use of in this way. The boy was a gentleman, and was as chivalrous at heart as he was honest.

He turned at once in response to her quick whisper and offered her his arm.

"There's an old well at the back of the ruin," he said. "Come and see it. Mind the stones."

"That was splendid of you," she said approvingly, as they moved away together. "Are you always so prompt? But I know you're not. I shouldn't have asked you, only I took you for Mr. Devereux. You are very like him at the back."

"Never heard that before!" he responded bluntly. "Don't believe it, either, if you will forgive my saying so."

She laughed, a merry, ringing laugh.

"Oh, don't you like Mr. Devereux?"

"Yes, he's all right." Phil seldom spoke a disparaging word of any of his comrades. "But I haven't the smallest wish to be like him," he added.

Audrey laughed at him again, freely, musically. She found this young officer rather more entertaining than the rest.

They reached the other side of the shrine. Here, in a *débris* of stones and weeds, there appeared the circular mouth of an old well, forgotten like the shrine and long disused.

Audrey examined the edge with a fastidious air, and finally sat down on it. The place was flooded with moonlight.

"I wish I were a man," she said suddenly.

"Good Heavens! Why?"

He asked the question in amazement.

"I should like to be your equal," she told him gaily. "I should like to do and say to you just exactly what I liked."

Phil considered this seriously.

"You can do both without being my equal," he remarked at length in his bluntest tone, "that is, if you care to condescend."

"Goodness!" laughed Audrey. "That's the only pretty thing I have ever heard you say. I am sure it must be your first attempt. Now, isn't it?"

He laughed.

"And it wasn't strictly honest," proceeded Audrey daringly. "You know you don't think that of any woman under the sun."

He did not contradict her. He had a feeling that she was fooling him, but somehow he rather liked it.

"What about the women under the moon?" he said. "Perhaps they are different?"

She nodded merrily.

"Perhaps they are," she conceded. "Certainly the men are. Now, you are about the stodgiest person I know by daylight or lamplight except—except—" She stopped. "No, I don't mean that!" she said, with an impish smile. "There is no exception."

Phil was frowning a little, but he looked relieved at her amendment.

"Thank you!" he said brusquely. "I shall never dare to come near you after that."

"Except by moonlight?" she suggested, with the impudent audacity of a child.

What reply he would have made to that piece of nonsense he sometimes wondered afterward, but circumstances prevented his making any. The words had only just passed her lips when she sprang to her feet with a wild shriek of horror, shaking her arm with frantic violence.

"A snake!" she cried. "Take it away! Take it away! It's on my wrist!"

Phil Turner, though young, was accustomed to keep his wits about him, and, luckily for the girl, her agony did not scare them away. He had seized her arm in a fierce grip almost before her frenzied appeal was uttered. A small snake was coiled round her wrist, and he tore it away with his free hand, not caring how he grasped it. He tried to fling the thing from him, but somehow his hold upon it was not sufficient. Before he knew it the creature had shot up his sleeve.

The next instant he had shaken it down again with a muffled curse and was trampling it savagely and vindictively into the stones at his feet.

"Are you hurt?" he asked, wheeling sharply.

"No," gasped Audrey, "no! But you—"

"Yes, the little beast's bitten me," he returned. "You see—"

"Oh, where, where?" she cried. "Let me see! Quick, quick! Something must be done. Can't you suck it?"

He pushed up his sleeve.

"No; can't get at it," he said. "It's just below the elbow. Never mind; it isn't serious!"

He would have tweaked his sleeve down again, though he was pale under his sunburn. But Audrey stopped him, holding his bare arm between her hands.

"Don't be a fool!" she gasped vehemently. "If you can't, I can—and I will!"

Before he could stop her she had stooped, still holding him fast, and put her lips to the tiny puncture in his flesh, on which scarcely more than a speck of blood was visible.

Phil stiffened and stood still, every nerve rigid, as if something had transfixed him. At last, hurriedly, jerkily, he spoke:

"Mrs. Tudor—for Heaven's sake! I can't let you do this. It wasn't poisonous, ten to one. Don't! I say, Audrey—please don't!"

His voice was imploring, but she paid no heed. Her lips continued to draw at the wound, while he, half-distracted, bent over her, protesting, scarcely conscious of what he said, yet submitting in spite of himself.

There came the sound of running feet, and he guessed that her scream had given the alarm. He stood up with mingled agitation and relief, and an instant later was face to face with her husband.

"I—couldn't help it!" he stammered. "It was a snake-bite."

People were crowding round them with questions and exclamations. But Tudor gave utterance to neither. He only put his hand on his wife's shoulder and spoke to her.

"That will do, Audrey," he said. "There's a doctor here. Leave it to him."

At his words Audrey straightened herself, quivering all over; and then, unnerved by sheer horror, she put out her hands with an unconscious groping gesture, and fainted.

CHAPTER IV

AN UNCONVENTIONAL CALL

Audrey had been an only girl at home, and had run wild all her life amongst a host of brothers. She had seen next to nothing of the world previous to her marriage, consequently her knowledge of its ways was extremely slender.

That she had grown up headstrong and extremely unconventional was scarcely to be wondered at.

It had been entirely by her own choice that she had married Eustace Tudor. She had just awakened to the fact that the family nest, like the family purse, was of exceedingly narrow dimensions; and a passion for exploring both mentally and physically was hers.

They had met only a couple of months before he was due to sail for India, and his proposal to her had been necessarily somewhat precipitate. She had admired him wholeheartedly for he was a soldier of no mean repute, and the glamour of marriage had done the rest. She had married him and had, for nearly six weeks, thereafter, been supremely happy. True, he had not made much love to her; it was not apparently his way, but he had been full of kindness and consideration. And Audrey had been content.

But, arrived in that Indian Frontier station where all the world was gay, she had become at once the centre of attraction, of admiration; and, responding to this with girlish zest, she had begun to find something lacking in her husband's treatment.

It dawned upon her that, where others worshipped with open devotion, he did not so much as bend the knee. And, over and above this serious defect, he was critical of her actions and inclined to keep her in order.

This made her reckless at first, even defiant; but she found he could master her defiance, and that frightened her. It made her uncertain as to how far it was safe to resist him. And, being afraid of him, she shrank a little from too close or intimate a companionship with him.

She told herself that she valued her liberty too highly to part lightly with it; but the reason in her heart was not this, and with all her wilfulness, her childish self-sufficiency, she knew that it was not.

On the morning that followed the moonlight picnic she deliberately feigned sleep when he rose, lest he should think fit to prohibit her early ride. She had not slept well after her fright; but she had a project in her mind, and she fully meant to carry it out.

She lay chafing till his horse's hoof-beats told her that he was leaving the house behind him; then she, too, rose and ordered her own horse.

Phil Turner, haggard and depressed after a night of considerable pain, was sitting up in bed with his arm in a sling, drinking tea, when a fellow-subaltern, who with two others shared the bungalow with him, entered, half-dressed and dishevelled, with the astounding news that Mrs. Tudor was waiting in the compound to know how he was.

Phil shot upright in amazement.

"Good Heavens, man! She herself?" he ejaculated.

His brother officer nodded, grinning.

"What's to be done? Send out word that you're still alive though not too chirpy, and would she like anything to drink on the veranda? I can't go, you know; I'm not dressed."

"Don't be an ass! Clear out and send me my bearer."

Phil spoke with decision. Since Mrs. Tudor had elected to do this extraordinary thing, it was not for him to refuse to follow her lead. He was too far in her debt, even had he desired to do so.

His bearer, therefore, was dispatched with a courteous message, and when Phil entered the veranda a quarter of an hour later he found her awaiting him there.

"This is awfully kind of you," he said, as he grasped her outstretched hand. "I was horribly put out about you! You are none the worse?"

"Not a mite," she assured him. "And you? Your arm?"

He made a face.

"Raleigh was with me half the night, watching for dangerous symptoms; but they didn't develop. He cauterized my arm as a precaution—a beastly business. He hasn't been round again yet, but I believe it's better. Yes, it was a poisonous bite. It would have been the death of me in all probability, but for you. He told me so. I—I'm awfully obliged to you!"

He coloured deeply as he made his clumsy acknowledgments. He did not find it an easy task. As for Audrey, she put out her hands swiftly to stop him.

"Ah, don't!" she said. "You did a far greater thing for me." She shuddered and put the matter from her. "I'm sure you ought not to be up," she went on. "I shouldn't have waited, only I thought you might feel hurt if I went away after you had sent out word that you would see me. I think I'll go now. Good-bye!"

There came the jingle of spurs on the veranda, and both started. The colour rose in a great wave to the girl's face as she saw who it was, but she turned at once to meet the newcomer.

"Oh, Eustace," she said, "so you are back already from the parade-ground!"

He did not show any surprise at finding her there.

"Yes; just returned," he said, with no more than a quiet glance at her flushed face.

"How are you, Phil? Had any sleep?"

"Not much," Phil owned, with unmistakable embarrassment. "But Raleigh says I'm not going to die this time. It was good of you—and Mrs. Tudor—to look in. Won't you have something? That lazy beast Travers isn't dressed yet!"

"Oh, yes, he is!" said Travers, appearing at that moment. "I'll punch your head for you, my boy, when we're alone! Hullo, Major! Come to see the interesting invalid? You'll have some breakfast, won't you? Mrs. Tudor will pour out tea for us."

But Tudor declined their hospitality briefly but decidedly, and Audrey was obliged to support him.

Travers assisted her to mount, expressing his regret the while; and when they were gone he turned round to his comrade with a grin.

"The major seems to be in a genial mood this morning," he remarked. "Had they arranged to meet here?"

But Phil turned back into the bungalow with a heavy frown.

"The major's a bungling fool!" he said bitterly.

CHAPTER V

THE BARRIER

Tudor was very quiet and preoccupied during breakfast, but Audrey would not notice it; and when at length she rose from the table she laid her fingers for a second on his shoulder in a passing caress.

He turned instantly and took her hand.

"Just a moment, Audrey!" he said gravely.

She stopped unwillingly, her hand fidgeting ineffectually to be free.

He rose, still holding it in a quiet, strong grasp. He was frowning slightly.

"I only want to say," he said, "that what you did this morning was somewhat unusual, though you may not have been aware of it. Please don't do it again!"

Her cheeks flamed, and she met his eyes defiantly. She left her hand in his rather than prove her weakness, but quite suddenly she was trembling all over. It was a moment for asserting her freedom of action, and she fully meant to do so; but she was none the less afraid.

"I was aware of it," she said, speaking very quickly before his look could disconcert her. "But then what I did last night was unusual, too. Also what Phil Turner did for me. You—you don't seem to realise that he saved my life!"

"I think you discharged your debt," Tudor returned, with a certain dryness that struck her unpleasantly.

"What else could I have done?" she demanded stormily. "If you had been in my place—"

He stopped her.

"I was not discussing that," he said. "I have not blamed you for that. Under the circumstances, you did the best thing possible. But I can't say the same of your conduct this morning; and since you knew that what you did was highly unconventional, I blame you for it. I hope you will be more careful in the future."

Audrey was chafing openly before he ended.

"You treat me like a child," she broke in, the instant he paused. "You don't give me credit for any judgment or discretion of my own."

He raised his eyebrows.

"That is hardly remarkable," he said.

She snatched her hand from him at last, too exasperated for the moment to care what she did or how she did it.

"It is remarkable," she declared, her voice quivering with wrath. "It—it's intolerable. And there's something else that struck me as remarkable, too, and that is that you didn't think it worth while even to thank Phil for—for saving my life last night. I think you might have expressed a little gratitude, even—even if you didn't feel it."

The bitter words were uttered before she realised their full bitterness. But the moment she had spoken them she knew, for his face told her.

A dead silence followed her outburst, and while it lasted she was casting about wildly for some means of escape other than headlong flight. Then, as if he read her impulse in her eyes, he moved at last and turned aside.

She did not hear his sigh as she made her escape, or even then she might have scaled the barrier that divided them, and found beyond it a better thing than the freedom she prized so highly.

CHAPTER VI

MRS. TUDOR'S CONFESSION

"Come in and sit down, Mrs. Tudor. Mrs. Raleigh isn't at home. But she can't be long now. I have been waiting nearly half an hour."

Phil Turner hoisted himself out of the easiest chair in the Raleighs' drawing-room as he uttered the words, and advanced with a friendly smile to greet the newcomer.

"Oh, isn't she in?" said Audrey. "I am afraid I took her for granted at the door."

"We all do," he assured her. "It is what she likes best. Do you know, I haven't seen you for nearly a fortnight? I called, you know, twice; but you were out."

Audrey laughed inconsequently.

"Why don't you treat me as you treat Mrs. Raleigh?" she said. "Come in and wait, next time."

Phil smiled as he handed her to the chair he had just vacated.

"The major isn't so kind to subalterns," he said. "He would

certainly think, if he didn't say it, that it was like my cheek."

Audrey frowned over this.

"I don't see what he has to do with it," she declared finally. "But it doesn't signify. How is your arm?"

"Practically convalescent, thanks! There's nothing like first aid, you know. I say, Mrs. Tudor, you weren't any the worse? It didn't hurt you?"

He looked down at her with anxiety in his frank eyes, and Audrey was conscious suddenly that he was no longer a mere casual acquaintance. Perhaps she had been vaguely aware of it before, but the actual realisation of it had not been in her mind till that moment.

She laughed lightly.

"Of course not," she said. "How could it? Don't be so ridiculous, Phil."

His face cleared.

"That's right," he said heartily. "Don't mind me. But I couldn't help wondering. And I thought it was so decent of you to come round and look me up on that first morning."

Audrey's smile faded.

"I am glad you thought it was decent, anyhow," she said, with a touch of bitterness. "No one else did."

"Oh, rot, Mrs. Tudor!"

Phil spoke hastily. He was frowning, as his custom was when embarrassed.

She looked up at him and nodded emphatically.

"Yes, it was—just that," she said, an odd little note of passion in her voice. "I never thought of these things before, but it seems that here no one thinks of anything else."

"Don't take any notice of it," said Phil. "It isn't worth it."

"I can't help myself," said Audrey. "You see—I'm married!"

"So is Mrs. Raleigh." Phil spoke with sudden heat. "But she doesn't care."

"No, I know. But her husband is such an old dear. Everything she does is right in his eyes."

It was skating on thin ice, and Phil at least realised it. He made an abrupt effort to pull up.

"Yes, I'm awfully fond of Major Raleigh," he said. "By the way, he's an immense admirer of yours. Your promptitude the other night quite won his heart. He complimented your husband upon it."

"Did he? What did Eustace say?"

There was more than curiosity in Audrey's voice.

"I don't know."

Phil's eyes suddenly avoided hers. He spoke in a dogged, half-surly tone.

Audrey sat and looked at him for a moment. Then lightly she rose and stood before him.

"Tell me, please!" she said imperiously.

He made a sharp gesture of remonstrance.

"Sorry," he said, after a moment, as she waited inexorably. "I can't!"

"Oh, but you can!" she returned. "You're not to say you won't to me."

He looked down at her.

"I am sorry!" he said less brusquely. "But it can't be done. It isn't worth a tussle, I assure you, nor is it worth the possible annoyance it might cause you if you had your way. Look here, can't we talk of something else?"

She laid her hand impulsively on his arm.

"Tell me, Phil!" she said.

He drew back abruptly.

"You put me in a beastly position, Mrs. Tudor," he said. "I hate repeating things. It isn't fair to corner me like this."

"Don't be absurd!" said Audrey. Her face was flushed and determined. She was bent upon having her own way in this, at least. "I shall begin to hate you in a minute."

But Phil could be determined, too.

"Can't help it," he said; but there was genuine regret in his voice. "You'll have to, I'm afraid."

He was scarcely prepared for the effect of his words. She flung away from him in tempestuous anger and turned as if to leave the room. But before she reached the door some other impulse apparently overtook her. She stopped abruptly with her back to Phil, and stood for what seemed to him interminable seconds, fumbling with her handkerchief.

Then, before he had fully realised the approaching catastrophe, her self-control suddenly deserted her. She sank into a chair with her hands over her face and began to cry.

Now, Phil was young, and no woman had ever thus abandoned herself to tears in his presence before. The sight sent a sharp shock through him that was almost like a dart of physical pain. It paralysed him for an instant; but the next he strode forward, convention flung to the winds, desirous only to comfort. He reached her and bent over her, one hand upon her shaking shoulder.

"I say, Mrs. Tudor, don't—don't!" he urged. "What is the matter? You're not crying because I wouldn't do as you asked me? You couldn't care all that for such a trifle?"

His voice was husky with agitation. He felt guiltily that it was all his fault, and he could have kicked himself for his clumsiness.

She did not answer him, nor did her sobs grow less. It was the pent-up misery of weeks to which she was giving vent, and, having yielded, it was no easy matter to check herself again.

Phil became desperate and knelt down by her side, almost as distressed as she.

"I say," he pleaded—"I say, Audrey, don't cry! Tell me what is wrong. Let me help you. Give me a chance, anyhow. I—I'd do anything in the world, you know. Only tell me."

He drew one of her hands away from her face and held it between his own. She did not resist him. Her need of a comforter just then was very great. Her head was bowed almost against his shoulder and it did not occur to either of them that they were transgressing the most elementary laws of conventionality.

"You can't help me," she sobbed at last. "No one can. I'm just lonely and miserable and homesick. I hate this place and everyone in it except—except you—and a few others. I wish I were back in England. I wish I'd never left it. I wish—I wish—I'd never married."

Her voice came muffled and piteous. It was the cry of a desolate child. And all the deep chivalry in Phil's soul quivered and thrilled in response. Before he knew it, tender, consoling words had sprung to his lips.

"Don't cry, dear; don't cry!" he said. "You'll feel better about it presently. We all go through it, and it's beastly, I know, I know. But it won't last. Nothing does in this chancy world. So what's the good of fretting?"

She could not tell him. Her trouble was too immense at that moment to bear discussion. But he comforted her. She liked the feel of his hand upon her shoulder; the firm, friendly grasp of his fingers about her own.

"I sometimes think I can't go on," she whispered through her tears. "It's like being in prison, and I want to run away. Only I can't—I can't. I've got to bear it all my life."

A slight sound from the open window followed this confidence, and Phil looked up sharply. Audrey had not heard it, and she did not notice his movement.

Her head was still bent; and over it Phil, glaring like a tiger, met the quiet, critical eyes of the girl's husband.

He rose to his feet the next instant, but he did not utter a word.

As for Tudor, he stood quite motionless, quite inscrutable, for the space of seconds, looking gravely in upon them. Then, to Phil's unspeakable amazement, he turned deliberately and walked away. There was thick matting on Mrs. Raleigh's veranda, and his receding footsteps made no sound.

CHAPTER VII

AN UNPLEASANT INTERVIEW

"There!" said Audrey, a few seconds later, "I've been a perfect idiot, I know; but I'm better now. Tell me, do I look as if I had been crying?"

She raised her pretty, woebegone face to his and smiled very faintly.

There was something unmistakably grim about Phil at that moment, and she wondered why.

"Of course you do," he said bluntly.

Audrey got up and peered at herself uneasily in a mirror.

"It doesn't show much," she said, after a careful inspection. "And, anyhow"—turning round to him—"I don't know what you have to be cross about. It—it was all your fault!"

Phil groaned and held his peace. She would know soon enough, he reflected.

Audrey drew nearer to him.

"Tell me what he said to Major Raleigh, Phil," she said rather tremulously.

He shrugged his shoulders and yielded.

"He only said that he wished your discretion equalled your promptitude in emergencies," he said.

"Oh," said Audrey. "Was that all? Well, I think you might have told me before."

Phil laughed grudgingly. The situation was abominable, but her utter childishness palliated it. How was Tudor going to treat the matter? he wondered. What if he—

A sudden thought flashed across Phil's brain, and his face

grew set. Of course it had been his fault, since she said so. It remained therefore for him to extricate her, if he could. He turned to her.

"Look here, Mrs. Tudor," he said, in a judicious, elder-brotherly tone, "I think it's a mistake, don't you know, to let yourself get depressed over—well, little things. I know what it is to feel down on your luck. But luck turns, you know, and—and—he's a good sort—a bit stiff and difficult to get on with, but still—a good sort. You won't think me rude if I leave you now? I didn't expect Mrs. Raleigh to be so long, and I'm afraid I can't wait any longer. I've got to dress for mess."

"Goodness!" said Audrey, with a glance at the clock. "Does it take you two hours? No, don't scowl! I'm only joking, so you needn't be cross. Good-bye, then! Thank you for being kind to me."

Her hand lay in his for a moment. She was smiling at him rather sadly, notwithstanding her half-bantering words.

Phil paused a second.

"I'm confoundedly sorry!" he said impulsively. "Don't cry any more."

She shook her head and withdrew her hand.

"Who says I've been crying?" she said lightly. "Go away, and don't be silly!"

He took her at her word and departed.

At the gate of the compound he met Mrs. Raleigh, but he refused to turn back with her.

"I really must go; I've got an engagement," he said. "But Mrs. Tudor is waiting for you. Keep her as long as you can. I believe she's a bit down—homesick, you know." And he hurried away, breaking into a run as soon as he reached the road.

He went straight to the Tudor's bungalow without giving himself time to flinch from the interview that he had made up his mind he must have.

The major *sahib* was in, the *khitmutgar* told him and Phil scribbled an urgent message on his card and sent it to him. Two minutes later he was shown into his superior officer's presence, and he realised that he stood committed to the gravest task he had ever undertaken.

Major Tudor was sitting unoccupied before the writing-table in his smoking-room, but he rose as Phil entered. His face was composed as usual.

"Well, Mr. Turner?" he said, as Phil came heavily forward.

Phil, more nervous than he had ever been before, halted in

front of him.

"I came to speak to you, sir," he said with an effort, "to—to explain—"

Tudor was standing with his back to the light. He made no attempt to help him out of his difficulties.

Phil came to an abrupt pause; then, as if some inner force had suddenly come to his assistance, he straightened himself and tackled the matter afresh.

"I came to tell you, sir," he said, meeting Tudor's eyes squarely, "that I have nothing to be ashamed of. In case"—he paused momentarily—"you should misunderstand what you saw half an hour ago, I thought it better to speak at once."

"Very prudent," said Tudor. "But—it is quite unnecessary. I do not misunderstand."

He spoke deliberately and coldly. But Phil clenched his hands. The words cut him like a whip.

"You refuse to believe me?" he said.

Tudor did not answer.

"I must trouble you for an answer," Phil said, forcing himself to speak quietly.

"As you please," said Tudor, in the same cold tone. "I have a question to put first. Had I not chanced to see what took place, would you have sought this interview?"

The blood rose in a hot wave to Phil's head, but he did not wince or hesitate.

"Of course I shouldn't," he said.

Tudor made a curt gesture as of dismissal.

"Out of your own mouth—" he said, and turned contemptuously away.

Phil stood quite still for the space of ten seconds, then the young blood in him suddenly mounted to fever pitch. He strode up to his major, and seized him fiercely by the shoulder.

"I won't bear this from any man," he said between his teeth. "I am as honourable as you are! If you say—or insinuate—otherwise, I—by Heaven—I'll kill you!"

The passionate words ceased, and there followed a silence more terrible than any speech. Tudor stood absolutely motionless, facing the young subaltern who towered over him, without a sign of either anger or dismay.

Then at last, very slowly and quietly, he spoke:

"You have made a mistake. Take your hand away."

Phil's hand dropped to his side. He was white to the lips. Yet he would not relinquish his purpose at a word.

"It hasn't been for my own sake," he said, his voice still shaking with the anger he could not subdue.

Tudor made no response. He stood with his eyes fixed steadily upon Phil's agitated face. And, as if compelled by that searching gaze, Phil reiterated the assertion.

"If I had only had myself to consider," he said, "I shouldn't have—stooped—to offer an explanation."

"Let me remind you," Tudor said quietly, "that I have not asked for one."

"You prefer to misunderstand?" said Phil quickly.

"I prefer to take my own view," amended Tudor. "If you are wise—you will be satisfied to leave it so."

It was final, and, though far from satisfied, Phil felt the futility of further discussion. He turned to the door.

"Very well, sir," he said briefly, and went out, holding his head high.

As for Tudor, he sat down again before his writing-table with an unmoved countenance, and after a short interval took up his correspondence. There was no anger in his eyes.

CHAPTER VIII

AT THE DANCE

Audrey saw no more of Phil Turner for some days. She did not enjoy much of her husband's society, either. He appeared to be too busy to think of her, and she in consequence spent most of her time with Mrs. Raleigh. But Phil, who had been one of the latter's most constant visitors, did not show himself there.

It did not occur to Audrey that he absented himself on her account, and she was disappointed not to meet him. Next perhaps to the surgeon's wife, she had begun to regard him as her greatest friend. Certainly the tie of obligation that bound them together was one that seemed to warrant an intimate friendship. Moreover, Phil had been exceptionally kind to her in distress, kinder far than Eustace had ever been.

She was growing away from her husband very rapidly, and she knew it, mourned over it even in softer moments; but she felt powerless to remedy the evil. It seemed so obvious to her that he did not care.

So she spent more and more of her hours away from the bungalow that had been made so dainty for her presence, and Eustace never seemed to notice that she was absent from his side.

He accompanied her always when she went out in the evening, but he no longer intruded his guardianship upon her, and deep in her inmost heart this thing hurt his young wife as nothing had ever hurt her before. She had her own way in all matters, but it gave her no pleasure; and the feeling that, though he might not approve of what she did, he would never remonstrate, grew and festered within her till she sometimes marvelled that he did not read her misery in her eyes.

She met Phil Turner again at length at a regimental dance. As usual her card was quickly filled, but she reserved a waltz for him, and after a while he came across and asked her for one.

"You were very nearly too late," she told him. "Why didn't you come before?"

He looked awkward for a moment. Then—

"I was busy," he said rather shortly. "I'm one of the stewards."

He scrawled his initials across her card and left her again. Audrey concluded in her girlish way that something had made him cross, and dismissed him from her mind.

When at length he came to claim her she was hot and tired and suggested sitting out.

He frowned at the idea, but, upon Audrey waxing imperious, he yielded. They sat out together, but not in the cool dark of the veranda as she had anticipated, but in the full glare of the ballroom amidst all the hubbub of the dancers.

Audrey was annoyed, and showed it.

"I am sure we might find a seat on the veranda," she said.

But Phil was obstinate.

"I assure you, Mrs. Tudor," he said, "I looked in there just now, and every seat was occupied."

"I don't believe you are telling the truth," she returned.

He raised his eyebrows.

"Thank you!" he said briefly.

Something in the curt reply caught her attention, and she gave him a quick glance. He was looking remarkably handsome in his red and gold uniform with the scarlet cummerbund across his shirt. Vexed as she was with him, Audrey could not help admitting it to herself. His brown, resolute face attracted her irresistibly.

She allowed a considerable pause to ensue before she went to the inevitable attack. Somehow, notwithstanding his surliness, she had not the faintest desire to quarrel with him.

"You're very grumpy tonight," she remarked at length in her cheery young voice. "What's the matter?"

He started and looked intensely uncomfortable.

"Nothing—of course!" he said.

"Why of course? I wonder. With me it's the other way round. I am never cross without a reason."

Audrey was still cheery.

He smiled faintly.

"I congratulate you," he said.

Audrey smiled also. Fully exposed as was their position, there was no one near enough to overhear.

"Well, don't be cross any more, Phil," she said persuasively. "Cheer up, and come to tiffin with me tomorrow. Will you? I shall be quite alone."

Phil's smile departed instantly. He glanced at her for a second, and then fixed his eyes steadily upon the ground between his feet.

"You're awfully good!" he said at last. "But—thanks very much—I can't."

"Can't?" echoed Audrey, with genuine disappointment. "Oh, I'm sure that's nonsense! Why can't you? You're not on duty?"

"No," he said, speaking slowly, "I'm not on duty; but—fact is, I'm going up to the Hills shooting for a few days and—I shall be busy, packing guns and things. Besides—"

"Oh, do stop!" she broke in, with sudden impatience. "I know you are only making up as you go along. It's very horrid of you, besides being contemptible. Why can't you say at once that you are not coming because you don't want to come?"

Her quick pride had taken fire at sound of his deliberate excuse; and, as was its wont upon provocation, her anger flamed high at a moment's notice.

Phil did not look at her. His expression was decidedly uneasy, but there was a certain grimness about him that did not seem to indicate the probability of any excessive show of docility in face of a browbeating.

"I don't say it," he said doggedly at length, "because, besides being rude, it wouldn't be strictly true."

"I shouldn't have thought you would have had any scruples of that sort," rejoined Audrey, hitting her hardest because he had managed to hurt her. "They haven't been very apparent tonight."

Phil made no protest, but he was frowning heavily.

She leant slightly towards him, speaking behind her fan.

"Be honest just for a second," she said, "if you can, and tell me; are you tired of calling yourself a friend of mine? Are you trying to get out of it? Because, if you are, it's quite the easiest thing in the world to do so. But once done—"

She paused. Phil was looking at her at last, and there was something in his eyes that startled her. A sudden pity rushed over her heart. She felt as she had felt once long ago in England when a dog—an old friend of hers—had been injured. He had looked at her with just such eyes as those that were fixed upon her now. Their dumb pleading had been almost more than she could bear.

Involuntarily she laid her hand on his arm, music and dancers all forgotten in that moment of swift emotion.

"Phil," she whispered tremulously, "what is it? What is it?"

He did not answer her by a single word. He simply rose to his feet, as if by her action she had suggested it, and whirled her in among the dancers.

He kept her going to the very last chord, she too full of wonder and uncertainty to protest; and then he led her straight through the room to where Mrs. Raleigh stood, surrounded by the usual crowd of subalterns, muttered an excuse, and left her there.

CHAPTER IX

DREADFUL NEWS

It was nearly a week later that Audrey, riding home alone in a rickshaw from a polo-match, was overtaken by young Gerald Devereux, a subaltern, who was tearing along on foot as if on some urgent errand. Recognising her, he reduced his speed and dropped into a jog-trot by her side.

"You haven't heard, of course?" he jerked out breathlessly. "Beastly bad news! Those hill tribes—always up to some devilry! Poor old Phil—infernal luck!"

"What?" exclaimed Audrey. "What has happened to him? Tell me, quick, quick!"

She turned as white as paper, and Devereux cursed himself for a clumsy fool.

"It may not be the worst," he gasped back. "Dash it! I'm so winded! We hope, you know, we hope—but it's usually a knife and good-bye with these ruffians. Still, there's a chance—just a chance."

"But you haven't told me what has happened yet," cried Audrey, in a fever of impatience.

He answered her, still running by her side "The Waris have got him; rushed his camp at night and bagged everything. The coolies were in the know, no doubt. Only his *shikari* got away. He has just come in wounded with the news. I'm on my way to tell the Chief, though I don't see what good he can do."

"You mean you think he is murdered?" gasped Audrey, through white lips.

He nodded.

"Afraid so, poor beggar! Well, so long, Mrs. Tudor! We must hope for the best as long as we can."

He put his hand to his cap, and ran on, while Audrey, with a set, white face, was borne to her bungalow.

Her husband was sitting on the veranda. He rose as she alighted and gave her his hand up the short flight of steps to his side.

"You are rather late," he said in his grave way. "I am afraid you will have to hurry."

They were dining out that night, but Audrey had forgotten it. She stared at him as if dazed.

"What is it?" he asked. "Nothing wrong?"

She gasped hysterically.

"Oh, Eustace, an awful thing—an awful thing!" she cried. "Mr. Devereux has just told me—"

Her voice broke, and her lips formed soundless words. She groped vaguely for support with one hand.

Tudor put his arm round her and led her, tottering, indoors.

"All right; tell me presently," he said quietly. "Sit down and keep still for a little."

He put her into an armchair and left her there. In a few seconds he returned with some brandy and water, which he held to her lips in silence. Then, setting down the glass, he began to rub her nerveless hands.

Audrey submitted passively at first to his ministrations, but presently as her strength returned she sat up.

"You haven't heard?" she asked him shakily.

"I have heard nothing," he answered. "Can you tell me now?"

"Yes—yes!" She paused a moment to steady her voice. Then—"It's Phil!" she faltered. "He has been taken prisoner—murdered perhaps—by those dreadful hill men! Oh Eustace"—lifting her face appealingly—"do you think they would kill him? Do you? Do you?"

But Tudor said nothing. He made no attempt to comfort her, and she turned from him in bitter disappointment. His lack of sympathy at such a moment was almost more than she could bear.

"How did Devereux know?" he asked, after a pause.

She shook her head.

"He said something about a *shikari*. He was going to tell the colonel; but he didn't think it would be any use. He said—he said—"

She broke off, quivering with agitation. Her husband took the glass from the table again and made her drink a little. She tried to refuse, but he insisted.

"You have had a shock. It will do you good," he said, in his level, unmoved voice.

And Audrey yielded to the mastery she had scarcely felt of late.

The spirit helped to steady her, and at length she rose.

"I am going to my room, Eustace," she said, not looking at him. "I—can't go out tonight. Perhaps you will make my excuses."

He did not answer her, and she threw him a swift glance. He was standing stiff and upright. His face was stern and composed; it might have been a stone mask.

"What excuse am I to make?" he asked.

Her eyes widened. The question was utterly unexpected.

"Why, the truth—of course," she said. "Say that I have been upset by the news, that—that—I hadn't the heart—I couldn't—Eustace,"—appealing suddenly, a tremor of indignation in her voice—"you don't seem to realise that he is one of my greatest friends. Don't you understand?"

"Yes," he said—"yes, I understand!"

And she marvelled at the coldness—the deadly, concentrated coldness—of his voice.

"All the same," he went on, "I think you must make an effort to accompany me to the Bentleys' tonight. It might be thought unusual if I went alone."

She stared at him in sudden, amazed anger.

"Eustace!" she exclaimed. "How can you be so cruel, so cold-blooded, so—so heartless? How can you expect such a thing of me—to sit at table and hear them all talking about it, and his chances discussed? I couldn't—I couldn't!"

He did not press the point. Perhaps he realised that her nerves in their present condition would prove wholly unequal to such a strain.

"Very well," he said quietly at length. "I will send a note to excuse us both."

"I don't see why you should stay at home," Audrey said, turning to the door. "I would far rather be alone."

He did not explain his motive, and she went out of his presence with a sensation of relief. She had never fully realised before how wide the gulf between them had become.

She remained shut up in her room all the evening, eating nothing, face to face with the horror of young Devereux's brief words. It was the first time within her memory that death had approached her sheltered life, and she was shocked and frightened, as a child is frightened by the terrors of the dark.

Very late that night she crept into bed, dismissing her *ayah*, and lay there shivering and forlorn, thinking, thinking, of the cruel faces and flashing knives that Phil had awaked to see. She dozed at last in her misery, only to wake again with a shriek of nightmare terror, and start up sobbing hysterically.

"Why, Audrey!" a quiet voice said, and she woke fully, to find her husband standing by her bed.

She turned to him impulsively, hiding her face against him, clinging to him with straining arms. She could not utter a word, for an anguish of weeping overtook her. And he was silent also, bending over her, his hand upon her head.

Gradually the paroxysm passed and she grew quieter; but she still clung closely to him, and at length with difficulty she began to speak.

"Oh, Eustace, it's all so horrible! I can't help seeing it. I'm sure he's dead, or, if he isn't, it's almost worse. And I was so—unkind to him the last time we were together. I thought he was cross, but I know now he was only miserable; and I never dreamt I was never going to see him again, or I wouldn't have been so—so horrid!"

Haltingly, pathetically, the poor little confession was gasped out through quivering sobs and the face of the man who listened was no longer a stony mask; it was alight and tender with a compassion too great for utterance.

He bent a little lower over her, pressing her head closer to his heart; and she heard its beating, slow and strong and regular, through all the turmoil of her distress.

"Poor child!" he said. "Poor child!"

It was all the comfort he had to offer, but it was more to her than any other words he had ever spoken. It voiced a sympathy which till that moment had been wholly lacking—a sympathy that she desired more than anything else on earth.

"Don't go away, Eustace!" she begged presently. "It—it's so dreadful all alone."

"Try to sleep, dear," he said gently.

"Yes, but I dream, I dream," she whispered piteously.

He laid her very tenderly back on the pillow, and sat down beside her.

"You won't dream while I am here," he said.

She clasped his hand closely in both her own and begged him tremulously to kiss her. By the dim light of her night-lamp she could scarcely see his face; but as her lips met his a great peace stole over her. She felt as if he had stretched out his hands to her across the great, dividing gulf that had opened between them and drawn her to his side.

About a quarter of an hour later Eustace Tudor rose noiselessly and stood looking down at his young wife's sleeping face. It was placid as an infant's, and her breathing was soft and regular. He knew that, undisturbed, she would sleep so for hours.

And so he did not dare to kiss her. He only bowed his head till his lips touched the coverlet beneath which she lay; and then stealthily, silently, he crept away.

CHAPTER X

A CHANGE OF PRISONERS

Heavens, how the night crawled! Phil Turner, bound hand and foot, and cruelly cramped in every limb, hitched himself to a sitting posture and began to calculate how long he probably had to live.

There was no moon, but the starlight entered his prison—it

was no more than a mud hut, but had it been built of stone walls many feet thick his chance would scarcely have been lessened. It was merely a question of time, he knew, and he marvelled that his fate had been delayed so long.

To use his comrade's descriptive language, he had expected "a knife and good-bye" full twenty hours before. But neither had been his portion. He had been made a prisoner before he was fully awake, and hustled away to the native fort before sunrise. He had been given *chupatties* to eat and spring water to drink, and, though painfully stiff from his bonds, he was unwounded.

It had been a daring capture, he reflected; but what were they keeping him for? Not for the sake of hospitality—of that he was grimly certain. There had been no pretence at any friendly feeling on the part of his captors. They had glared hatred at him from the outset, and Phil was firmly convinced, without any undue pessimism, that they had not the smallest intention of sparing his life.

But why they postponed the final deed was a problem, that he found himself quite unable to solve. It had worried him perpetually for twenty hours, and, combined with the misery of his bonds, made sleep an impossibility.

Sleep! The very thought of it was horrible to him. It had never struck him before as a criminal waste of the precious hours of life, for Phil was young, and he had not done with mortal existence. There were in it deeps he had not sounded, heights he had never scaled. He was not prepared to forego these at the will of a parcel of murderous ruffians who chanced to object to the white man's rule. He had friends, too—friends he could not afford to lose—friends who could not afford to lose him.

Doubtless his murder would be avenged in due course; but— He grimaced wrily to himself in the darkness, and tried once more to ease his cramped limbs.

From outside came the murmur of voices. He could just see the shoulder of one of his guards at the entrance and the steel glint of a rifle-barrel. He gazed at the latter hungrily. Oh, for just a sporting chance—to be free even in the midst of his enemies with that in his hand!

A shadow fell across the entrance, and he saw the rifle no more. He saw the two Wari sentinels salaaming profoundly, and he began to wonder who the newcomer might be—a personage of some importance apparently.

There followed an interval of some minutes, during which Phil began to chafe with feverish impatience. Then at last the shadow became substance, moving into his line of vision, and a man, wrapped in a long, native garment and wearing a *chuddah* that concealed the greater part of his face, glided into the hut on noiseless, sandalled feet.

He held a naked knife in his hand, and Phil's heart began to thud unpleasantly. It taxed all a man's self-control to face death in cold blood, trussed hand and foot and helpless as an infant. But he gripped himself hard, and faced the weapon without flinching. It would not do to let these murderous ruffians see a white man afraid.

"Hullo!" he said contemptuously. "Come to put the finishing touch, I suppose? You'll hang for it, you infernal, treacherous brute; but that's a detail you border thieves don't seem to mind."

It eased the tension to hurl verbal defiance at his murderer, and there was just the chance that the fellow might understand a little English. But when his visitor stooped over him and deliberately cut his bonds, he was astounded into silence.

He waited dumfounded, and a muscular hand gripped his shoulder, holding him motionless.

"You'll be all right," a quiet voice said, "if you don't make a confounded fool of yourself."

Phil gave a great start, and the hand that gripped him tightened. Through the gloom he made out the outline of a grim, bearded face.

"Control yourself!" the quiet voice ordered. "Do you think I've done this for nothing? We are alone—it may be for five minutes, it may be for less. Get out of your things—sharp, and let me have them."

"Great Jupiter—Tudor!" gasped Phil.

"Yes—Tudor!" came the curt response. "Don't stop to jaw. Do as I tell you."

He took his hand from Phil's shoulder and stood up, backing into the shadows.

Phil stood up, too, straightening himself with an effort. The suddenness of this thing had thrown him momentarily off his balance.

"Quick!" commanded Tudor in a fierce whisper. "Take off your clothes. There isn't a second to lose."

But Phil stood uncertain.

"What's the game, Major?" he asked.

Tudor's hand gripped him again and violently.

"You fool!" he whispered savagely. "Don't stand gaping there! Can't you see it's a matter of life and death? Do you want to be killed?"

"No, but—"

Phil broke off. Tudor in that frame of mind was a stranger to him, but he was none the less one who must be obeyed. Mechanically almost he yielded to the man's insistence and began to strip off his clothes.

Tudor helped him with an energy that neither fumed nor faltered. Mute obedience was all he required. But when he dropped the garment he wore from his own shoulders, Phil paused to protest.

"I am not going to wear that!" he said. "What about you?"

"I can look after myself," Tudor answered curtly. "Get into it—quick! There is no time for arguing. You're going to wear these, too."

He pulled the ragged, black beard from his face and the *chuddah* from his head.

But Phil's eyes were opened, and he resisted.

"Heavens above, sir!" he said. "Do you think I'm going to do a thing like that?"

"You must!" Tudor answered.

He spoke quietly, but there was deadly determination behind his quietude. They faced one another in the gloom, and suddenly there ran between them a passion of feeling that blazed unseen like the hidden current in an electric wire.

For a few seconds it burnt fiercely, silently; then Tudor laid a firm hand on the younger man's shoulder.

"You must," he said again. "The choice does not rest with you. It is made already. It only remains for you to yield—whatever it may cost you—as I am doing."

Phil started as if he had struck him.

"You are wrong, sir," he exclaimed. "On my oath, you are wrong. You don't understand. You never have understood. I—I—"

Tudor silenced him summarily with a hand upon his lips.

"I know, I know!" he said. "There is no time for this. Leave it and go. If it is any comfort to you to know it, I think no evil of you. I realise that what has happened had to happen, was in a sense inevitable, and I blame myself alone. Listen to me. This disguise will take you through all right if you keep your mouth shut. You are a priest, remember, preaching the Jehad, only I've done all the preaching necessary. You have simply to walk straight through them, down the hill till you come to the pass, and then along the river-bed till you strike the road to the Frontier. It's six miles away, but you will do it before sunrise. No, don't speak! I haven't finished yet. You are going to do this not for your own sake or for mine. You think you are going to refuse, but you are not. As for me, your going or staying could make no difference. I have come with a certain object in view, but I shall remain, whether I gain that object or not. That I swear to you most solemnly."

He turned away with the words and began to loosen his sandals. Phil watched him dumbly. He was face to face with a difficulty of such monstrous proportions that he was utterly nonplussed. From the distance came the sound of voices.

"You had better go," observed Tudor, in steady tones. "The guards are coming back. It will hasten matters for both of us if we are discovered like this."

"Sir!" Phil burst out suddenly. "I—can't!"

Tudor wheeled swiftly. It was almost as if he had been waiting for that desperate appeal. He caught up the native garment and flung it over Phil's shoulders. He dragged the beard down over his face and secured the *chuddah* about his head. He did it all with incredible rapidity and a strength that would not be gainsaid.

Then, holding Phil fast in a merciless, irresistible grasp, he spoke:

"If you attempt to disobey me now, I'll kill myself with my own hands."

There was no mistaking the resolution of his voice, and it wrought the end of the battle—an end inevitable. Phil realised it and accepted it with a groan. He did not utter another word of protest. He was conquered, humiliated, powerless. Only when at last he was ready to depart he stood up and faced Tudor, as he had faced him on the day that the latter had refused to give him a hearing.

"I've given in to you," he said; "but it's to save your life, if possible, and for no other reason. You can think what you like of me, but not—of her! Because, before Heaven, I believe this will break her heart."

He would have said more, but Tudor cut him short.

"Go!" he said. "Go! I know what I am doing—better than you think!"

And Phil turned in silence and went out into the world-wide

starlight.

CHAPTER XI

THE AWAKENING

The sun was already high when Audrey awoke. She started up, refreshed in body and mind. Her first thought was of her husband. No doubt he had gone out long before. He always rose early, even when off duty.

Then she remembered Phil, and her face contracted as all the trouble of the night before rushed back upon her. Was he still living? she wondered.

She stretched out her hand to ring for her *ayah*. But as she did so her eyes fell upon a table by her side and she caught sight of an envelope lying there. She picked it up.

It was addressed to herself in her husband's handwriting, and, with a sharp sense of anxiety, she tore it open. The note it contained was characteristically brief:

I hope by the time you read this to have procured young Turner's release, if he still lives—at no very great cost, I beg you to believe. I desire the letter that you will find on my writing-table to be sent at once to the colonel. There is also a note for Mrs. Raleigh which I want you to deliver yourself. God bless you, Audrey.

E.T.

Audrey looked up from the letter with startled eyes and white cheeks. What did it mean? What had he been doing in the night while she slept? How was it possible for him to have saved Phil?

Trembling, she sprang from her bed and began to dress. Possibly the note to Mrs. Raleigh might explain the mystery. She would ride round with it at once.

She went into Tudor's room before starting and found the letter for the colonel. It was addressed and sealed. She gave it to a *syce* with orders to deliver it into the colonel's own hands without delay.

Then, still quivering with an apprehension she would not own, she mounted and rode away to the surgeon's bungalow.

Mrs. Raleigh received her with some surprise.

"Ah, come in!" she said kindly. "I'm delighted to see you, dear; but, sure, you are riding very late. And is there anything the matter?"

"Yes," gasped Audrey breathlessly. "I mean no, I hope not. My husband has—has gone to try to save Phil Turner; and—and he left a note for you, which I was to deliver. He went away in the night, but he—of course he'll—be back—soon!"

Her voice faltered and died away. There was a look on Mrs. Raleigh's face, hidden as it were behind her smile, that struck terror to Audrey's heart. She thrust out the letter in an anguish of unconcealed suspense.

"Read it! Read it!" she implored, "and tell me what has happened—quickly, for I—I don't understand!"

Mrs. Raleigh took the letter, passing a supporting arm around the girl's quivering form.

"Sit down, dear!" she said tenderly.

Audrey obeyed, but her face was still raised in voiceless supplication as Mrs. Raleigh opened the letter. The pause that followed was terrible to her. She endured it in wrung silence, her hands fast gripped together.

Then Mrs. Raleigh turned, and in her eyes was a deep compassion, a motherly tenderness of pity, that was to Audrey the confirmation of her worst fears.

She did not speak again. Her heart felt constricted, paralysed. But Mrs. Raleigh saw the entreaty which her whole body expressed, and, stooping, she took the rigid hands into hers.

"My dear," she said, "he has gone into the Hills in disguise, up to the native fort beyond Wara, as that is where he expects to find Phil. Heaven help him and bring them both back!"

Audrey stared at her with a stunned expression. Her lips were quite white, and Mrs. Raleigh thought she was going to faint.

But Audrey did not lose consciousness. She sat there as if turned to stone, trying to speak and failing to make any sound. At last, convulsively, words came.

"They will take him for a spy," she said, both hands pressed to her throat as if something there hurt her intolerably. "The Waris—torture—spies!"

"My darling, my darling, we must hope—hope and pray!" said the Irishwoman, holding her closely.

Audrey turned suddenly, passionately, in the enfolding arms and clung to her as if in physical agony.

"You may, you may," she said in a dreadful whisper, "but I can't—for I don't believe. Do you in your heart believe he will ever come back?"

Mrs. Raleigh did not answer.

Audrey went on, still holding her tightly:

"Do you think I don't know why he wrote to you? It was to put me in your care, because—because he knew he was never coming back. And shall I—shall I tell you why he went?"

"Darling, hush—hush!" pleaded Mrs. Raleigh, her voice unsteady with emotion. "There, don't say any more! Put your head on my shoulder, love. Let me hold you so."

But Audrey's convulsive hold did not relax. She had been a child all her life up to that moment, but, like a worn-out garment, her childhood had slipped from her, and she had emerged a woman. The old, happy ignorance was gone for ever, and the revelation that had dispelled it was almost more than she could bear. Her newly developed womanhood suffered as womanhood alone can suffer.

And yet, could she have drawn the veil once more before her eyes and so have deadened that agonising pain, she would not have done so.

She was awake now. The long, long sleep with its gay dreams, its careless illusions, was over. But it was better to be awake, better to see and know things as they were, even if the anguish thereof killed her. And so she refused the hushing comfort that only a child—such a child as she had been but yesterday—could have found satisfying.

"Yes, I can tell you—now—why he went," she said, in that tense whisper which so wrung Mrs. Raleigh's heart. "He went—for my sake! Think of it! Think of it! He went because I was fretting about Phil. He went because—because he thought—that Phil's safety—meant—my happiness, and that *his* safety—his—his precious life—didn't—count!"

The awful words sank into breathless silence. Mrs. Raleigh was crying silently. She was powerless to cope with this. But Audrey shed no tears. It was beyond tears and beyond mourning—this terrible revelation that had come to her. By-andby, it might be, both would come to her, if she lived.

She rose suddenly at length with a sharp gasp, as of one seeking air.

"I am going," she said, in a clear, strong voice, "to the colonel. He will help me to save my husband."

And with that she turned to the veranda, and met the

commanding-officer face to face. There was another man behind him, but she did not look at him. She instantly, without a second's pause, addressed the colonel.

"I was coming to you," she said through her white lips. "You will help me. You must help me. My husband is a prisoner, and I am going into the Hills to find him. You must follow with men and guns. He must be saved—whatever it costs."

The colonel laid his hand on her shoulder, looking down at her very earnestly, very kindly.

"My dear Mrs. Tudor," he said, "all that can be done shall be done, all that is humanly possible. I have already told Turner so. Did you know that he was safe?"

He drew her forward a step, and she saw that the man behind him was Phil Turner himself—Phil Turner, grave, strong, resolute, with all his manhood strung up to the moment's emergency, all his boyhood submerged in a responsibility that overwhelmed the lesser part of him, leaving only that which was great.

He went straight up to Audrey and took the hands she stretched out to him. Neither of them felt the presence of onlookers.

"He saved my life, Mrs. Tudor!" he said simply. "He forced me to take it at his hands. But I'm going back with some men to find him. You stay here with Mrs. Raleigh till we come back. We shall be quicker alone."

A great sob burst from Audrey. It was as if the few gallant words had loosened the awful constriction at her heart.

"Oh, Phil, Phil!" she cried brokenly. "You understand—what this is to me—how I love him—how I love him! Bring him back to me! Promise, Phil, promise!"

And Phil bent till his lips touched the hands he held.

"I will do it," he said with reverence—"so help me, God!"

CHAPTER XII

A WOMAN'S AGONY

All through the day and the night that followed Audrey watched and waited.

She spent the terrible hours at the Raleighs' bungalow,

scarcely conscious of her surroundings in her anguish of suspense. It possessed her like a raging fever, and she could not rest. At times it almost seemed to suffocate her, and then she would pace to and fro, to and fro, hardly knowing what she did.

Mrs. Raleigh never left her, caring for her with a maternal tenderness that never flagged. But for her Audrey would almost certainly have collapsed under the strain.

"If he had only known! If he had only known!" she kept repeating. "But how could he know? for I never showed him. How could he even guess? And now he never can know. It's too late, too late!"

Futile, bitter regret! All through the night it followed her, and when morning came the haggard misery it had wrought upon her face had robbed it of all its youth.

Mrs. Raleigh tried to comfort her with hopeful words, but she did not seem so much as to hear them. She was listening, listening intently, for every sound.

It was about noon that young Travers raced in, hot and breathless, but he stopped short in evident dismay when he saw Audrey. He would have withdrawn as precipitately as he had entered, but she sprang after him and caught him by the arms.

"You have news!" she cried wildly. "What is it? Oh, what is it? Tell me quickly!"

He hesitated and glanced nervously at Mrs. Raleigh.

"Yes, tell her," the latter said. "It is better than suspense."

And so briefly, jerkily, the boy blurted on his news:

"Phil's back again; but they haven't got the major. The fort was deserted, except for one old man, and they have brought him along. They are over at the colonel's bungalow now."

He paused, shocked by the awful look his tidings had brought into Audrey's eyes.

The next instant she had sprung past him to the open door and was gone, bareheaded and distraught, into the blazing sunshine.

How she covered the distance of the long, white road to the colonel's bungalow, Audrey never remembered afterwards. Her agony of mind was too great for her brain to register any impression of physical stress. She only knew that she ran and ran as one runs in a nightmare, till suddenly she was on the veranda of the colonel's bungalow, stumbling, breathless, crying hoarsely for "Phil! Phil!"

He came to her instantly.

"Where is he?" she cried, in high, strained tones. "Where is my husband? You promised to bring him back to me! You promised—you promised—"

Her voice failed. She felt choked, as if an iron hand were slowly, remorselessly, crushing the life out of her panting heart. Thick darkness hovered above her, but she fought it from her wildly, frantically.

"You promised—" She gasped again.

He took her gently by the arm, supporting her.

"Mrs. Tudor," he said very earnestly, "I have done my best."

He led her unresisting into a room close by. The colonel was there, and with him a man in flowing, native garments.

"Mrs. Tudor," said Phil, his hand closing tightly upon her arm, "before you blame me, I want you to speak to this man. He can tell you more about your husband than I can."

He spoke very quietly, very steadily, almost as if he were afraid she might not understand him.

Audrey made an effort to collect her reeling senses. The colonel bent towards her.

"Don't be afraid of him, Mrs. Tudor," he said kindly. "He is a friend, and he speaks English."

But Audrey did not so much as glance at the native, who stood, silent and impassive, waiting to be questioned. The agony of the past thirty hours had reached its limit. She sank into a chair by the colonel's table and hid her face in her shaking hands.

"I've nothing to ask him," she said hopelessly. "Eustace is dead—dead—dead, without ever knowing how I loved him. Nothing matters now. There is nothing left that ever can matter."

Dead silence succeeded her words, then a quiet movement, then silence again.

She did not look up or stir. Her passion of grief had burnt itself out. She was exhausted mentally and physically.

Minutes passed, but she did not move. What was there to rouse her? There was nothing left. She had no tears to shed. Tears were for small things. This grief of hers was too immense, too infinite for tears.

Only at last something, some inner prompting, stirred her, and as if at the touch of a hand that compelled, she raised her head.

She saw neither the colonel nor Phil, and a sharp prick of wonder pierced her lethargy of despair. She turned in her chair, obedient still to that inner force that compelled. Yes, they had gone. Only the native remained—an old, bent man, who humbly awaited her pleasure. His face was almost hidden in his *chuddah*.

Audrey looked at him.

"There is nothing to wait for," she said at length. "You need not stay."

He did not move. It was as if he had not heard. Her wonder grew into a sort of detached curiosity. What did the man want? She remembered that the colonel had told her that he understood English.

"Is there—something—you wish to say to me?" she asked, and the bare utterance of the words kindled a feeble spark of hope within her, almost in spite of herself.

He turned very slowly.

"Yes, one thing," he said, paused an instant as she sprang to her feet with a great cry, then straightened himself, pushed the *chuddah* back from his face, and flung out his arms to her passionately.

"Audrey!" he said—"Audrey!"

CHAPTER XIII

HAPPINESS AGAIN

By slow degrees Audrey learnt the story of her husband's escape.

It was Phil's doing in the main, he told her simply, and she understood that but for Phil he would not have taken the trouble. Something Phil had said to him that night had stuck in his mind, and it had finally decided him to make the attempt.

Circumstances had favoured him. Moreover it was by no means the first time that he had been among the Hill tribes in native guise. One sentinel alone had returned to guard the hut after Phil's departure, and this man he had succeeded in overpowering without raising an alarm.

Then, disguising himself once more, he had managed to escape just before the dawn, and had lain hidden for hours among the boulders of the river-bed, fearing to emerge by daylight. But in the evening he had left his hiding-place, and found the fort to be occupied by British troops. The Waris had gone to earth before their advance, and they had found the place deserted.

He had forthwith presented himself in his disguise and been taken before Phil, the officer-in-command.

"But surely he knew you?"

"Yes, he knew me. But I swore him to secrecy."

She drew a little closer to him.

"Eustace, why?" she whispered.

His arm tightened about her.

"I had to know the truth first," he said.

"Oh!" she murmured. "And now—are you satisfied?"

He bent and kissed her forehead gravely, tenderly.

"I am satisfied," he said.

"Well, didn't I tell you so?" laughed Phil, when they shook hands later.

Audrey did not ask him what he meant, for, with all his honesty, Phil could be enigmatical when he chose. Moreover, it really didn't much matter, for, as she tacitly admitted to herself, fond as she was of him, he no longer occupied the place of honour in her thoughts, and she was not vitally interested in him now that the trouble was over.

So when, a few weeks later, Phil cheerily packed his belongings and departed to Poonah, having effected an exchange into the other battalion stationed there, only his major understood why, and was sorry.

CPSIA information can be obtained at www.ICGtesting.com
Printed in the USA
LVOW132008100513

333282LV00001B/280/A